HUNTING PROMETHEUS

THE UNDERWORLD SAGA, BOOK EIGHT

Eva Pohler

Eva Pohler Books
20011 Park Ranch
San Antonio, Texas 78259
www.evapohler.com

Book Layout ©2017 BookDesignTemplates.com

Book Cover Design by B Rose Designz

Hunting Prometheus/ Eva Pohler. -- 1st ed.
Paperback ISBN 978-1-958390-42-9

For my brother.

Contents

"Humans have but one spin, one go, one bright moment and then the flame goes out."

--HADES

CHAPTER ONE

Secrets Revealed

After Therese had blown out her candles and had opened the presents of her favorite bath and body products from her aunt and uncle and Mr. and Mrs. Stern, she went outside to the two giant Elms in the back of what was now her aunt and uncle's property, searching for her favorite red birds—her parents. She couldn't understand their song without the help of Hermie and Hestie to translate, but she had a feeling they were singing her a happy birthday wish. Besides, their words were less important than their presence. Their gift of immortality—even if they couldn't be human—had been the best gift anyone had ever given her.

And she had received many amazing gifts, she thought, as she clutched the lockets around her neck. One had come from Athena, with the inscription: "The most common way people give up their power is by believing they have none." The other had been a Christmas present from her Aunt Carol, and it contained a photo of her parents on one side and a photo of Carol, Richard, and Lynn on the other. She rarely took the lockets off.

She'd also received a crown of invisibility from Artemis. It wasn't as powerful as Hades's helm. The crown could only hide one from mortals. But it had come in handy over the years, especially when Jen had still lived at home.

Perhaps the most useful was the traveling robe from Aphrodite. The first one had been ripped to shreds years ago, during Therese's challenge with the Hydra, but Aphrodite had given her another one after the twins were born. It had helped Therese get around when she was in a hurry, and it had also helped her to take Than and the twins to visit the Underworld from time to time—though it had been almost a year since they'd been. She would go more often if she didn't feel as though she was in the way. The gods were busy and rarely seemed to have time for Therese and her family.

And of course, her animal companions—Clifford, Jewels, and Stormy—had been granted immortality, which had been a wonderful thing; though, she had to admit it only reminded her of what she and Than had lost. Now *Jen* road Stormy across the skies, and Therese rarely saw him. And she worried about who would take care of Clifford and Jewels once Therese and Than and the twins were in the Elysian Fields of the Underworld, living eternity in blissful oblivion.

She blinked away her tears. Thirty-seven. She was thirty-seven years old. She and Than had both aged and were reminded of it every time they saw the ever-youthful Hip and Jen, Pete and Tizzie, and the others. In fact, Therese now looked the same age as Persephone, and Than looked more like Hades's brother than his son. Maybe that was another reason they didn't visit the Underworld often.

She was brought from her reverie when she heard the twins around the corner on the deck at the side of the house. They seemed unaware of Therese as they sat at the table where Therese used to sit with her father to watch the deer, chipmunks, and wild horses that came out at sunset.

"So, what did Morpheus say to you, exactly?" Hestie was asking.

"The gods are fighting," Hermie replied. "And Mom and Dad are in danger. I think he said we all are."

Therese held her breath.

"Let's both pray to him tonight and see if we can find out more," Hestie suggested.

Then Lynn spoke up. "You're in danger? And why would you *pray* to Morpheus?"

Lynn had met Morpheus many times when he'd visited in human form, and she knew he was their cousin.

"Uh, um," Hermie stuttered. "Lynn. I didn't hear you follow us out."

"It's a video game," Hestie said.

"Why are you lying to me?" Lynn insisted. "Why are you in danger?"

"It's cold out here. Don't you guys want to come inside?" It was Bobby.

"Lynn overheard us talking about Morpheus," Hermie said. "We don't know what to say."

"Why would the twins *pray* to your nephew?" Lynn asked.

"I don't think they meant *pray* literally," Bobby said. "That's a new slang word. People say, 'I'll pray to you later,' and what they mean is, "I'll text you later.'"

"Hmm," Lynn said—and it sounded to Therese like she wasn't buying it. "But you still haven't said why you're in danger."

Therese realized the time had come for Lynn to know the truth. It wasn't fair for the adults to keep putting their children in these sticky situations.

***

Thanatos watched on helplessly as Carol, Richard, and Therese told Lynn about his family. They'd waited until after the Sterns had left, though it would have been nice to have had Bobby's help.

"This is a lame joke," Lynn said.

"It's not a joke," Carol said gently. "Look, I understand how you feel. It was hard for your father and me to believe it at first, too."

"We should have told you sooner," Richard added. "But we didn't know how."

Therese put a hand on Lynn's shoulder. "And we didn't want to hurt your relationship with Hermie and Hestie."

Lynn was taller than Therese and the same height as Hestie. Her hair was curlier than theirs, and darker, as was her skin, but she shared their same facial features—pouty lips, green eyes, slender nose, and dimples. "You really expect me to believe that Than was once the god of death? His parents are Hades and Persephone? And, for a while, you were a god, too? This is crazy." Lynn collapsed on the couch beside her mother.

"It's true." Therese took the chair opposite her.

"Then why aren't you still gods?" Lynn asked.

Than sat on the arm of Therese's chair. "We gave that up so we could raise Hermie and Hestie here."

"Are they gods too?" Lynn asked.

"Demigods," Hermie said.

Lynn's eyes widened.

Than cleared his throat to buy some time to figure out how to phrase what he was about to say. He didn't want to go into too much detail, but he wanted Lynn to believe and to understand. "There was a war on Mount Olympus, and part of the peace treaty was Zeus's condition that no more gods could be made. Therese was pregnant with the twins at the time."

Hestie sat down on the couch beside Lynn. "Gods don't become immortal until they're born."

"So, we were born *mortal*," Hermie added.

Therese said, "And the only way we could be with them was for us to become mortal, too."

Than heard the subtle quiver in Therese's voice and hated that she wouldn't be anything but joyful on her birthday. He knew she missed their life among the gods. He wouldn't have guessed all those years ago, when he was first getting to know her, that she would one day long to live in the Underworld. He'd thought her love of animals and of the

Colorado mountains and of sunsets and of pine trees would make her miserable in his father's realm. He'd been wrong.

"My best friend, Jen Holt, married Than's brother, Hip," Therese said. "Hypnos. He's the god of sleep. Jen became the goddess of abused children. And they have a son named Morpheus, the god of dreams."

"The Sterns and Bobby know about the gods," Hestie explained.

"Pete Holt is married to our Aunt Tizzie," Hermie put in.

"Wait, what?" Lynn asked. "I thought Pete Holt was dead."

Therese glanced up at Than, who inwardly groaned.

Hermie's face turned red. "Oops."

"He took over my duties as Death," Than explained. "I gave him my immortality."

"So, Pete isn't *dead*, he's *Death*," Lynn repeated. "And he's married to Tizzie. And she's, what? The goddess of death?"

"Um," Hestie looked to Therese for help.

"She's a Fury," Therese said.

Than covered his mouth in frustration. He didn't want to overwhelm the poor girl.

"A Fury?" Lynn repeated. "You mean, like the avengers of hell?"

"She's a lot nicer in person," Hermie said.

Than could almost see the wheels turning in poor Lynn's head. He really hoped the conversation wouldn't lead to the two red birds who were perched outside near the window.

Lynn scratched her head. "So, if Zeus said there could be no more gods while you were pregnant with the twins, how could Jen and—what's her husband's name?"

"Hypnos," Than said.

"Hip for short," Hermie added.

"How could Jen and Hip's child be a god and not yours?" Lynn asked Therese.

"It's a long story," Therese replied. "But, basically, they had leverage."

Lynn furrowed her brows. "So, let me get this straight. Than's parents are the rulers of the Underworld."

"Yes, sweetheart," Carol said.

"And all those gods in the stories you've told to me—they all exist? Like Zeus and Athena and Aphrodite and Poseidon? They're all real?"

"Yes," Therese said.

"What about Santa Claus and the tooth fairy? Are they real, too?"

"Why are you so angry?" Richard asked Lynn.

"Because you've been lying to me all my life."

Carol put an arm around her. "I'm so sorry, sweetheart. Can you forgive us?"

"Just tell me this." Lynn turned to Hestie. "Why is your family in danger?"

"In danger?" Carol repeated, her eyes suddenly wide with worry.

"It was just a dream," Hermie said. "We don't know if any of it's real."

"I'm sure it's nothing," Therese said, but Than knew she was lying.

***

During the drive home from their grandparents' house, Hermie wasn't surprised when his mother turned from the front passenger seat and said, "Tell me what's going on with Morpheus."

"Um, we don't know," Hermie said. "We're going to ask him tonight."

"Maybe it's time," their dad said to their mom.

"Time for what?" Hestie asked.

"Let's talk inside," their mother said.

Hermie sighed. "How long is this going to take? I made plans to meet with my friends online at nine o'clock."

"You made plans on Mom's birthday?" Hestie chided.

"I asked her first," Hermie replied. "Mom said we'd be home between eight and eight-thirty, and when I asked if we were doing anything after that, she said no."

"This is important," their father said, as he pulled the truck into their gravel drive and headed for the garage.

"So is my game. I made a commitment to my team to be there. It's World of Warcraft. I'm the tank. They'll die without me."

"This might be more important," Hestie said gently.

"This game is important to me and my friends. They're counting on me. I don't like to let people down. The talk can wait, can't it? We'll be finished by ten or ten thirty."

"We've waited sixteen years." His mom unfastened her safety belt. "We can wait another couple of hours."

Hermie tried not to let the guilt bother him as he played, but he failed, and his whole team died after an hour into the game. At least it hadn't been a total waste. They'd had fun while it had lasted, and he hadn't let them down in that.

His family was waiting for him in the living room. Apparently, they'd begun without him. He fell into one of two armchairs across from the sofa, where his parents sat frowning, with Clifford and Noodle in their laps. Hestie was already in the other armchair with Kitty, and the expression on his sister's face could only be described as perplexed.

"What did I miss?" Hermie asked.

As an answer, his canary, Chidori, chirped from her cage, "You have a destiny."

Of course, only he and Hestie heard it. To his parents, Chidori's tweets were unintelligible.

"An important destiny," Chidori chirped again.

Hermie's Grampa Hades had told him years ago that he had a destiny, so it was no surprise. Even if he had no idea what that destiny was or how he was to fulfill it, he hadn't thought much about it. It was

Hermie's belief that it would happen, whether he tried to do anything about it or not. The Fates were never wrong.

His father raked a hand through his dark, wavy hair. "When you were still a baby, Apollo had a vision of you two when you came to be about the age you are now."

"Is it safe to say this out loud?" his mother interrupted.

His father shifted on the couch. "They need to know. I'll make it quick."

His mom nodded—reluctantly it seemed to Hermie.

"So, what was the vision?" Hestie asked.

"Apollo saw you with Prometheus," their father replied.

Hermie cleared his throat, trying to hide the skepticism in his voice. "The Titan who made humankind?"

"That's right," his mother said. "And he also gave us fire against Zeus's wishes, because he loved his creation more than the gods."

Hestie stroked Kitty. "I've always thought that was pretty cool."

"But to Zeus, it was a betrayal. As punishment, Prometheus was chained to a mountain," his father said. "And Zeus's eagle ate out his liver every morning."

"And the liver grew back every evening," Hermie said. "We already know the story."

"And you know that Hercules set him free?" their mother asked.

Hestie and Hermie nodded.

"Where is he now?" Hermie asked.

"No one knows," his father said. "He went into hiding centuries ago."

"Did Apollo say why Prometheus was with *us*?" Hestie asked.

"No." Their mother helped Clifford down from her lap. "We don't know if *he* comes to *you*, or *you* find *him*."

"Obviously, *he* comes to *us*," Hermie said. "Right? We have no idea where he is."

"Nothing in this is obvious, Son," his father said. "And you need to know about another, much older, prophecy."

"Is this the one you told me about tonight, while Hermie was playing his game?" Hestie asked.

"Yes," their mother said.

His father helped Noodle, who wanted to follow Clifford, from his lap. "It's one that Prometheus told Zeus, while he was still Zeus's prisoner."

Hestie brushed her long hair from her eyes. "He said that Metis would have a son by Zeus, and that son would one day overthrow him."

"That's why Zeus swallowed Metis in the first place, and why Athena later had to be let out by Hephaestus and his ax," Hermie said.

"And then, centuries later, why Metis had to be rescued by the Athena Alliance," Hestie added.

"That's right," their father said.

"I know the story, but I didn't know Prometheus was the one who told Zeus," Hermie admitted.

"There's more," Hestie said. "When we were only a year old, Metis disguised herself as Hera and tricked Zeus. She got pregnant using dark magic."

"With a son?" Hermie asked.

"We don't know for sure," their mother said, "but that's what the Olympians suspect."

"Metis disappeared after the Olympians imprisoned Uranus for trying to wage war on them," their father went on.

"Uranus took over his father's body and nearly swallowed your Uncle Hip," their mother explained.

Their father added, "Zeus probably fears that her son and Prometheus will team up to take over the throne."

"Why would Prometheus do that?" Hermie asked. "You said he cares more about us than the gods."

"I wouldn't have suspected him if it weren't for Apollo's vision," their father said.

"Maybe Prometheus tries to stop Metis's son," Hestie offered.

"Maybe," their mother said. "The point is, we don't know where he stands. We only know that one day soon, the two of you will be in his company—whether as his prisoners or his allies, we just don't know. We need you to train."

"We shouldn't have waited this late," their father said.

"Time got away from us," their mother added. "We've been so busy. If I hadn't overheard you tonight at Grammie's talking about Morpheus, we probably would have put this off until it was too late."

"We may have already," their father said. "Don't make any plans tomorrow. We need to teach you two how to fight."

"You've been teaching us our whole lives," Hestie pointed out.

"We know how to use a sword and shield," Hermie added.

"You even taught us how to wrestle," Hestie said.

"How to punch, how to kick. What more is there?" Hermie asked.

"We never taught you how to kill," their father said.

CHAPTER TWO

A Warning from Morpheus

That night, Hermie searched for Morpheus in his dreams. So far, his winged cousin was nowhere to be found. Hermie was running on…where was he? He stopped and looked around. He was on a ship on the wide, blue sea. Was it an aircraft carrier? It was the ship from *The Avengers* movie. But there was no one around and nothing to do.

Too bad. It would have been nice to see Scarlet Johansson.

Hermie searched all around the deck. No computers. No video games. Not even a swimming pool. What kind of cruise was this? His parents had wanted him to go with them, but he'd rather stay home. Everything he needed to see and do could happen right on his desk, where the best computer ever made—built by Hermie himself—existed. Not only was it made of the best components, but Hermie had created his own programs, too.

Yes, it was one badass computer.

But, if Scarlet Johansson ever showed up, Hermie could be persuaded to stay on the cruise.

He saw a stack of cards on a nearby table. Maybe they were Magic the Gathering or Yugioh cards. He couldn't play without an opponent, but he could look through the cards and think of what strategies he would use with whatever was in the deck.

Shoot. These were regular playing cards. Should he pass the time with a game of Solitaire? What were his options?

Wait a minute. He needed to find Morpheus.

Hermie jumped up from the table, the cards flying everywhere. "Morpheus! Hey, Morpheus! Where are you?"

Suddenly, the theme song from *Scooby-Doo* blasted over the speakers. Gee whiz.

Hermie decided to look below deck. As he descended a ladder, he found himself entering the Underworld. He recognized the Phlegethon—also known as the River of Fire. He followed the winding light down an otherwise dark tunnel.

To no one in particular, he said, "Am I really in the Underworld?"

"No," came a familiar voice behind him.

Hermie turned. "Morpheus?"

His bright, silver wings were folded behind him. Silver-rimmed black eyes peered from a lustrous, bronze face. Though not as tall as Hermie, Morpheus was stouter, his bare chest ripped like that of a bodybuilder.

Not that Hermie didn't have muscles of his own. He enjoyed working out with his father in the basement. It was one of the few things they ever did together.

"Go on. Do the test, like you always do," Morpheus said patiently.

Hermie took a deep breath. "Figment, I command you to show yourself!"

Morpheus lifted his palms. "See?"

Relieved, Hermie shook his cousin's hand. "Thanks for meeting me. I can't remember everything you told me last night. What are the gods fighting about? Why is my family in danger?"

Morpheus rolled his eyes. "Looks like I got in trouble for nothing. You really can't remember what I said? Now I'll have to hear it from my dad again."

"Just tell me."

"Write it down this time," Morpheus said. "As soon as you wake up. Got it?"

Hermie nodded.

"Zeus's spies think they finally spotted the son of Metis," Morpheus said. "So, Zeus went to Apollo and asked him to reveal any visions he'd had about the future, even if they didn't seem relevant."

Hermie lowered his head. "So, Zeus knows about Apollo's vision of me and my sister."

"With Prometheus. Yeah."

"Great. So now what? What did you overhear?"

"My dad thinks Zeus wants to kill you and Hestie."

Hermie's mouth went dry.

"Try not to freak out," Morpheus added.

"Easier said than done," Hermie managed to say. "Why would killing *us* help Zeus?"

"I guess Zeus thinks the vision means that you and your sister are going to help Prometheus and Metis's son overthrow him."

"That's ridiculous."

"Tell me about it."

Hermie folded his arms across his chest. "So, what should we do?"

"I don't know. Hide?"

"Hide? Morpheus, that's not helpful. Not at all. How can you hide from Zeus?"

"I don't know, cuz. Sorry to say it, but I think you're screwed."

***

Hestie opened her eyes and sat up in bed. From the dim light streaming through her windows, she could tell it was early morning—the sun had barely dawned. Hermie would still be asleep, but this couldn't wait. She pulled on a pair of shorts and rushed down the hall to his room.

"Hermie! Wake up!" She jostled his shoulder. "This is important!"

Hermie frowned and rolled over.

"Wake up! We need to talk!"

He blinked and wiped his mouth. "Huh?"

"Wake up!"

"Wait a minute." He sat up. "Get me a pen and that notepad over there."

Hestie quickly remembered that Morpheus had told her to write down her dream, too. "Oh, yeah."

She handed over the pen and paper and then rushed back to her own room and sat at her desk. She wrote down everything she could recall. She'd been in the mall with Lynn, checking out the newest styles at Forever 21, and Got7 had been there. And, of course, Lynn hadn't known who Got7 was, so Hestie had had to educate her about Korean pop music. In the dream, others in the mall had noticed the band members and were pointing and chasing after them. Before Hestie could ask JB or Youngjae to take a selfie with her, they were scattering through the mall in all directions.

Hestie had run after them. She had caught sight of Jinyoung rounding a corner, but when she caught up to him, he'd vanished.

She'd cried out, "Jinyoung! I want to interview you for my Youtube channel!"

"Shouldn't you be looking for *me*?"

She'd turned to find Morpheus.

"Oh, yeah."

That's when he'd told her to write everything down as soon as she woke up. He'd told her about Prometheus and his prophecy about Metis and Zeus's son. He'd told her about Uranus taking over Aether's body and nearly killing Uncle Hip. He'd told her about Apollo's vision of her and her brother—all things she'd already known. But then he'd said that Zeus wanted to kill her and Hermie!

She ran back to her brother's room. "What the truck are we gonna do?"

Hermie dropped his pen and rubbed his head. "Let's go back to sleep and ask Mom and Dad when we wake up."

"Go back to sleep? You're crazy! We need to figure this out *now*!"

***

Hypnos disintegrated and dispatched to the Fields of Asphodel to confront his son. He'd tried to reach out to him telepathically but hadn't gotten a reply and wasn't sure whether Morpheus was ignoring him or unable to hear him.

Even though slumber was Hip's primary duty, requiring him to fly around the globe day in and day out, he oversaw the Dreamworld, too—not because he didn't think Morpheus could handle it, but because he worried about his safety. Zeus and the others knew Morpheus was close to Than's twins, and Hip feared Zeus had spies who manipulated Morpheus in their dreams, where they collected their intel. What was worse, Morpheus collected intel of his own while he visited the dreams of the other gods. Hip had caught him doing it on more than one occasion.

He would much rather be with Jen during one of her few off-duty moments for a little roll in the hay or playing Night Frisbee with Morpheus, Ariadne, and Asterion than delivering a scolding; but tensions were high now that Zeus was hot on Metis's trail.

Morpheus lay among the flowers, half on his belly and half on his side, his wings spread over him like a blanket. Although he wasn't granted the ability to disintegrate outside of the Dreamworld, he was permitted a single godly form in addition to the one lying here.

Hypnos was constantly amazed by how much his son had grown and learned in the brief fifteen years since he'd been adopted. A mortal boy of four from Africa with no surviving family members, no possessions of his own—not even a name (everyone had called him *Muggie*, which meant *tiny bug*)—he had transformed more dramatically than any other being Hip knew. Morpheus was full grown and would probably keep his youthful appearance for many centuries to come. One couldn't know for certain, since the gods aged at different rates, but most deities developed quickly at infancy and then aged so slowly, once they were fully grown, that they didn't seem to age at all.

Hip tapped his son's shoulder. "Tell me where you are. We need to talk."

Half asleep with hooded eyes, the boy said, "With Iris. Rainbow."

"Where?"

Morpheus closed his eyes and shrugged.

Frustrated, Hip lay down beside his son, closed his eyes, and sought him out in the Dreamworld.

***

Her golden wings were smaller than his silver ones, but Iris was still faster than Morpheus. Maybe it had something to do with how small she was. Not quite three feet tall, she was nearly half his size. As Morpheus chased Iris up the rainbow, he was dimly aware of his father calling out to him over by the Gates of Horn.

"Where in the Upperworld are you?" his father cried out. "We need to talk!"

Iris giggled and flew up to the clouds with her full pitcher. Morpheus jumped up into the bright sky after her, making note of the land below.

It was the Amazon rainforest. Was that Venezuela below? Morpheus was still learning his geography.

"I'm in the sky above what I think is Venezuela," he said to his father at the Gates of Horn.

Instantly, his father was in the sky beside him.

Iris glanced down at Morpheus from where she was pouring her pitcher into the clouds.

"I'll come right back!" he called up to her. "And when I do, you better tell me the name of that flower. I mean it!"

Morpheus followed his father toward the forest, where they hovered out of earshot of Iris.

"What's that all about?" his father asked him.

Morpheus blushed. He'd been after Iris all week to reveal the name of her favorite flower. He wanted to paint her a picture of it to keep in her room on Mount Olympus. He figured it would always remind her of him. "Nothing. What's up?"

His father took his hand, and they god traveled to Morpheus's room in the Underworld.

"You disobeyed me again," his father said.

"Pops, I'm worried about them, that's all."

His father crossed his arms and scratched his chin. "You're making it worse by interfering."

"How? Shouldn't Hermie and Hestie know they're in danger? That Zeus wants to kill them?"

His father's brows shot up. "What makes you say that?"

"I may have overheard you talking to Mom."

"Zeus is not trying to kill them. Oh, Morpheus. What have you done?"

"What do you mean?" Morpheus was getting worried now.

"You heard something you didn't understand, and now you've put the twins in danger."

"If Zeus isn't trying to kill them, why would they be in danger?"

"Don't you think Hermie and Hestie are talking about this? Don't you think Zeus will suspect them to be working with Prometheus, as Apollo predicted?"

Morpheus hadn't thought of that. "Go put them back into the deep boon of sleep. I can fix this. I'll tell them not to talk."

"I'm trying. Hermie's nearly out again, but Hestie is resisting me."

Morpheus noticed his father's face turn grim.

"Pops? What's wrong?"

"Ares and his sons. They've just arrived at Than and Therese's house. Come on!"

CHAPTER THREE

Prisoners

Hestie opened her eyes and sat up in bed, the morning light streaming in through her windows. She had a serious case of déjà vu. Hadn't she already been awake?

Her rats, Katniss and Prim, were sleeping soundly in their cages, or she might have asked them.

She got up for what she knew was the second time and marched down the hall to Hermie.

The paper where he'd written down his dream lay on the nightstand, and the one on which she'd written hers was right beside it. She wasn't imagining things.

"Hermie?" She tapped his back.

He opened his eyes. "What's wrong?"

"We need to go downstairs and talk to Mom and Dad."

Hermie pulled off his covers and climbed out of his bed, not caring that he was only wearing underwear.

"Well, okay," she muttered, glancing away.

She waited for him to use the restroom and pull on a pair of jeans. Then they went downstairs together.

Hestie was first alarmed when she didn't hear Clifford or Noodle running toward her to tell her good morning and to ask if she would take them for a walk outside. It was a daily ritual.

She was next alarmed when she saw Kitty curled on the sofa, sobbing.

"Where's Clifford and Noodle?" Hestie asked her.

"Trapped outside," Kitty replied.

"What?" Hermie rushed to the back door to let the dogs in. "What happened?"

Chidori tweeted, "Bad guys. Bad guys."

"Phobos and Deimos," Clifford barked. "They were here."

"They took your parents away," Kitty said between sniffs.

"They did?" Noodle whined.

"Oh, no!" Clifford barked.

"It all happened so fast," Jewels said from her sandbox.

Hestie couldn't breathe as she ran to her parents' room. Hermie and the dogs were fast on her heels, crying out for them.

Their parents weren't in the bedroom. They weren't in the bathroom or closet, either. They weren't in the basement or the garage, but both vehicles were there. They weren't on the back deck or on the front porch.

Hestie phoned her Grammie, asking if she'd seen them.

"You mean they left without telling you?" Grammie asked.

Hestie didn't want to worry her grandparents, so she said, "Oh, wait. Here's a note. They ran into town for some shopping. Thanks anyway, Grammie. Bye."

Hermie prayed out loud to their family in the Underworld for help. Hestie silently did the same. They waited for several minutes, which felt more like hours, and when they heard nothing, Hestie began to cry again.

"What do we do?" she asked her brother.

"Tell Carol and Richard the truth," Clifford barked.

"We can't worry them." Hermie took a puff from his rescue inhaler. "Let's call Bobby Holt. Maybe he'll have an idea." Hermie took a second puff.

When Bobby didn't answer, Hestie called Mrs. Stern.

"Wouldn't you know it? His phone's here in the house, and he's out in the barn," Mrs. Stern said. "I can have him call you when he comes inside."

"Thank you," Hestie said before hanging up.

"Let's go down there now," Hermie said.

"What can Bobby Holt do?" Hestie asked, wondering if they were wasting precious time.

"You got any better ideas?"

She didn't.

They finished getting dressed and headed on foot down the road to the Sterns' ranch. They were fast on their feet and had reached the pen in less than ten minutes.

"Bobby?" Hermie said through the barn door. "Are you in there?"

Hestie was trying to catch her breath, realizing how out of shape she was.

Bobby emerged, in dusty jeans and boots, his flannel shirt dirty with mud and hay. His blond bowl-shaped hair clung to his forehead and dripped with sweat.

"What's up, you two?" Bobby asked with a smile. "Are you ready for a job after all?"

Hestie and her brother had worked for the Sterns on and off over the years, grooming the horses and cleaning out the barn. They usually did it during the summers, mainly because their parents didn't give them a choice, and recently Bobby had asked if they'd be interested in part-time work all year long. As much as Hestie enjoyed the horses, she had too much going on during school, especially with her fashion and make-up channel on Youtube. And Hermie had never developed an interest in riding.

Lynn had worked for the Sterns regularly until club volleyball had taken over her life four years ago.

"That's not why we're here," Hermie said. "Our parents are missing."

"Clifford said that Phobos and Deimos took them," Hestie added.

"And no one will answer our prayers," Hermie said.

"Oh, no." Bobby put his hands on his hips. "Why would Ares's sons take your parents?"

"We were wondering if you would ask him," Hermie said.

"Please?" Hestie bit her lip to keep back her tears.

"Of course, I will. But I don't know if it will do any good." Bobby closed his eyes and bowed his head. "Ares, if you can hear me, and if our friendship ever meant anything to you, please help me out. Than and Therese have gone missing, and Clifford says your boys took them. Can you tell me what's going on?"

Hestie looked around anxiously, half-expecting Ares to show up.

Bobby opened his eyes, and when nothing happened, he said, "Come on, Ares. You're like a brother to me. Can't you spare one dang minute from your busy schedule? One *minute*?"

Hestie flinched when the god of war appeared beside Bobby.

"What happened to our parents?" Hermie asked.

Ares narrowed his eyes and looked down at them, his short red hair the same color as Hestie's and standing in the wind like a ball of fire.

"They've been taken to Mount Olympus," he said.

***

Therese blinked, unable to believe that she and Than were back on Mount Olympus. Phobos and Deimos, who looked so young to Therese—the same age as her children—had placed magical cuffs on her and Than's wrists and ankles, and they stood in the center of the great hall, surrounded by the gods. Therese studied their grim faces. Only Poseidon, Hades, and Than's siblings weren't there.

Persephone cried out to Zeus, "Must you treat them like criminals?"

Demeter attempted to comfort her daughter, but Persephone pulled away, approaching the center of the room to stand by her son. Demeter took Hecate by the hand and frowned.

"It's for the safety of all," Zeus commanded from his throne.

"We're no threat to you," Than said, his eyes wide.

"Please," Therese appealed to Zeus. "What have we done to deserve this?"

"Nothing," Athena said from Zeus's right. "You've done nothing to deserve this."

Athena's gray eyes were blazing, and her dark hair hung around her shoulders. She wasn't wearing armor today, but she appeared ready to fight—for what, Therese wasn't sure.

"It's an unfortunate and necessary evil," Zeus said.

"Why?" Than asked.

Therese noticed that Hermes couldn't even look at her, and both Persephone and Aphrodite were in tears. Apollo kept clenching his jaw, as if he would say something but couldn't. And the face of Hephaestus was so red, Therese thought he might explode with anger. Only Hera was smiling.

It was Artemis who approached them. "My brother had a vision concerning your twins. He saw them with Prometheus."

Hades, Hypnos, and Jen arrived, and everyone turned to Hades, whose face was even redder than that of Hephaestus.

"What's the meaning of this?" Hades demanded. "Why are you holding my children captive?"

"Leverage," Hera replied with a cruel smile.

"My father believes that Than's kids will lead us to Prometheus," Ares, who stood at Hera's left, explained matter-of-factly.

"And taking Than and Therese as our prisoners ensures their cooperation," Hera added.

Therese met Jen's look of shock and horror. Her mouth had fallen open, her brown eyes wide with fear. Therese knew her best friend would do anything to help her, but there didn't seem to be anything she could do about this.

Tears fell from Therese's eyes. She'd tried so hard to protect her kids, and here she was helpless to save them.

She glared at Zeus. "You didn't have to resort to this! We would have done anything to serve you! You're our king!"

Zeus frowned. "Dear, Therese. I hope you understand that I can't afford to take any chances. My worst nightmare is on the horizon. *Our* worst nightmare."

"Always so impulsive and bull-headed!" Hades accused. "Why couldn't we discuss our strategies civilly? What happened to your promise of democracy?"

"We're in a state of emergency," Zeus said calmly. "And I don't know who my allies are. You can hardly blame me for wanting to take extra precautions."

Ares whispered something to his mother and vanished.

Poseidon burst through the front door. "What did I miss?"

Hades caught him up and then strolled across the floor to Zeus's throne. "Why must *my* family always pay for *your* sins?"

"Aren't we family, too, brother?" Zeus said with narrowed eyes. "And I committed no sin to bring this on. I was tricked."

"Like Persephone was tricked when Melinoe was conceived?" Hades said brazenly.

"Watch your tone," Zeus warned. "I am still your king. You wouldn't be here if I hadn't rescued you from our father. None of you would!"

But Hades didn't back down. "When Metis was freed, you lost any ounce of wisdom you ever possessed."

"How dare you!" Zeus bellowed.

"How dare *you*!" Hades shouted back. "This act against my children, this is an act of war!"

"If you lift one finger to sabotage me, brother, I won't hesitate to kill them," Zeus said, pointing to Than and Therese.

Hades turned his back on Zeus and looked at Therese and Than. Therese was trying not to cry, but she was *so angry,* and she felt *so helpless.*

Through her tears, she noticed a look exchanged between Hades and Poseidon. It was brief and nearly unreadable, but she was sure it meant something.

"When will you release my children?" Hades spun around to face Zeus.

"After I've returned Metis to my belly, along with her son."

Therese glanced at Athena. The goddess's face had paled.

***

Hermie waited for Ares to explain and then said, "We have no idea how to find Prometheus. Do you?"

"If I did, we wouldn't need *you,*" the god of war replied.

"Do you have a photo of him?" Hermie asked. "Hestie could post it to her Youtube channel and ask if anyone has seen him."

"What's a Youtube channel?" Ares asked.

"It's like television," Hestie said. "That's actually a great idea, Hermie. I have over five hundred thousand followers all over the world, and each of my videos gets over a million views. Maybe someone has seen him."

"And I can hack into all the government data bases to see if there's a match," Hermie added. "He may be living under another alias."

"I don't have a photograph," Ares said. "Prometheus went into hiding before photography was invented."

"Oh," Hermie said. "Right."

"What about Hecate?" Hestie suggested. "Couldn't she do a location spell or something?"

"Now, *that's* a good idea," Ares said. "I wonder why she didn't think of it herself."

Hestie's face paled. Hermie didn't have to read her mind to know she was worried she'd gotten their friend in trouble. Maybe Hecate hadn't offered to help locate Prometheus for a reason.

"I've got to get back to Mount Olympus," Ares said to Bobby.

"Thanks for coming," Bobby said, shaking the god's hand.

"Sorry it wasn't to deliver better news." Ares turned to the twins. "And your parents are safe, I assure you. Zeus doesn't want to hurt them, or you."

"So, he doesn't want us *dead?*" Hermie asked.

Ares lifted his brows. "Of course not. Did someone tell you that?"

"No," Hestie said. "We're just scared."

"Zeus doesn't want to kill you. He just wants your help. He won't hurt your parents, either, unless you or anyone in your Underworld family makes him your enemy. And I'm sure that's not going to happen, right?"

"Right," Hermie said.

"Hecate will be free to talk to you soon," Ares said. "Zeus has declared us in a state of emergency, and all the gods are with him now."

"That's why no one else answered our prayers," Hestie murmured.

"Don't do anything foolish," Ares warned. "Hunt down Prometheus. Nothing else. Don't go to the Underworld to solicit help there. Don't try to rescue your parents. That's a sure way of getting them killed."

Ares vanished.

CHAPTER FOUR

Hecate's Spell

With reluctant promises from Bobby not to tell anyone what Ares had said, Hestie left the Sterns' ranch and headed home with her brother to figure out what to do next.

Their animals were eager to hear what had happened, so after Hestie and Hermie filled them in and consoled them as best as they could, they sat around the living room together trying to come up with a plan.

Hestie hugged one of the pillows from the couch and tried her best to keep from crying. She had to be strong for the animals. Kitty was already a mess.

"Are you sure we shouldn't talk to Grammie and Gramps?" Hestie asked her brother. "Maybe they can help us."

Hermie sat in the armchair closest to the fireplace. "Help us how? They don't have powers. It'll just worry them and make our situation worse."

"How can it get worse?" Hestie asked.

"We're going to have to leave home. You know that, right? Prometheus isn't going to come knocking on our door."

"I know, but…"

"And you really think Grammie and Gramps will be good with that?"

Hestie shrugged. She supposed her brother was right. They wouldn't understand.

"Who's going to take care of us while you're gone?" Noodle asked.

Clifford barked at the poodle. "They've got enough to worry about right now. We'll manage."

"No. Noodle's right," Hestie said. "We're going to have to ask Lynn to help."

"And what are we going to tell her?" Hermie asked. "The truth?"

"I think so," Hestie said. "Hopefully, she can keep a secret."

"Man, this sucks," Hermie complained.

Hestie noticed a few tears escape her brother's eyes.

"I guess the only thing we can do is keep praying to Hecate and hope that she answers," Hestie said.

Hermie headed upstairs.

"Where are you going?" Clifford barked.

"To my computer," Hermie said. "I'm going to find out everything I can about Prometheus."

***

Thanatos sat beside Therese on a couch in Demeter's rooms, with Demeter, his mother, and Hecate. Cubie, the Doberman, and Galin, the polecat, lay at his feet. His father had left in a hurry—Than had no idea why—and his mother was pacing the room. Jen and Hip had spoken to them briefly, promising to find a way out. Meanwhile, Than and Therese still wore the magical cuffs at their ankles and wrists, which prevented them from leaving Mount Olympus, and there were guards on both sides of Demeter's door. Cupid stood on the inside, and Phobos and Deimos guarded the outside. Extra security had also been positioned at the gates of Mount Olympus.

Persephone wrung her hands as she paced. "If only I could return to the Underworld for even a few minutes."

"Quit saying that," Demeter said from where she sat in the corner at her golden table—almost the same gold hue as Demeter's hair. "Our agreement with Hades is ancient and unbreakable."

"But Hecate could go," Persephone said.

"I'm ready to serve, my lady," Hecate said.

"No one can leave without Zeus's permission," Cupid reminded them.

Demeter stood up. "Am I to be a prisoner, too?"

"You can leave anytime," Cupid said. "But you'll have to get Zeus's permission first. He'll want to know where you're going and how long you'll be gone."

"This is ridiculous," Persephone complained. "Does Zeus have my husband on such a leash?"

"Should he?" Cupid asked.

Than wanted to say that if he were Hades, the first thing he'd do is conjure the helm and attempt to communicate with Hermie and Hestie, since the Underworld gods had been forbidden to speak with them. Or, he'd use it to listen in on the conversations of the other gods, to find out who was and was not his enemy.

But he couldn't share these thoughts out loud. He could only pray to his mother and father and hope that his prayers were heard.

Suddenly, Demeter's door opened, and Ares entered.

"Hecate," he said. "Zeus wants a word with you."

***

Hermie was reading an article on his computer screen at his desk when Hestie entered his room, followed by Clifford, Noodle, and Kitty. Hestie plopped onto Hermie's bed, where the animals joined her, Kitty curling up on her favorite spot—his pillow.

"This is impossible," Hestie moaned.

Hermie nearly jumped from his chair when someone else appeared—right beside his desk.

"Don't lose heart." It was Hecate.

Hestie climbed to her feet and threw her arms around the goddess. "I'm so glad you're here! Are our parents okay?"

"Yes. They're fine. They're being kept in Demeter's rooms. They're comfortable and surrounded by family. What about the two of you? I can only imagine how frightened you've been."

Hestie slumped back on Hermie's bed, tears sliding down her cheeks again.

"We're okay," Hermie said.

"Just scared," Hestie said.

"And not really sure what we're supposed to do," Hermie added.

"I'm here to help," Hecate said. "Hello, Clifford."

The goddess leaned over and pet the dogs and Kitty.

"Long time no see," Clifford barked. "How are Cubie and Galin?"

"Sad about all of this, but otherwise well. I'll tell them you said hello."

To Hermie, Hecate was the most beautiful of the goddesses. Her long white and black hair was stunning, and her dark eyes were mesmerizing.

"Are you going to teach us a location spell to help us find Prometheus?" Hestie asked.

"That's exactly what I'm going to do," she said. "I've written everything down on this slip of paper."

"Thank goodness!" Kitty purred.

"The spell is best read over a bright light. It makes the magic more illuminating," Hecate added.

Hermie furrowed his brow. "Can't you stay and perform the spell yourself?"

Hecate mussed his hair and smiled. "It may take you a while to gather all the ingredients."

Hermie blushed at the goddess's show of affection.

"How long?" Hestie asked.

"Weeks, months? I don't know. Most of the items will be easy. You'll need a map of the world, four blue candles, a silver bowl, water, and incense made of jasmine, lotus, thyme, or mesquite."

"We've got a silver bowl," Hermie said. "And a world map."

"Mom's got dried thyme in the pantry," Hestie said. "Will that work?"

Hecate shrugged. "It would be better to buy incense sticks, because they burn slowly. You can find them at the drug store."

"What else do we need?" Hermie asked.

"This is the hard part," Hecate warned. "For the location spell to be accurate, you'll need something that Prometheus has personally touched."

Hestie slumped over and covered her face with her hands.

Hermie lifted a finger in the air. "He touched *you* at some point, didn't he?"

Hecate shook her head. "You can't use a living being."

"Why not?" Hestie asked.

"Because it must be burned in the spell," Hecate said. "And before you ask why I wouldn't sacrifice myself, since I'm immortal, it has nothing to do with being afraid of being burned alive. Believe me. I've experienced that more than once in my lifetime."

"Really? Why?" Hermie asked.

"I traded places with many a witch unjustly sentenced to burn at the stake."

"Oh, my gods," Hestie said. "That's awful."

"And if you used me in this location spell, the magic would point to *my* location, not to Prometheus's. So, you must use a nonliving object for this to work."

Hestie fell back on the bed, her head barely missing the wall behind her. "This is impossible."

"How can we do that, Hecate?" Hermie asked, feeling as hopeless as his sister. "That sounds harder than finding Prometheus himself."

"I have a few ideas," Hecate said. "But none that are easy."

Hermie crossed one leg over the other and sat back in his chair. "We're listening."

"The first torch," Hecate said. "It was a giant fennel stalk given to Prometheus by Aether, who got the fire from Helios."

Hestie sat up. "I thought Prometheus stole the fire from Mount Olympus."

"That's how the story is often told," Hecate said. "But that's not how it happened."

"Anyway," Hermie said, "where can we find the first torch?"

"I don't know," Hecate said.

Hermie thought he was going to be sick. "Okay."

"But Aether might," Hecate said.

"You want us to pray to Aether?" Hestie asked.

Hecate shook her head. "I'll question him and get back to you."

"Wait a minute." Hermie recalled something he'd just been reading in an article. "What if we create an original flame?"

"What are you talking about?" Hestie asked.

"The fire for the torch relay for the Olympics," Hermie explained. "They create an original flame using mirrors, and it's passed from torch to torch. If, for some reason, it goes out, they can't just relight it with a lighter. They create another original flame with mirrors, because they at one time believed the flame came directly from Prometheus."

Hecate seemed to consider it. "That's not a bad idea, but I just don't know, because an original flame comes from Helios, not Prometheus."

Hermie sighed and bit his lip, trying to rein in his frustration.

"But I'll talk to Helios and see what he says," Hecate added.

"What were your other ideas?" Hestie asked.

"Pandora's jar," Hecate said. "Prometheus knew it was a trick and took the jar away from Pandora, but his brother Epimetheus got it back for her."

"Wait. I thought it was a box," Hermie said.

"Bad translation," Hestie put in. "It was a big jar made of clay. Zeus gave it to Pandora and told her not to open it. He knew she wouldn't be able to resist."

"I'm familiar with the story," Hermie said. "But I thought it was a box. Pandora was the first woman, made to bring down mankind after Prometheus gave them fire, right?"

"I hate how women are used as a curse in all the early stories," Hestie complained.

Hecate winked. "You and me both, sister."

"Where's the jar now?" Hermie asked.

Hecate shrugged. "I don't know."

Hestie fell back on the bed again, this time catching Noodle on the leg with her shoulder. Noodle winced and moved over.

"Sorry, buddy." Hestie stroked the poodle. "You okay?"

Noodle licked her cheek. "You just surprised me."

"But maybe Epimetheus knows," Hecate said. "I'll go to the Titan Pit in Tartarus and question him, as well as Aether and Helios. This may take me several days."

"What should we do in the meantime?" Hermie asked.

"Go buy lots of maps, blue candles, and incense sticks," Hecate said.

Hestie sat up again. "Why? I thought we only needed four candles and *one* map?"

"The spell may not work on the first try. It's best to be prepared for the worst." Hecate gave them each a hug. "I'll return as soon as I can."

"Wait. Hecate?" Hermie said. "If you had all these ideas for using the location spell, why didn't you start working on this a long time ago? Why wait until now?"

Hecate's face turned white. "I, I'm not at liberty to say."

The goddess vanished.

Hermie glanced at his sister, whose mouth had dropped open, too.

"That was weird," Hestie said.

***

Hestie and Hermie cooked a frozen pizza for dinner and spent the rest of the day researching—she on her laptop and he on his desktop, but they hadn't come up with any more ideas on where to begin their hunt for Prometheus. Bobby called to check on them, and they reassured him that they were fine, for now. He made them promise to call him if they needed anything—anything at all.

That night, Hestie tried her best to get some rest. Between the dogs whining in their sleep, the restless pacing of her rats in their cage, and her own bad dreams, the night was miserable.

The next day, she went downstairs to let the dogs out and to eat a slice of cold leftover pizza. She gave the dogs their kibbles and Chidori her seed and water. She checked on Jewels in her sandbox and turned the heat lamp back on. Then she went upstairs to Hermie's room, where he was bent over his own screen, with Kitty in his lap.

"Let's try the spell with your idea of the original flame," she said.

He looked up from his computer. "Hecate said she didn't think that would work."

"What have we got to lose?"

He bit his lip. "I guess we could make a supply run and give it a try."

Hestie frowned. Hermie wasn't yet a licensed driver. He'd had no interest in learning. Hestie had a learner's permit but still needed more practice.

Then Hestie said, "Desperate times call for desperate measures, I guess. Come on. I'll drive."

"We could ask Bobby to go for us," Hermie suggested.

"Let's not bother him over something this simple," Hestie said. "Let's wait until we really need him."

Clifford begged to go along for the ride, but Hestie told him he needed to stay in case Hecate came looking for them. Plus, he was the only one she trusted to watch over the other animals when no human was at home.

***

Hermie was terrified in the passenger seat of their mom's old Lamborghini as Hestie slowly backed out of the garage and down their long, curvy driveway. His hands hurt from clenching his fists so hard that his knuckles had turned white. He wouldn't say it out loud, but this may very well be the most dangerous part of his and his sister's path to fulfilling their destiny.

Once she was on the road and heading toward Lemon Dam, she slammed on the brakes, throwing them both forward against their safety belts.

"What the heck?" he asked her before using his inhaler.

"Sorry," she said. "I thought I saw a cat on the road, but it's just a rock."

"Maybe we should call Bobby," Hermie said.

"No, it's okay. I got this."

Hermie was glad when they had bought their supplies and were safely back home. Finally, his heart could slow back down to its normal pace and he could breathe without an inhaler.

They took the slip of paper Hecate had given them with the spell written on it and carried the rest of the ingredients to the table on their back deck. Noodle and Clifford followed, but Kitty didn't want to be anywhere near fire.

Hestie lit the incense with a lighter and put it in a jar, smoking end up. Then she took the paper with the spell written on it and read aloud:

Light four blue candles and place them at each cardinal point around a silver bowl, filled three-quarters with clear water.

Hestie flicked the lighter and lit the four blue candles, which she'd placed around the silver bowl.

Then she read:

Burn incense made of jasmine, lotus, thyme, or mesquite, and allow the smoke to wash over the bowl.

Hestie used her palms to manipulate the smoke from the incense so that it passed over the bowl of water. Then she read:

Place an object, or part of an object, once touched by Prometheus over the flame of the candle at the northern point, until the object catches fire. Then, using the flame from the burning object, set fire to a world map.

Hermie used a magnifying glass to direct the light of Helios onto a scrap of paper.

Once it caught fire, he said, "An original flame."

He took the original flame and held it to the world map until the map caught fire. "Now what?"

Hestie read:

Drop the object and the burning map into the bowl of water.

Hermie bent his brows. "Are you sure?"

"That's what it says."

Hermie put the last bit of the scrap of paper with the original flame and the burning map into the bowl. He was surprised when the map continued to burn.

"Now what?" he asked.

Hestie read:

When the flames die, stir the water in the bowl clockwise with your finger four times, and ask the water to reveal the location of Prometheus.

Hermie bent over the bowl and watched the map shrivel down to a very small scrap before the flames ceased and there was nothing but smoke coming from the bowl.

"Isn't the water going to be hot?" he asked, not wanting to burn his finger.

"Let me do it."

Hestie bent over the water and cautiously dipped her finger into it. As she stirred, she said, "Please show me the location of Prometheus."

Hermie was astonished when the only unburnt piece of the world map floated to the surface.

"It's Lemon Reservoir," Hestie said with a huge sigh of disgust. "It didn't work."

"Unless Prometheus is here."

Hestie frowned. "I doubt that. I guess we'll have to wait and see if Hecate has any luck finding an object Prometheus has touched."

Hermie thought over everything they had done, to be sure they'd followed the steps correctly. Then something else occurred to him. "Didn't Hecate say to read the spell over a bright light?"

"Isn't the sun the brightest light there is?"

"Not *under* a bright light. She said *over* a bright light."

"Oh, yeah!" Hestie said. "Let me grab a flashlight, and we can try again!"

CHAPTER FIVE

Double Meanings

Hypnos was relieved when Hecate appeared in Hades's main chamber to report on the twins.

"They're safe," Hecate said.

"Thank goodness." Jen squeezed Hip's hand. Then to Hecate, she said, "What did you find out?"

Hecate studied Hades, who sat on his throne rubbing his beard. He gave her a nod to proceed.

Before she spoke, Pete appeared asking if he could help, but Hades sent him away.

"I can't afford to involve too many in this affair," Hades said after Pete had gone. "Business must go on as usual, so as not to draw any suspicion."

"Suspicion already abounds, my lord," Hecate said.

"Which is precisely why we can't afford to add to it," Hades said. "No one beyond this room must know of my dealings with Metis. Not yet. Now tell us about the twins."

"They're upset, as you might imagine," Hecate said. "But they're doing everything they can to figure out how to find Prometheus."

"You gave them the spell?" Hip asked, feeling hopeful. Maybe the twins would be able to pull through this mess after all.

"Yes. And I told them how to use it, but I don't think they'll try it until after I return."

Hecate went on to explain her plans to talk with Aether about the first torch, to Helios about the original flame, and to Epimetheus about Pandora's jar.

"I want to go with her," Hip said to his father. He had to help, however he could.

"That will require approval from Zeus," Hades said bitterly.

"I'm happy to plead my case to him," Hip said. "I hope I earned his trust and respect after all I went through fifteen years ago, when Uranus nearly swallowed me."

"It wouldn't hurt to try, would it?" Jen asked.

"When you approach Zeus, don't sound too eager, Hypnos. We can't afford to raise any red flags." Then Hades added, "How goes it in the Dreamworld? Have you managed to make contact yet with Poseidon or Athena?"

"Not yet," Hip said. "I may need to send Morpheus on a vacation if I'm to get anywhere. He thinks I question his abilities."

"We can't afford for him to know what we're up to," Hades reminded him. "Especially with him so friendly with Iris."

"I couldn't agree more," Hip said.

Morpheus was too young and enthusiastic to be trusted with such grave information in the Dreamworld.

"Maybe Morpheus could be sent down to help Hermie and Hestie," Hecate suggested.

Jen's eyes widened. "I'm not sure that's a good idea."

It was a great idea, in Hip's opinion, but he didn't want to contradict his wife.

"That's just the thing Zeus would go for," Hades said. "You can use it as a bargaining chip. Tell him you'll give up Morpheus for the opportunity to accompany Hecate when she interviews Aether and Epimetheus."

Hip could tell Jen wasn't happy, but he had to agree with his father. Morpheus would be safe with his cousins, because Zeus wanted them to succeed in finding Prometheus; and, with the Dreamworld all to himself, Hip could seek out allies for his father without his son's interference.

***

Hestie found a flashlight in a kitchen drawer and returned outside to the back deck, where Hermie and the dogs were waiting.

"Give me the paper," she said.

"Let me do it." Hermie held out his hand for the flashlight.

Hestie arched a brow. "Hand it over, bud. I'm the one who got the flashlight."

Hermie rolled his eyes and gave Hestie the spell.

Hestie turned on the flashlight and held the slip of paper over the beam of light.

"There's other writing on here," she said. "Do not read this…"

She stopped. The final words of the sentence were *out loud*.

Hermie leaned over her shoulder.

Do not read this out loud.
Do not discuss this out loud.
Prometheus is not your enemy.

"Why…?" Hestie began and then stopped.

Hermie said nothing but shook his head.

If they couldn't discuss it out loud, how were they supposed to figure out what it meant? And why couldn't Hecate just tell them so? Why would she resort to this secretive method?

Were they being watched by someone who *was* their enemy? If so, who?

Hermie pulled his phone from his front jean pocket.

"Who are you calling?" she asked.

"No one. I'm texting."

"Who?"

Her phone buzzed. She pulled it from her back pocket.
A text from Hermie read:

This is how we'll discuss it.

She smiled and texted back.

Great idea!

Hermie texted:

I wonder why she couldn't tell us this in person.

Hestie texted:

I know. Right? Is someone watching us?

Hermie texted:

I guess so. Leave out details in texts, too. Just in case.

Hestie texted:

We can trust her, can't we?

Hermie texted:

Yes.

Hestie texted:

I guess this means we don't have to be afraid of him whenever we find him.

Hermie texted.

Yeah.

Then he added:

I'm hungry.

Hestie laughed. That was something he could have just said out loud, but she went with it:

Cook another pizza?

He replied:

Sounds perfect.

It was one of the few things they knew how to cook and one of the few things they always had on hand.

While the pizza was in the oven, an idea came to Hestie out of the blue. "Hey, I thought of something!"

"Well? I can't read your mind."

"Yeah. True. So, Pandora was the first woman, right?"

"Right."

"And if Prometheus tried to stop her from opening the jar, he must have touched her, don't you think?"

"Likely. Why? We don't know where Pandora is. How is this helpful?"

"But we *do* know where she is!" Hestie gave her brother a huge grin.

"We do?"

"Lucy! The first woman, remember? We just learned about her. She's supposed to be on exhibit in some museum. Look it up, and we'll go and borrow one of her bones for the spell!" Hestie couldn't hold back her enthusiasm. This plan was going to work.

"Those aren't her real bones," Hermie said. "They're replicas. Those won't do squat."

Hestie suddenly felt very deflated. She fell on one of the chairs at the kitchen table. "What the truck? I thought that was a good idea, bench."

"Quit talking like that. You don't sound cool."

"Shut the truck up. I don't care." She was mad now.

The timer went off for the pizza, but Hestie made no move to get it out of the oven. Her appetite was ruined.

As Hermie put on the oven mitts and opened the oven door, he said, "We might be able to find out where they keep the real bones. They won't be on display. They'll be in a secure lab. Doesn't mean we can't find a way in."

Hestie ran upstairs for her laptop and brought it back down to the kitchen. While the pizza cooled, she Googled Lucy, the first woman.

She scrolled through several articles before she discovered the location. From the *Institute of Human Origins* website, she read: "The 'real' Lucy is stored in a stainless steel safe in the Paleoanthropology Laboratories of the National Museum of Ethiopia in Addis Ababa."

"Ethiopia?" Hermie repeated.

Hestie's smile returned. "We need a plan, bud, because it looks like we're going to Africa."

"Aphrodite's traveling robe!" Hermie said. "Google what time it is in Ethiopia right now."

Hestie laughed. "This is crazy, but okay." She typed *Ethiopia time* into the search bar. "Dude, it's like three in the morning."

"No, that's good! Don't you see? We can travel to Ethiopia while most people are asleep there, scope out the lab from the outside, and come up with a plan. If anyone sees us, we'll disappear."

"You mean right now? Tonight?" Her heart pumped faster in her chest—with excitement and fear.

"Well, we should eat our pizza first," he said before taking a bite.

***

Morpheus stood before his father in the fields of asphodel at a loss. "Are you serious?"

"Absolutely."

Morpheus took a deep breath. "If you want to punish me, can you pick something else?"

"You're not being punished. You'll still have your powers. I thought you'd be happy to spend time with your cousins."

"Helping them hunt for Prometheus isn't exactly a vacation," Morpheus pointed out.

"Okay, you're right. I shouldn't have called it that. I just know from experience that sometimes it's nice to have a break from our regular duties."

Morpheus studied his father. "What's this really about, Pops?"

"I need you focused on their safety. If anything were to happen to them…"

"So, it's true that Zeus wants them dead?" Morpheus scrutinized his father's face.

"What? No! I told you once before."

"But I overheard you talking to Mom about it," Morpheus said. "I know what I heard."

"Listen to me, kiddo. You're way off. Not sure how you got that idea."

"Then why do I need to protect the twins if they're not in danger?"

"They're mortal," his father said. "They're always in danger."

"What about when they're sleeping?" Morpheus asked. "Could I maybe spend some time with Iris then?"

His father laughed. "Oh, Sonny. You're more like me than I ever thought possible."

Morpheus laughed too. "We are a lot alike, aren't we, Pops?"

"That's a fact, Sonny boy."

"So, that's a yes, then? On visiting Iris?"

"Uh, no. Sorry."

Morpheus's smile fell. "Seriously? And what do I do while the twins are sleeping?"

"Watch over them."

***

Hermie looked over his sister's shoulder at her laptop screen, which showed the view using Google Earth of Addis Ababa, Ethiopia and the paleoanthropology laboratory.

Hestie pointed to the screen. "See this park in front, surrounded by that cluster of trees? This is what we should imagine while we're god traveling."

Hermie took a deep breath and slowly let it out. He wasn't feeling very confident about using Aphrodite's robe without at least one of their parents. They'd never god traveled without them.

"What if we screw up and end up lost?" he asked.

"Then we just come straight home and try again."

"And what if we land somewhere dangerous—like in the middle of the sea or in an active volcano or in something even worse, like a prison?"

"Wait. How is a prison worse than a volcano?" she asked.

"An active volcano would kill us instantly. We would *suffer* in a prison."

"Oh, stop, Hermie," his sister laughed. "Stop imaging every terrible scenario. We've got this. It's gonna be fine."

Hermie wasn't so sure he agreed, but he said, "If you say so."

He couldn't help his cautious nature. And he supposed his sister, who was opposite to him in this regard, couldn't help her reckless, impulsive one. He hoped they could meet somewhere in the middle without dying.

"I'll get the robe." Hestie jumped from her chair and then returned in less than a minute from their parents' room, robe in hand.

"I'm gonna have to start calling you Jesse Quick." Hermie laughed.

"Only because you want to be called the Flash."

"True."

"You want a costume so bad, don't you, nerd?"

"You want one too, so shut up."

Hestie grinned as she put on the robe. "I guess this will have to do. Ready?"

"Not really." He looked over at Clifford, who was watching them with a worried look on his face. "We'll be right back, boy, okay? And if we're not, get help from Bobby Holt."

"Stop being negative," Hestie said. "We *will* be right back, guys."

Hestie grabbed Hermie's hand, and before he could blink, he was surrounded by nothing but pressure. He closed his eyes, unable to breathe, and within seconds, the pressure dissipated, and he'd landed on solid ground. He opened his eyes to darkness.

Hestie tapped on the flashlight app on her phone, shining it around the park in front of the Ethiopian museum and lab. "See? No problem."

"We need to find a window, so we can scope out the inside of the museum."

"This way. Come on."

Hermie followed his enthusiastic sister across the damp grass to the dark buildings, illuminated by a single streetlamp.

She pressed her face to the front glass door. "I don't see anyone. We can go right in. Come on."

Before he could warn her about alarms and security cameras, she'd grabbed his hand and traveled them inside, where his worst nightmare came true. The sound of the alarm was earsplitting. He grabbed her hand and traveled them out, but he hadn't thought it all the way through. What was his destination? The only thing he could think of was the palace in the Underworld.

And, boom, he fell on his knees from the sudden shift of pressure, and from his sister frantically pulling at him.

"What have you done!" she accused.

"Me? You're the one who jumped right in without even thinking and almost got us killed!"

"What's this about?" Hades asked from his throne. "Why have you come here?"

"It was an accident," Hermie explained. He'd never seen his grandfather so angry.

"Leave immediately," Hades said. "Zeus will suspect..." He stopped, crossed the room, and stood before them. "Listen to me quickly. Do not discuss this with Morpheus. We don't want him to leak anything to Iris by mistake."

Hermie was confused.

"Discuss what?" Hestie asked before Hermie could.

"I want you to find Prometheus," Hades said, "but I don't want you to lead Zeus to him."

Hermie's mouth fell open. "But..."

"Why not?" Hestie asked.

"There's no time to explain," Hades said.

In the next instant, Hermie found himself standing in his driveway in Colorado beside his sister, who had the same look of confusion on her face that he was sure he wore on his own.

***

Therese had just returned from using Demeter's facilities when the door burst open, and Zeus stormed inside.

"Why did the twins travel to the Underworld?" he demanded of Than, who sat, dumbfounded on Demeter's couch. "I forbade it! They disobeyed me!"

"I don't know what you're talking about," Than said.

"Did they have a clandestine meeting with Hades?" Zeus accused.

"I doubt it was meant to be clandestine," Therese said as she joined Than on the couch, trying to hide her trepidation.

"Hades has that palace warded," Zeus pointed out. "It's impossible for me to see what transpires in his realm, which is why the twins are forbidden from going there."

"I'm sure this was just some misunderstanding," Than said.

Therese glanced at her husband's worried face. "I bet they were attempting to god travel."

"Yes," Zeus said. "They went to Ethiopia, looking for Pandora's remains to use with Hecate's location spell."

"That was smart," Than said.

"They traveled into a high-security laboratory and sounded off the alarms," Zeus said.

"Oh," Therese said. "Not so smart."

"I'm sure they panicked," Than said. "I can't imagine that Hermie and Hestie would intentionally disobey you, Lord Zeus."

"Were they in the Underworld long?" Therese asked.

Zeus shook his head. "Hades had the grace to send them back home immediately."

"Then you have nothing to worry about. I'm sure of it," Than said.

"I wish *I* was sure, too, Thanatos," Zeus muttered as he left the room.

Therese turned to Than. "I hate not being there with them."

"I know. Me, too." He stroked her hair.

"We gave up our immortality to protect them, and now we're stuck up here on Mount Olympus anyway."

Than leaned in and gently kissed her. At least they were together, she thought, as she clutched his hair in her fists and pressed her mouth harder against his. She couldn't imagine trying to endure the worry and the fear without him.

"I love you," she said against his lips.

Persephone burst into the room wearing a gleeful smile. She was followed by Cubie and Galin.

Than and Therese sat up.

"Good news?" Therese asked, trying to hide her embarrassment as she combed Than's disheveled hair back into place.

"Zeus is sending Morpheus to watch over Hermie and Hestie!"

"What?" Than asked. "Really?"

"I wonder why," Therese said. "Maybe he feels bad for yelling at us."

"Hip was just here," Persephone explained. "It was his idea—or maybe Hecate's. I don't know which. But isn't that wonderful?"

"Hecate's," Cubie said.

"Morpheus will have his powers?" Than asked. "He'll go as a god, right?"

Persephone nodded. "This must bring you some comfort, doesn't it, my son? I can't bear to see you so miserable."

"Yes, it does. Thanks, Mother."

Persephone kissed Than on the cheek and gave Therese her brilliant smile. "I'm going to sleep for a while. I need a few more words with Hip. I'll see you two later."

So, Hip was taking over the Dreamworld. Of course, he would, Therese thought. But something else occurred to her as Cubie and Galin settled on the floor at her feet. Maybe there was another reason, other than helping Hermie and Hestie, that Hip wanted Morpheus in the Upperworld. Unfortunately, she couldn't risk discussing her suspicions with Than on Mount Olympus, but she hadn't forgotten the look that had passed between Hades and Poseidon, and she couldn't help but think that something dangerous was afoot.

***

Morpheus flew up into the bright sky toward Iris's rainbow. He hadn't asked his father's permission to say goodbye to her on his way to see the twins, but, as he'd often heard his mother say, sometimes it's better to ask for forgiveness later.

Iris emerged from the high arch of colors, pitcher in hand.

"Hey, there, gorgeous," Morpheus said.

She didn't look at him but fled up toward the clouds. "I heard you were leaving us."

"Already?" He chased after her. "Wow. Word travels fast."

"Who's going to bother and annoy me while you're gone?" she asked, still not looking at him as she emptied her pitcher into the clouds.

He took her by the shoulders and turned her to face him. "I knew it. You're in love with me. Just admit it."

She smiled her cute, sweet, beautiful smile, and his heart melted. "I'm still thinking about it."

"Ah, now you're just lying to yourself."

She broke away to take her empty pitcher down to the sea below. Like a puppy, he followed.

"All right, then," he said, when she'd said nothing more. "Goodbye, Iris."

She looked up at him. "Moonflower."

It took him a minute to figure out what she'd meant. "Oh, really? I never would have pegged you for a nighttime bloom lover."

"They keep the dark side of the earth illuminated with their reflection of moonlight," she said sweetly. "That's what I love about them."

Morpheus wanted to kiss her so badly that he could taste it. They hadn't had their first kiss yet, and he didn't want to rush it, but who knew when he'd see her again?

He closed his eyes and leaned in but was met with resistance. He opened his eyes to find her index finger pressed against his lips.

"When you come back," she said.

He smiled. "You're gonna make me wait for it, huh?"

"Maybe it will hurry you along." She flashed him a smile before she flew away with her full pitcher, back up into the clouds.

"I knew she loved me," he whispered to himself.

Then he took off to Colorado to find his cousins.

CHAPTER SIX

Subterfuge

Hestie followed her brother into the house and removed the traveling robe. "You could have gotten Mom and Dad killed. Ares said…"

"I didn't do it on purpose."

She sank onto the sofa. "I know. Sorry."

A moment later, her phone buzzed. It was a text from Hermie.

How do we do what he asked?

Hermie didn't have to use names for her to know what he meant. She had the same question: How were they supposed to find Prometheus without leading Zeus to him?

I have no idea.

Hestie had barely hit send when there was a knock at the door, followed by, "It's me, Morpheus. Can I come in?"

He was the only god they knew that knocked when he visited, which was usually only a few times a year, plus holidays.

Hermie ran to the door and opened it. "Hey, Morpheus! I'm glad you're here!"

Clifford and Noodle greeted him as well. Kitty stayed on her pillow on the couch. Chidori chirped from her cage, and Jewels peeked over the edge of her sandbox.

"Hey!" Morpheus said in his friendly way.

Hestie stood up. "Do you know if our parents are okay?"

He shrugged. "As far as I know. I guess my dad would have told me if they weren't before he sent me here."

"*Sent* you?" Hermie asked.

Morpheus gave them a huge grin. "Check out your guardian angel. Huh? Yah?" He unfolded his wings and turned in a slow circle, showing himself off.

Hestie frowned. "But I thought this was supposed to be *our* destiny—me and Hermie's."

"No, this is great," Hermie said. "With his help, good stuff could happen, like us not dying."

"I agree!" Clifford barked.

"I told you," Hestie sneered. "We *aren't* gonna die."

"Actually, the prophecy regarding our destiny was never clear about that," Hermie pointed out.

"Guys!" Morpheus interrupted. "Guys, guys, guys! Please! Is this how it's going to be? The two of you bickering the whole time? My dad told me that Zeus is *not* trying to kill you. Let's have some fun!"

"This is serious, Morpheus," Hestie warned. "Our parents' lives are still on the line."

"I have to agree with Hestie on this," Hermie said. "This isn't about having fun. It's about saving our parents and fulfilling our destiny. It's serious stuff, man."

Hestie wanted to add that it had become even more serious now that they'd been warned by Hades to keep Zeus from following them. She still had no clue how they'd manage that. It wasn't like they had the helm of invisibility.

And she also wondered why Hades would ask such a thing. Wasn't Zeus their king?

"Well, at least you agree about something," Morpheus said. "Where do we start?"

"What?" Hermie glanced at Hestie. "We thought you were here to tell *us* that."

"No, man. I'm here to follow your lead."

Hestie told them their plan to find Pandora and how it had backfired. "We need to go back to Africa. We need to find a way into that museum without triggering the alarm."

***

Hypnos flew along the colorful spectrum of the Dreamworld, searching for Athena. He sensed she was sleeping, and that didn't happen often enough for him to squander this chance.

He found her in a dream in which she was besting Poseidon at a foot race over some nameless hills at Delphi. Poseidon, of course, was only a figment, and he was losing.

Athena boasted, "You need to spend less time in the water and more on land, uncle! You're losing your edge!"

Hypnos remained on the sideline, invisible to the gray-eyed goddess, as he manipulated the figment to pull ahead.

"Not as slow as you think, wise one!" the figment, as Poseidon, gloated.

Athena's face darkened, and she picked up her pace. Hip transformed the figment into Metis's likeness and had her turn to face her daughter.

Athena came to a halt. "Mother? Is that really you?"

"Hello, Athena."

Athena's eyes were wide, her jaw open. Then her lips turned up into a smile of glee as she embraced her mother. Before the figment could say another word, however, Athena's brows furrowed.

Hip worried the goddess of wisdom was going to call him out.

"Mother, where have you been? I've searched for you for years—for *fifteen* years. I've been mad with worry!"

Hip sighed with relief.

"I'm sorry, darling."

"And you took my shield, didn't you? It had to be you!"

Hip wasn't sure if Metis *had* taken the shield, but he commanded the figment to go with it.

"Yes, dear," the figment said. "For good reason."

"Why would you do this to me? Abandon me when I had only just saved you from Zeus's belly? You'd been out not a year when you left me."

Tears had formed in Athena's eyes. Hip created a similar expression on the face of the figment playing her mother.

"I'm sorry, darling," she said again. "I didn't abandon you. I'm trying to save you—all of you—from a cruel, selfish leader."

"Are you referring to my father?" Athena's face paled.

"Yes, darling. You know how he mistreated me—both of us—when he swallowed me."

"But you loved him, remember?" Athena pointed out. "You didn't want to come out when we bound Zeus to set you free."

"I'd been traumatized, my darling. It was not easy to accept my freedom. I was frightened. But it didn't take long for me to wake up and realize how I'd been victimized—how both of us had been abused by the very god who should have protected us."

"It was a defensive move on his part," Athena said. "He wanted to protect the crown."

"At our expense," the figment said. "His crown came first."

"Do you blame him for that?"

"Yes. And you should, too."

Athena frowned.

"You excuse far too much when it comes to your father," the figment added. "He turned you to stone and planned to give you a forgetting potion using black magic so you'd forget about me, remember? Poseidon took you prisoner in that underwater contraption—that tube surrounded by electric eels."

Athena bowed her head. "I haven't forgotten."

"But you've forgiven," the figment said. "And I haven't. I can't. What Zeus did to us was inexcusable. And he's done other horrible things to others. Consider what he did to Hades and to his family."

"Hades has forgiven him, too," Athena said.

"Are you certain?" the figment asked.

Athena blanched. "Why do you ask such a thing?"

"What would you say if I told you that I hope to solicit Hades's support?"

Athena's face went from white to red. "Support in what, Mother? In dethroning Zeus?"

"I didn't agree with Uranus's ways, with the mortal lives he carelessly destroyed, with what he did to Aether, and with what he was prepared to do to Hypnos, but he opened a door of opportunity for us."

"You really mean to do this?" Athena's jaw had dropped open, and her eyes were wide with fear.

"I have a son—Zeus's son—and he's destined for greatness. He's a good boy, unlike his father. He's not ambitious or proud. He doesn't want to be a king. He doesn't care about power."

"What does he care about?" Athena challenged.

"Justice. Equality. An end to pain and suffering. The moral good."

Athena's hands became fists at her sides. "Please don't make me choose, Mother."

"It's too late. What's done is done. And it began with that cruel act of your father's. Do you choose him over me? Do you choose impulsive, selfish tyranny over justice and wisdom?"

Athena covered her face and wept. After a long moment of inconsolable crying, she wiped her eyes and said, "No. No, I don't. I choose justice and wisdom, Mother. I choose you."

***

"What time is it in Ethiopia?" Hermie asked Hestie.

She went to her laptop and searched it up. "It's almost 5:00 p.m."

Hermie felt a nudge of panic. "We better hurry. The museum may be closing soon."

"What?" Hestie asked. "I thought you said we should go at night, when no one's there."

"That was to scope the place out," Hermie said. "And now, thanks to you, we know there's an alarm system. We'll have to go during business hours."

"So, what's the plan?" Morpheus asked.

"We'll use the crown of invisibility," Hermie said after swallowing the lump in his throat. He wasn't looking forward to this mission.

Hestie threw her arms around his neck. "Great idea! Why didn't I think of that?"

"Are you sure about this?" Clifford barked.

"You really don't need the crown with me along," Morpheus pointed out. "With me by your side, you'll be invisible."

"That's the thing," Hermie said through a dry throat. "We're going to have to split up."

"I don't like the sound of that!" Chidori chirped.

***

Even though Hip knew that it had been Uranus, and not Aether, calling the shots fifteen years ago, when Hip had been trapped in Hephaestus's old trick chair, it still gave him the willies to see the god of the upper air again. His cave hadn't changed. There was still the couch and the bed with the table in between, with bowls of olives and nuts and a bottle of wine. The god seemed melancholy, and Hip felt rather sorry for him. When Hecate asked Aether about the first torch, the old god shrugged and admitted that only Prometheus knew where it was, if it still existed.

Strike two. Helios had already warned them that using an original flame for the location spell was not likely to work. At least their visit to him hadn't been as futile as their call on the god of the upper air. The sun god had vowed to watch over Hermie and Hestie as best he could in their hunt for Prometheus. And he'd promised that his sister, Selene, would guard them whenever the twins were on the dark side of the world.

Hip had a feeling it wasn't devotion to Zeus that had prompted Helios to make such promises. There had never been much love between the sun Titan and the king of the Olympians. No, Hip thought. Something else was going on. Helios had always loved Prometheus. And perhaps he loved Metis, too.

Now Hip and Hecate headed back to the Underworld, to the Titan Pit, to question Epimetheus.

Entering the Titan Pit was not something that happened often, and, when it did, it was a major production involving lots of powerful gods. Hades was the only one who could sanction it, and he wouldn't do it without all three Furies present and at least one other god as powerful as he. In this case, it was Poseidon who'd been called upon to help.

The god of the sea was late, as usual, but no one dared complain, since it was as a favor to them that he was there at all.

"Does Zeus know what we're doing?" Poseidon asked Hades after the horses and chariot had been attended to and the gods were making their way along the Phlegethon into Tartarus.

"He knows we're doing all we can to find Prometheus," Hades replied.

Hip and Hecate took up the rear, with his sisters and their familiars in the middle. Tizzie glanced back at him with an arched brow. She wasn't aware of the goings on between their father and Metis, or of the plan to recruit Poseidon, but he could tell she suspected it. He only hoped his father's ambitions weren't as obvious to the rest of the pantheon.

When they reached the pit, an awkward chill crept down Hip's back. Almost every deity behind that door wanted to kill him and his family. It hardly seemed like the best place to visit.

***

As Hermie entered the national museum in Ethiopia beneath the protection of the invisibility crown, he still wasn't sure which job was the scariest—his or his sister's.

He waited in the lobby for Hestie to do her thing. He imagined she was screwing up the courage. He watched her, standing alone at the ticket counter. Except for the woman on the other side of the counter, the lobby was empty of people.

That was no good. They'd been counting on a bit of a crowd.

Fortunately, a few minutes later, after Hestie had purchased her ticket, a group of elementary-school-aged children in matching t-shirts swarmed into the lobby from the main exhibit hall. Now would be the perfect time for Hestie to make her move.

Come on, sis, Hermie thought. You can do it.

The school kids were almost to the exit when Hestie cried, "Help me! That man took off with my little brother! Somebody stop him!" She said it first in English, and then in Amharic, the official language of Ethiopia. When that didn't get people buzzing, Hestie shouted again, this time in another language Hermie understood but didn't know the name of.

The lobby broke into a chorus of chaos. Two security guards made their way toward Hestie. It was Hermie's turn to move.

"Lock the doors!" one of the guards ordered.

Hermie held the crown securely on his head as he made his way through the aggravated crowd, following the signs to the lab. He'd studied the building's layout online, but his heart was pounding, the blood was running fast through his body, and he could barely breathe much less think. Morpheus followed him.

They were walking fast—well, technically, Morpheus was flying, but they were moving against the flow of traffic, as everyone else made their way to the lobby to learn what was going on. There weren't many people, but the rooms and passages were small and dark. Hermie noticed another security guard among them. He hoped this meant the lab was left unguarded.

They descended two flights of steps and had to negotiate through several exhibits before they reached the lab, which was labeled "Archives." They found the door locked. Luckily, Hermie had Morpheus to god travel him inside—Hestie was wearing Aphrodite's traveling robe, just in case she needed to bail.

Hermie found a series of cabinets and drawers, some labeled and some not. He couldn't find anything clearly marked as the bones of Lucy. Morpheus searched, too. There was one person sitting at a desk eating sausages, but he didn't notice anything unusual, so far.

In the back of the room, Hermie found a deep stainless steel safe. He motioned to Morpheus to open it. When they opened the door, they found a drawer containing what Hermie thought *had* to be the bones of Pandora. There was no other collection of bones in the room that he could find in a large enough quantity to belong to the first human. He searched for a label—anything to confirm—and finding none, decided to tuck one of the finger bones into his pocket. Time was running out. He worried for his sister.

He gave Morpheus a nod, and the god of dreams took his hand and god traveled them outside. Hermie waited in the garden, clinging to the crown, full of relief and happiness that he'd made it out okay, and hoping all would go as planned for Hestie.

***

Hip took a deep breath as Hades unlocked the adamantine chains and unbolted the ten locks on the door to the Titan Pit. Then Hades conjured the helm and disappeared beneath its protection as he cranked the handle and pushed the door in, which was an improvement. The door used to swing out, making the gods on the outside more vulnerable to a deluge of angry prisoners.

Poseidon stood with his trident, ready to paralyze any offending prisoner bent on escape. The Furies stood with their familiars behind him, creating a barricade in the narrow passageway. In front of Poseidon, Hip stood behind Hecate and followed her inside.

Not much of the Phlegethon flowed in this deepest pit of Tartarus, but enough to create shadows. Hip was surprised that the prisoners hadn't clamored toward them in a massive stampede of angry reproach. Instead, they appeared bored, depressed, and barely alive at all as he followed Hecate down the narrow winding passage into the pit.

Hip hardly recognized the prisoners, though he knew every one of them there. Cronos lay on his side, picking his nails. Atlas seemed to be staring at nothing. Most of them lay with their eyes closed, praying for sleep. Hip had never granted it to them, but he did so now—whatever it took to keep them docile.

Only Uranus got up and approached them with a barrage of filthy insults. They ignored him and moved on.

They found Epimetheus lying on his back staring blankly at the dark walls of the pit.

Hecate stepped toward him and called him by name.

The Titan didn't move. Hecate called to him again. Slowly, the Titan sat up and looked first at Hecate and then at Hip. His brows lifted, and he asked, "To what do I owe the pleasure?"

"Pandora's jar," Hecate said. "Do you know where it is?"

"Of course, but why do you care?" he asked.

"We need it," Hecate said.

Epimetheus laughed, cursed them, and lay back down on the rock.

"Tell us and I'll put you in the deep boon of sleep," Hip offered. "I'll even give you sweet dreams for good measure."

The Titan sat up. Tears had come to his eyes, and he looked at Hip with what could only be described as longing.

Then Epimetheus wiped his eyes and said, "No."

"What do you care if we find the jar?" Hecate asked him.

"I care nothing for the jar," the Titan replied. "But I can't bear to give satisfaction to my captors."

"Epimetheus!" Hades's voice exploded from beneath the helm, causing Hip to jump. "Tell us, or the Furies will beat it out of you."

Epimetheus's mouth twitched and his eyes widened in fear. He turned to Hip and said, "On second thought, perhaps I'll take your deal."

Hip gave him a grim smile. "Tell us, and I'll fulfill my part of the bargain immediately."

At that moment, several of the Titans who hadn't gone to sleep climbed to their feet and headed in their direction.

"Don't speak, Epimetheus, you fool!" Menoetius hollered. "Not without bargaining something for the rest of us, or I'll swallow you myself!"

Hip glanced around at the approaching circle of Titans. The space between them thinned, and the pit felt smaller. He looked at Hecate before saying, as calmly as he could muster, "Sweet dreams for everyone. Now go to sleep!"

Immediately, the army of raging Titans settled down and found a spot of rock on which to rest. They didn't fall into the deep boon of sleep as easily and as quickly as a mortal would; but, because they longed for it more than anything save their freedom, they fell fast enough.

Hip was surprised and felt less afraid as he turned to Epimetheus and said, "You were saying?"

***

Hestie felt like an eternity had passed since she'd entered the national museum in Ethiopia. While two guards searched the building for her supposed little brother and his kidnapper, a third asked the same questions over and over, as if he suspected her. Who was she? Where was she from? Why was she here? Where were her parents? Had she come with anyone else besides her brother? How old was he? What were their names?

She hadn't been as prepared as she had needed to be. She was young, female, and sobbing. She thought she'd have the guards eating out of her hands—but no.

Apparently, there were more than old bones in the collection. Very valuable art and royal regalia was on display. The guard seemed to think she was working with a thief, which was true.

Again, she said, "Please save my little brother. He's only five years old, and he's everything to me!"

And, again, the guard asked, "Why are you here? Where are your parents?"

Finally, Morpheus, in the guise of a five-year-old white boy, ran through the lobby toward her. They threw their arms around each other, putting on a show for the guard.

"Johnny! What happened?" she asked him.

"I don't know! The mean man ran away and let me go!" Morpheus said in a much younger voice.

Hestie had expected the guard to be relieved and happy for their little reunion, but he screwed up his face and told them to follow him.

Morpheus and Hestie exchanged worried glances. Follow him where?

"Now," Hestie said, grabbing her cousin's arm.

They god traveled to the garden outside to look for Hermie.

"Over here!" he said, removing the crown.

The guard from the museum called out to them from the front door, shouting at them to stop.

Morpheus took their arms and god traveled them home. They landed in their living room, where Clifford and Noodle, and even Kitty, jumped for joy.

"Thank the gods!" Hermie said, out of habit.

"You're welcome." Morpheus grinned.

C H A P T E R   S E V E N

Pandora's Jar

Therese sat across from Than at Demeter's table. They were alone, except for Cupid, who was stationed across the room near the door. They still wore the magical cuffs on their ankles and wrists, but she'd gotten used to them and barely noticed them anymore.

They were enjoying a light lunch of cucumber sandwiches, having heard nothing but good things about Hermie and Hestie and how hard they were working to find Prometheus.

"Your mother sounded pretty impressed," Therese said, referring to their conversation with Persephone earlier that day. "She said they had *initiative.*"

"They could have sat around waiting for Hecate," Than said. "It took guts for them to look for Pandora on their own."

"Well, Morpheus was with them."

"Not the first time," Than reminded her.

"True." Therese shook off the memory of Zeus's anger when he'd suspected a clandestine meeting between her children and Hades. She sipped her coffee and tried to keep her anxiety at bay. Everything was going to be okay. Wasn't it?

Aphrodite entered the room, and the look on her face was grave. Therese dropped her sandwich back onto her plate and tried to breathe.

"What's happened?" Than asked.

Aphrodite sat on the chair between them. "Your children are playing a very dangerous game."

"What are you talking about?" Therese asked, afraid of the answer.

Aphrodite slapped a piece of paper onto the table, causing Therese to flinch.

"What's that?" Than asked, looking it over. "Hecate's location spell? So?"

Aphrodite shot a bit of light from her hand to illuminate the backside of the page.

Than squinted at the writing.

"What?" Therese asked. "What is it?" Her heart felt as if it had stopped beating.

Aphrodite glared at her. "Read it yourself."

Than handed the paper over. The goddess backlit the page. New words appeared that hadn't been there before:

Do not read this out loud.
Do not discuss this out loud.
Prometheus is not your enemy.

"Our children can't be blamed for this," Than said. "They had nothing to do with it."

"Perhaps," the goddess said. "As for Hecate, well, she's obviously guilty of treason and will be punished accordingly."

"What's that supposed to mean?" Therese asked. "What punishment?"

"The Titan Pit, of course," Aphrodite said. "But not until after we've tortured her long enough to discover with whom she's collaborating."

"This isn't your style," Than said to his aunt. "You can't mean that."

Therese moaned. "Please have mercy on her, Aphrodite. Give her the benefit of the doubt. Maybe someone forced her."

"There must be an explanation," Than agreed.

"We'll find out soon enough," Aphrodite said. "The Furies are already getting started."

***

Hermie searched the entire house for Hecate's location spell but couldn't find it anywhere.

"You had it last," he said to Hestie. "Where is it?"

"I don't know. I thought I left it here on the table, next to my laptop."

"Should I go and ask Hecate to write it down again for you?" Morpheus offered.

Hermie frowned. He didn't like to bother the gods. He'd learned over the years that even though they lived forever, they were always busy. Conflict, drama, and sometimes even important matters consumed their lives.

"No," Hestie said. "I think I can remember it. Let's just get everything together and give it a try."

They took the candles, the silver bowl of water, and the incense with them to the back deck, where their grandparents were waiting on a branch overhead. Hermie hadn't had a chance to say hello before they tweeted in a frenzy and a panic, asking where Hermie and Hestie's parents were.

"Zeus has them on Mount Olympus," Hestie said, and then she and Hermie explained what had happened.

The two red birds were furious that the twins hadn't told them before.

"We're sorry," Hermie said.

"It's just that we've been doing everything we can to free them," Hestie added. "There's been no time to lose."

"That's no excuse," their grandfather chirped.

"We didn't want to worry you," Hermie finally admitted. "When there's nothing you can do about it."

That didn't go over well either, but Hermie finally turned to his sister, ignoring the chirping as best as he could, and said, "Let's get on with it."

Hermie placed the four candles at the cardinal points around the bowl, and Hestie lit the incense and then the candles.

Then Hestie washed the smoke from the incense over the silver bowl, filled three-quarters with water.

"Give me the bone," Hestie said.

Hermie dug it out of his pocket. His heart was pounding hard, and he prayed a little prayer to Hecate that he'd gotten the right bone.

Hestie held the finger bone to the flame of the candle on the northern point until it caught fire.

"Hand me the map," she said to Morpheus.

He handed it over to her—it didn't matter that it was still folded up—and she put the burning bone close enough to catch it on fire, too. Then she dropped both the bone and the map into the bowl and waited for the flames to die.

"Was it clockwise or counter-clockwise?' she murmured.

"Clockwise," Hermie said. "I remember it was clockwise."

Hestie dipped her finger into the water and, as she stirred, said, "Please show me the location of Prometheus."

A small piece of the map, maybe a square inch at most, popped up to the surface of the water.

Hermie took it from the bowl and squinted in the afternoon light. He didn't want to read it out loud, because of what Hades had said about keeping Zeus from following them, but he knew there was no way to prevent Morpheus from saying it, too. "Seoul. Seoul, South Korea."

Hestie clapped her hands. "I've been wanting to go there! Jinyoung, here I come!"

Hermie rolled his eyes. His sister's obsession with K-pop was annoying.

"I'm joking," Hestie assured him. "Come on, Hermie! I know we'll be too busy looking for Prometheus."

"You're saying that, but do you believe it?" Hermie asked.

Hestie frowned. "You're a jerk."

"Guys! Guys!" Morpheus said. "The spell worked. We should be happy, not fighting."

Hermie decided to come clean. "I'm not a hundred percent sure the spell worked."

Morpheus rolled his silver-rimmed eyes. "Bro! It worked! What are you talking about?"

"I'm not sure if that bone was Lucy's—or Pandora's."

"What?" Hestie's face turned red. "Did you just grab some random bone?"

Hermie felt small. "Kind of. Nothing was labeled. It seemed like the most logical choice, but before we go traipsing off to South Korea, maybe we should be a little surer of ourselves."

Hestie put her hands on her hips. "And how are we supposed to do that, bud?"

"I don't know yet," he said.

But one thing was for sure, Hermie thought. If they were to keep Zeus from following them, they had to think of a way to do the spell without giving away the location it revealed. And they had to do it without Morpheus knowing it.

***

Hip winced as his sisters tied Hecate to their torture table. Zeus bent over them, red-faced, with flaring nostrils and gritted teeth. Hades stood beside him, his jaw set, and Ares stood next to him, appearing calmer than any of them. His sons, Phobos and Deimos, hovered to Hip's right and left, adding to the overall feelings of fear and panic in his chest.

Hecate lay on the table with a blank look on her face, but she spoke to Hip telepathically. "If Zeus suspects we were working together, you won't be able to use the Dreamworld as planned. Act outraged, Hypnos. Spit on me. Do something!"

There was no way on Earth—or on any planet for that matter—that Hip would spit on Hecate. She'd been like a second mother to him. It took every ounce of his strength not to cry as his sisters unleashed their snake hair and transformed into the monstrous avengers of Tartarus.

He wondered how Meg felt as she straddled Hecate with her falcon perched on her shoulder, ready to peck out an eye.

"Tell us why you did what you did," Meg said, though it was without the usual hiss in her voice. "Why did you give a secret message to Than's twins?"

Hecate kept her expression blank.

"Answer the question!" Zeus roared.

Hecate said nothing.

"Why would you betray our king?" Alecto asked, but not in anger.

Hecate remained placid, staring blankly. Hip noticed she was careful to avoid eye contact with his sisters.

"Do it!" Zeus ordered. "Take out her eye!"

Hip couldn't believe that his father was going to allow one of his most loyal friends to be tormented, and it broke Hip's heart that his sisters were the ones being forced to carry it out.

Meg hesitated. "Please, Hecate."

Tizzie cracked her whip and shouted, "Do it!"

Her wolf howled as if in echo.

Hecate prayed to Hip. "*You* do it, Hypnos! You pluck out my eye! Now!"

Hip knew why and hated to admit to himself that it was a good idea. He had to appear on Zeus's side if he was to make any headway in the Dreamworld.

Shaking like a rag doll, Hip rushed to the table, conjured his knife, and, biting hard on his lip, carved out her eye with a trembling hand.

Blood pooled to the socket, and a long chord of nerves dangled like fish bait from it.

Hecate screamed and writhed with pain.

Tears flowed down Hip's cheeks. To cover his sorrow, he shouted, "Traitor!"

Hecate spoke to him telepathically as she moaned in pain. "Now offer the eye to Zeus!"

But when Hip turned to give him the eye, Zeus shook his head and wiped away a tear.

"This brings me no pleasure, Hecate," Zeus said, more calmly than before.

Hypnos got rid of the horrible, disembodied eye by making it disappear. Hecate would regenerate a new one.

At that moment, Hermes appeared beside Hecate, looking as white as a sheep. He bent over her and stroked her black and white hair before turning to his father. "Stop this. I beg of you. She would never betray you."

"But she has, Hermes," Ares said. "We have proof."

Phobos showed him the paper on which Hecate had written her spell. He added light to the back of the page, and the secret message appeared.

"Prometheus is not your enemy," Hermes read. Then he turned to his father. "Of course, she would say that. You know how she loved Prometheus."

"You don't find a secret message to be an obvious act of treason against me?" Zeus shouted, his anger rising.

Hermes turned to Hecate, still stroking her hair. "Did you do it, love? Did you put the message in your spell?"

Hip could see Hecate struggle to maintain her blank expression. For a moment, her mouth twitched into a frown, but she sucked in her lips and said nothing.

"Take out her other eye!" Zeus railed.

Hip could barely contain his anger over what was happening. He dared to glance at his father, who stood emotionless beside Zeus. Hip felt helpless and outraged and was on the verge of giving away their plans to make the violence stop.

Then all the anger he felt toward Zeus for everything he'd done to his family was directed at Hecate when he said, "Speak! Why did you betray our king?"

In his mind, Hecate said, "Good, Hypnos. Well done. Now disintegrate and go find Pandora's jar, and deliver it to the twins."

***

Morpheus wasn't feeling it. The twins had no idea what they were doing, so how was he supposed to help? As he watched Hermie and Hestie bicker yet again over whether they should journey to Seoul, he prayed to his father to let him come home.

He was shocked when his father appeared beside him on the back deck in Colorado.

"Pops!" he cried, as though he hadn't just seen him hours ago.

"Is that what I think it is?" Hermie asked, yawning.

He was referring to a clay pot that Morpheus's father was holding in his arms like a newborn baby.

"Pandora's jar," his father said.

"Where did you…" Hestie sank into a chair and promptly fell asleep.

Hermie crashed onto the deck—literally—and fell asleep at Morpheus's feet.

"You couldn't at least break his fall?" his father asked him.

Morpheus grinned. "He's fine. Can I come home now?"

"Sorry, kiddo. You're needed up here." He handed Morpheus the pot. "Gaia wants this back in one piece, so after you break off a fragment for the spell, be sure to use your powers to put it back together again. Then before you go searching for Prometheus, return this jar to her at Delphi in the cavern beneath the ruins of Apollo's temple, beneath the oracle's perch."

Before Morpheus could ask him why, his father vanished.

"Great," he muttered. Then to the twins, he said, "Wake up, guys," as he set the pot on the deck floor and chipped a tiny fragment from the lid.

Hermie groaned and climbed to his feet, rubbing his shoulder, where he fell. "So where did your dad find Pandora's jar?"

"He said Gaia had it. We have to take it back when we're done, so let's get going on that spell."

Hestie relit the candles—the incense was still burning. "There's another world map on the table by my laptop."

Morpheus god traveled and returned in less than two seconds with the map. He watched on as Hestie put the clay piece to the candle flame.

"Ouch!" she cried, dropping the fragment into the water. "It gets hot. I need some tongs from the kitchen."

Hermie fished the fragment from the bowl. "It won't catch fire while it's wet. Can you break off another piece?"

Morpheus sighed and cracked the lid in half. He handed over the smaller piece as Hestie returned from the house with a pair of tongs.

It seemed to take forever for the lid to catch fire, but when it finally did, Hestie used it to light the map, and then, like before, she dropped them both into the bowl. Their heads nearly bumped together as they bent over the bowl to watch. When the flames died down, Hestie dipped her finger into the water and stirred.

"Please show me the location of Prometheus."

A scrap of the map floated to the surface.

Hermie grabbed it eagerly, looked at it, and then—to Morpheus's surprise—swallowed it.

"What did you do that for?" Morpheus asked.

"Sorry. I'm starving. I don't know what came over me. With our parents gone, we haven't eaten much."

Morpheus remembered what that was like when he was three and four years old, before his parents adopted him. "Bro, let's get you some food."

"What did it say?" Hestie asked before blowing out the candles.

"Um, it said Beijing," Hermie said. "Beijing, China."

***

Hermie held Pandora's jar as Morpheus cupped a hand on his and his sister's shoulders and god-traveled them to Delphi, to the oracle's cave.

It had been close to noon in Colorado, but, here, it was approaching eight p.m. Darkness had fallen, and the ruins of Apollo's temple had been abandoned by the crowds of tourists that usually walked among them during the day. Hermie could recall being a tourist himself not quite a year ago, on another one of those family vacations he'd been forced to take. Luckily, they had god traveled then, too, so he hadn't had to waste countless hours traveling the conventional ways.

Now, as he followed Morpheus and Hestie down the pathway into the underground cavern, his bowels made a strange rumbling sound. He'd eaten too much lunch—all junk they had had on hand—too fast. It hadn't helped that a piece of burnt paper was digesting there, along with the chips, cookies, and questionable milk.

Hermie felt bad about swallowing the piece of map, but how else was he to hide the truth from Morpheus and the other gods? It hadn't said Beijing; it had said Seoul.

Which had surprised him, because it probably meant that he'd found the finger bone of Pandora.

"Can we get a little light, Morpheus?" Hestie asked. "Not all of us can see in the dark."

Morpheus glowed like a lightbulb and continued to lead the way down.

Hermie now had to figure out how to go to Seoul while making Morpheus and the other gods believe they were going to Beijing. At least both cities were in the same direction and relatively close to one another.

"How far down does this cavern go?" Hestie asked.

"I've never been here before," Morpheus said.

Hermie hadn't realized that this was Morpheus's first time down here, too. His chest felt tight, and he needed his inhaler, but he couldn't use it with his hands full.

"Are you sure Gaia is expecting us?" Hermie asked.

"That's what my dad said."

What if Gaia wasn't there, waiting for them? What if, instead, there were snakes, or wolves, or bears? Or what if this was a trap, and there was a monster, like Amphisbaena or Echidna, waiting to eat them?

"Hold up," Hermie said, putting down the jar. He pushed his hand into his jeans' pocket, snagged the inhaler, and brought it to his lips. He took two puffs and tried to breathe. Thankfully, he could get a whole breath. "Okay."

He picked up the jar and followed his sister down the dark path. He could breathe, but now his legs were wobbly.

"I've never met Gaia in person before," Morpheus admitted. "But my dad told me she's the one who released hope from Pandora's jar."

"That was a good thing, right?" Hestie asked.

"Yes," Hermie said. "You see, when Pandora opened it, misery, plague, famine, and disease were let out, but Zeus made her close the jar so people wouldn't have hope."

"That's so mean," Hestie said.

"After Pandora died," Morpheus said, "the jar came to Gaia. She knew what remained in the bottom, so she opened it."

"Was Zeus upset with her?" Hestie asked.

"He was okay with it," Morpheus said. "By then, he'd gotten over Prometheus's betrayal and loved humanity."

"According to legend," Hermie began, "Zeus considers himself a caretaker of mortals."

They continued deeper into the cavern. Hermie looked back and could no longer see the place through which they had entered.

"Ah, Pandora's jar," came a voice from the darkness.

"Are you Gaia?" Morpheus asked. "I haven't had a chance to meet you yet."

"Indeed, I am, Morpheus."

A figure came out of the darkness glowing like an ember. She had long auburn hair, dark brown eyes, and dark bronze skin—almost the same color as Morpheus's.

"These are my cousins," Morpheus began.

"Hermes and Hestia," Gaia said, taking another step closer. "What a pleasure to meet you face-to-face."

"Likewise," Hestie said.

"Aren't you our great-great grandmother?" Hermie asked, feeling better in the presence of the goddess.

"Yes," she said. "And as such, I have some advice for you."

Hermie reached out and handed her Pandora's jar. "That would be awesome, because we have no idea what we're doing."

She took the jar. "Avoid god travel. It's too dangerous. You have enemies watching your every move. Avoid flight, unless you have a chariot. Stay to the land and sea."

Then the goddess and the jar disappeared.

CHAPTER EIGHT

Stuck

Hestie followed Morpheus from the dark omphalos of ancient Greece and was glad when the fresh air of the night greeted her at the mouth of the cave. The stars were bright overhead, and the moon was large. For a second, she thought she saw the moon wink. Hestie blinked. She'd never met Selene. Did the moon Titan even know who she was?

Hermie used his inhaler again.

"Are you alright?" she asked him.

"Not really," he complained. "If we can't god travel, how are we supposed to get home?"

"I don't think you *are* going home," Morpheus said. "Not yet, anyway."

"So now what?" Hestie wondered out loud. "We find a way to Beijing?"

"The sooner we find Prometheus, the sooner your parents are freed," Morpheus put in.

"What about our animals?" Hermie took a second puff from his inhaler. "This could take days—more likely, weeks."

Hestie pulled out her phone. "I'll text Lynn."

"Be careful what you tell her," Hermie warned. "Say we had to go to Mount Olympus for a while."

Hestie tapped out the text. "Good idea." She wished she could send a message to the animals, to let them know she and Hermie were okay.

"Poor Clifford," Hermie said. "He's going to think the worst."

They hiked down the hill toward the small town below. None of them were sleepy, yet, so they decided to keep going.

"Man, do I hate walking," Morpheus said after a while. "Now that I think about it, this is the most I've walked since I've been a god."

"I hate it, too," Hermie said. "But I like running less."

"Can you remember much about your life before?" Hestie asked Morpheus.

"Yeah, but I don't like to think about it."

"Hey, have you ever heard of *The Flash*?" Hermie asked him.

"I've seen the figments take his form," Morpheus said. "And I know he's a fast comic book superhero, but that's about it."

For the next two hours, as they walked downhill from the mountains toward the sea, Hermie recounted all three seasons of *The Flash* TV show, and by the time he was caught up to the most current episode, they had reached the coastal city of Itea.

***

Under the protection of his father's helm, Hypnos god traveled to the Aegean Sea, just outside Poseidon's palace. Because it was heavily warded, he couldn't enter, even beneath the helm, so he waited for several hours until Amphitrite and her court of water nymphs returned from wherever they had gone. He followed them through the palace doors and swam directly to Poseidon's receiving room, hoping to find him before Amphitrite greeted him.

Poseidon sat on his throne speaking to a merman about a pirate ship that had been hijacking vessels in the Atlantic Ocean. Hip gave Poseidon a small dose of slumber, to make the god yawn, and after another few minutes, Poseidon dismissed his subject and announced to his guards that he was going to bed.

When Poseidon went to his bed chamber, Hypnos followed and put the god into the deep boon of sleep. Then he left the palace, glad to be out of water again, and returned home.

Back in the Underworld, where it intersected with the realm of dreams, Hip lay in the asphodel while his projection wandered through the prism of lights, searching for Poseidon. He found him sitting on the bank of the sea eating oysters.

"I've been waiting for you, Hypnos."

Hip blanched, unsure whether to reply. He was hidden, and Poseidon shouldn't be able to sense him. This was not supposed to happen.

"It was no coincidence that I became sleepy after Zeus had your friend tortured."

Hip revealed himself to Poseidon. "She was charged with committing treason."

"I would think you're next."

"If your brothers were to go to war, which would you support?" Hip's heart drummed faster than he wished it to.

"I've always felt loyal to Zeus, because he saved us from our father's belly."

Hip gritted his teeth and wished he had the power to wipe the dream from Poseidon's memory. There was a chance the sea god would forget, but there was no guarantee.

"On the other hand," Poseidon continued, "if the prophecy regarding the son of Metis is to come to pass, I wouldn't mind being on the winning side."

Before Hip could speak further with Poseidon, Hermes tapped him on the shoulder and pulled him from the dream. Hip sat up in the asphodel and squinted at his cousin. "What's wrong?"

"Zeus summons you to Mount Olympus."

Hip sighed. "Wonderful."

***

By the time they reached the harbor in Itea, Hermie was hungry again. They'd passed a bakery on the road next to the Hotel Galini. It was the only shop that appeared to be open this late at night.

There wasn't much activity on the harbor. Besides a beggar curled up on the dock with a foul-smelling blanket, there wasn't a visible soul around. The few ships that were docked were dark and quiet.

"I wonder if we'll be able to find a ride to Beijing," Hestie said.

"Too bad we can't fly," Morpheus said.

The beggar sat up and looked at her. "None of these ferries go that far," he said in English. "You'll have to book a private yacht in Patras."

"Are you sure?" Hermie asked him. "Isn't Patras in the opposite direction?"

"Don't take my word for it," the old man said. "Ask anyone."

"We'll have to wait until morning, anyway," Hermie said to Hestie and Morpheus. "Why don't we grab something to eat at that bakery next to Hotel Galini?"

"Do you have a spare coin for an old man?" the beggar asked.

Hermie fished out his wallet from his back pocket. He didn't have any coins, so he gave the old man two one-dollar bills. "They're American, so I'm not sure if they will help you."

"That's okay. There's a bank next to the bakery. I can exchange these for euros in the morning. Thank you."

"I guess that means we can't eat until morning," Hestie said.

"We may as well go and ask," Hermie said. "Maybe, since it's right by the bank, they'll make an exception."

On the way to the bakery, Morpheus stopped in his tracks.

"What is it?" Hestie asked.

"The duties of the Dreamworld," he said. "They're calling me. Something must be up with my dad."

"What do you mean? You're leaving us?" Hermie asked.

"I have no choice. Sorry, guys." With that, Morpheus disappeared.

"Great," Hermie said, needing his inhaler again. He took a puff.

"We'll be fine," Hestie said. "Come on."

Without Morpheus, Hermie felt less secure about what they were about to do. Could they really manage to sail to Seoul and hunt for Prometheus without him? Hermie prayed to his grandfather Hades, to his Uncle Hip, and to Hecate. He asked for guidance, but even hours later, after he and Hestie had checked into the Hotel Galini for a safe place to sleep, even after they'd gone to the bank for euros so they could pay the baker and the hotel, no guidance came.

He asked the clerk at the hotel if it was true that he and Hestie would have to go to Patras to find a boat that would take them to Beijing.

The clerk said yes in Greek, though he said it would be better to fly. He also said they should take the bus to Patras in one hour from a station down the road.

"I don't have much money left," Hermie told Hestie as they walked to the station. "I have enough for the bus, but not the boat. How can we book a private yacht with no money?"

"Maybe we should god travel," Hestie said.

"No way. It's dangerous. Enemies are watching our every move. We won't be able to save Mom and Dad if we're killed."

"Maybe we can offer to work on the boat in exchange for a ride."

"But we know nothing about sailing," Hermie pointed out. "No captain will hire us."

"Let's just get to Patras and figure it out from there."

The bus ride was long, boring, and tiresome. Hermie's phone had died, and he had no charger. For most of the trip, he stared blankly at the Greek countryside and coastline while he worried about everything that was probably going to go wrong.

When they finally arrived in Patras, they went to the nearest ferry station to ask about a boat to Beijing. Just as the old beggar had said, they were told they needed to book a private yacht, and the captain wouldn't arrive for many days.

"How many days?" Hestie asked the old woman behind the counter in Greek.

The woman wore her white hair pulled back in a colorful scarf. Her skin was very tanned and leathery from many years in the sun. "The only captain that will take you that far usually comes to port once a month—the second Monday of each month," the old woman behind the counter said. "He may be here in three days, or maybe not."

"That doesn't sound very reassuring," Hermie mumbled.

"Do we pay here to book it?" Hestie asked.

The woman shook her head. "Pay the captain. Look for *The Marcella*. She usually arrives on the other side of that ferry terminal."

As they walked along the harbor, Hermie said, "We don't have enough for a room. We'll have to curl up on the dock, like the old man in Itea, for who knows how long."

"At least it's not cold or raining," Hestie said.

He wondered how his sister could remain optimistic. He couldn't understand it, but he was glad for it. Her courage gave him courage.

They walked across the street and found an abandoned factory. There were blankets on the floor, a dirty cooking pan, a charred garbage can, and an old makeshift clothesline that strung across one corner, still holding a ratty t-shirt.

"Do you think someone's living here?" Hestie asked him.

"Someone obviously was at one time. It doesn't look like anyone's been here for a while, though. Look how dirty that pan is. And those blankets are pretty dusty. I don't think anyone's used them in a long time."

A rustling sound made them freeze as their eyes went wide. Then an old voice carried from around the corner, crying out for help. It sounded like an old man.

"Please," he begged in a feeble voice. "Help me."

Hestie headed in the direction of the voice, but Hermie grabbed her by the arm.

"What if it's a trap?" he whispered.

"What if he's dying?" she whispered back.

"Good point." As scary as it was, Hermie would rather err on the side of risking his own life than that of a helpless old man. "Just be careful."

Together, they crossed the factory to another room. Tin cans and other garbage littered the floor, and, on an old mattress, lay an even older man. He was thin, frail, and pale. Dark moons beneath his eyes and blue lips made him appear to be close to death. Hestie and Hermie knelt beside him.

"What can we do?" Hestie asked. "Should we call for an ambulance? Get you to a hospital?"

"I need water," he said.

"Wash out some of those tin cans and fill them with water at the fountain in the plaza," Hestie said.

"I don't think it's wise for you to stay here," Hermie said to his sister. "Come with me. We can both bring him the water."

Hestie leaned over the man. "We'll be right back. I promise."

The old man nodded as Hermie picked through the cans to find the best ones—those least caked over with gross dried food and mold. Hestie did the same. Then, together, they ran two blocks to the plaza to wash the cans and fill them with water. They returned in less than five minutes, but the old man was gone.

***

Hypnos sat on the golden trick chair Hephaestus had designed for Hera many centuries ago. It was the same chair on which Uranus had held Hip captive fifteen years ago, when Uranus had tried to take over Hip's body so that he could carry out his revolutionary plan. But today, the chair wasn't hidden in the sky god's cave; it was in the center of the main hall of Mount Olympus, and all the gods—or, most of them—were there staring at him.

Zeus stood on the dais before his throne, glaring down his nose at Hip. "Because of the pain and suffering you endured to restore Ares's leg and to save us from Uranus's plot, you will not be made to undergo the same interrogation methods as Hecate."

If Zeus's words had been meant to make Hip feel grateful or relieved, they failed. Hip wasn't sure how he should respond—with shocked offense that anyone would suspect him, with shameful self-reproach for having allied with a known traitor, or something else. Since he couldn't determine the best expression to wear, he kept it blank.

"Apollo has returned to help me in this matter," Zeus continued. "He will know if you're withholding the truth."

Hip was careful not to look at his father, or at Athena, or at Poseidon, even though it wasn't clear whether the latter had the intention of turning against Zeus. Instead, he returned Zeus's stare and waited for the inevitable. He had no regrets. He loved his family and would do anything for his father. He knew his father was on the side of right, and that this ruler before him had been selfish, impulsive, and a traitor to nearly every god in attendance at one time or another, especially to Hera.

Hip would have continued to serve Zeus and to maintain the status quo, but he had agreed with his father that the prophecy about the son of Metis could not be ignored and, instead, should be embraced as an opportunity for change. Change for the better.

Despite these feelings of confidence about his actions and intentions, Hip was worried about Jen and Morpheus. He hoped with all his being that Zeus wouldn't stoop to threatening his loved ones in exchange for cooperation. He hoped that only Hecate and he would have to endure Zeus's wrath. And he prayed that whatever that wrath would be, that it would be temporary, and that Hecate and Hip would be restored to their positions once his father and Metis's son brought about the change.

"Now tell me," Zeus began. "Why would Hecate secretly advise Than's children that Prometheus, my number-one enemy, is not *their* enemy?"

CHAPTER NINE

Unexpected Kindnesses

Hestie's mouth fell open. "Where did he go?"

Hermie turned, looking in all directions. "Something's not right."

Suddenly the tin cans full of water they'd been holding turned into golden bowls.

"What the…" Hestie stared wide-eyed at what smelled and looked like soup in one bowl and pudding in another.

"Are you seeing what I'm seeing?" her brother asked.

Hestie nodded.

Then the factory assembly line became a long golden banquet table with velvet-upholstered, wooden chairs around it. Platters of food appeared, along with two place settings. Gradually the rest of the old factory became gilded walls covered in silver wallpaper, illuminated by firelit wall sconces, and punctuated with historical paintings. The dusty floors became polished marble. And a crystal chandelier appeared hanging from the now coffered ceiling in the center of the room.

Hestie studied her brother's face. "What should we do?"

"This must be the work of one of the gods," he said. A little louder, he asked, "To whom do we owe our thanks?"

The old dying man appeared from around the corner, but as he took his slow, feeble steps in their direction, he, too, transformed. The old, wrinkled face became young and beautiful. Golden hair fell around feminine shoulders.

"Hestia?" She hadn't seen her namesake in over two years.

"Hello, Hestie," the goddess replied. "And Hermie."

"Why did you pretend to be the old man?" Hermie asked.

"I had to test you," she said. "Gods must be sure the recipients of their most lavish gifts are deserving. When you were willing to risk your lives to save someone you didn't know, you proved to be so."

"Have you seen our parents?" Hestie asked. "Are they okay?"

The goddess took Hestie's hand in her own and patted it. "They're with Demeter and are doing fine, my loves. I've come to thank you for helping my beloved brother, Zeus."

"Well, he didn't give us much of a choice," Hermie muttered.

Hestie wanted to kick him. "We haven't done much yet, but we're trying our best."

"Please, have a seat and nourish yourselves before you continue the long journey ahead."

As Hestie and her brother sat across from one another at one end of the long table, Hestia pointed to the back wall and created a hearth, complete with a cozy, crackling fire. Then she took the seat at the head of the table, between the two of them.

"No one will bother you in here," Hestia said. "There are clean beds in the next room and enough gold coins for you to afford the journey to Beijing. That *is* where you're headed, yes?"

"Yes," Hermie said. "Beijing. Hecate's location spell told us to go there to find Prometheus."

Hestie hoped Hermie wouldn't say too much more. She still worried about spies.

As if the goddess knew their worries, she said, "We're protected in this make-shift fortress I've created. It will last for as long as you need it, and you're safe in here. It's heavily warded. No one, not even a god, except me, can get in."

Hestie hadn't realized how tense she'd been. At Hestia's reassurances, her shoulders relaxed, and the knot between her shoulder blades loosened. "Thank you. We have so many questions, and so much to tell you. But we were worried that…"

"Wait," her brother said. "How do we know this is really Hestia? Before we tell her anything, we need proof."

"Smart boy," Hestia said. "Good for you. What shall I give as proof?"

Hestie searched her brother's face, hoping for a sign that he had an idea, because she was coming up empty. What could she possibly ask Hestia that anyone else wouldn't know?

Hermie cleared his throat. "I'm going to need a minute."

***

While Morpheus attended on the Dreamworld, he also flew through the sky searching for rainbows. When he found one dimly appearing after a recent rain over the Adriatic Sea, he went to it.

It had been two days since he'd last seen Iris, but it had felt much longer, mainly because, for the first time since he'd been pursuing her, she'd thrown him a bone. She'd told him her favorite flower, and, later today, he would paint it for her. Right now, he needed to see her beautiful face.

He hadn't quite reached the rainbow, when his mother appeared.

"You're back, from helping the twins?" she asked.

"The Dreamworld called to me," he explained. He didn't like the worried look on her face. "Are you okay?"

"I've had to take over your father's duties. He's being interrogated by Zeus."

Morpheus wasn't sure he'd heard his mother correctly. There was no way his father could ever do anything wrong. "What did you say?"

"Zeus has taken your father as a prisoner and is questioning him. Hecate was tortured earlier, and now she's in the Titan Pit. Morpheus, I need you to listen to me."

Morpheus could barely hear her. A strange ringing had filled his ears, and the hard beating in his chest added to his troubles. He took a deep breath, trying to calm himself. "Mom, what's going on?"

"The prophecy about Metis's son has the gods at odds with one another," she said. "Zeus doesn't know who's with him and who's against him. So, I want you to keep your nose clean, got it? I want you to focus on your duties and keep to yourself, understand?"

"What about Iris?" he said. "Can't I see her?"

His mother put a hand on his shoulder and rubbed it. Now that he was older, he didn't want to be held and touched by his mother like he once did, especially when they looked the same age. It was weird. When he was little, though, he couldn't get enough of it.

He pulled away. "She's my best friend."

"And she's Hera's closest companion," his mother said.

"Iris doesn't have anything to do with what's going on with Pops."

"You don't know that."

Morpheus felt like his heart was being ripped in two. "How can me being with her hurt anything?"

"Because there may come a time when you'll have to choose between your parents and your friend."

Heat rushed up his back, where his wings met, and traveled up to his cheeks. Sweat broke out on his forehead. "That's not gonna happen. And there's no contest, okay? I'd always choose you and Pops over anyone."

His mother kissed him on the cheek. "Okay, sweet boy. I just don't want you to get hurt. A mom can't help but watch out for her boy, understand?"

"Yeah, I know. I'll be careful. But let me just talk to her."

"Not for long, alright?"

His mother vanished. When he looked up into the darkening sky, he saw Iris hovering at the bottom of her rainbow with a pitcher full of water. He flew to meet her.

"Hey, you pretty thing, you," he said with a smile. "Miss me?"

"No contest, huh?" she asked. "You didn't even have to think about it?"

So, she *had* heard.

"They're my parents," he said.

"You're a grown man, aren't you? Or are you still a boy?" She carried the pitcher up to the clouds and emptied it.

"What do I look like to you?" He stood back and watched her give him a once over. He smiled when she blushed.

She turned away, back to the sea to refill her pitcher. He followed her.

When he caught up to her, she asked him, "Do you think your father has betrayed Zeus?"

"No way," he said. "He'd never do anything like that."

She met his gaze. "You're sure?"

"Absolutely. Don't you believe me?"

She carried her full pitcher back up into the clouds and emptied it again. He followed.

"Zeus will figure out that my dad's innocent soon enough," he said. "Then there won't be a problem. Meanwhile, I'm going to make you a gift."

"Does it have something to do with moonflowers?" she asked with a smile.

He laughed. "You'll have to wait and see."

He was about to leave, when she took his hand. He turned to face her.

"Morpheus, listen. Your mother's right. Until this all blows over, we shouldn't be seen together."

That wasn't what he'd wanted to hear. He leaned in close and pressed his lips to hers. "Fine."

She frowned. "Well, that was easy."

He smiled against her lips and whispered. "I'll see you in your dreams."

"But nowhere else?" she asked, frowning.

He threw his head back and laughed. "Perhaps my mom is overreacting."

***

As badly as Hip wanted the chance to say goodbye to Jen and to Morpheus, in case Zeus decided to throw him into the Titan Pit, he dared not make the request; he didn't want to give Zeus any ideas for ways to coax the information from him. To each of Zeus's questions ("What do you know about Hecate?" "Is there a plot against me?" "Do you know of any other traitors?" "Are you in league with them?"), Hip had replied, "You're my king. I won't usurp your crown." Hip had carefully chosen words that were true—words that Apollo could not reveal as lies.

But Zeus was not a fool. He could sense that Hip was avoiding something. The king sighed, growing tired of Hip's vague replies, and then he said what Hip had most feared: Zeus said, "Bring me Jen."

Hip couldn't breathe or speak. He opened his mouth and closed it, like a fish stranded on a beach. Before he could think of what to say without giving up his father, Apollo stepped forward.

"I can see a vision of the future," he said.

Zeus turned to his son. "What is it? What do you see?"

"This interrogation is a waste of time," Apollo said. "The son of Metis will soon be upon Mount Olympus. You should focus your efforts on finding him."

"What exactly do you see?" the king asked, his face pale.

"I see Metis's son at the gates of Mount Olympus before summer's end."

Zeus covered his face. "Please forgive me, Hypnos. I'm racked by insecurities. We must fortify Mount Olympus at once."

Hip sucked in his lips and finally breathed. Apollo's intervention could only mean one thing: The god of light, of healing, of music, and of truth was on his side. Without saying so, Apollo had just told Hypnos that they were allies.

***

As Hermie ate in the golden fortress in Patras, he searched his memory for something he could ask Hestia that would prove she wasn't an imposter trying to get information from him. Hestie kept glancing at him, as though she was counting on him to solve all their problems, and this was only adding more pressure and a sense of panic to his already tight chest. He tried to enjoy the food, but he'd cleaned his plate and couldn't recall eating it.

He took a puff from his inhaler.

"Was the food to your liking?" the goddess asked him.

"It was delicious," he said, to be courteous. "Thank you."

"Wait a minute," his sister said suddenly. "This reminds me of a story my grandmother told me, about the first time she met Psyche."

A light went off in Hermie's head. That was it. Persephone told them that she had only told Hestia the details of Psyche's family's betrayal, because she didn't want people to pity her, and she knew Hestia would be kind and gracious. "You're the only one she told, besides us, about Psyche's situation at home."

Hestia smiled. "That's right. Here's my chance to prove myself. Your grandmother told me that Psyche's sisters hated her. They were jealous of her beauty. But her father heard from Apollo's oracle that she was to be married to a dragon."

"Everyone knows that much," Hestie said. "Did our grandmother tell you anything more?"

"Yes," Hestia said. "When Psyche spilled the oil on Cupid after going against his wishes, he sent her home, but she wasn't welcomed there.

Her parents feared for their kingdom, and her sisters wanted her dead. Psyche begged Persephone to help her."

"That's right!" Hermie said, filling with confidence. Turning to his sister, he added, "This must be the real Hestia." Then he turned back to the goddess. "And you're sure we can't be overheard?"

"Yes, I'm certain," she said.

"Hecate sent us a secret message," Hestie began.

"She told us that Prometheus was not our enemy but that we weren't to talk about it," Hermie added.

Hestie wiped her chin with a napkin. "That made us realize there must be an enemy watching us."

"Then Gaia pretty much confirmed that suspicion when we returned Pandora's jar to her," Hermie said.

"She told us not to god travel and to stick to the land and sea," Hestie added.

"Gaia told you this?" Hestia's face reddened and her mouth became a thin line.

Hermie wondered why Hestia seemed so upset. "Do you have any idea who our enemies might be?"

Hestia stood up and glared down at them. "I wouldn't trust Gaia, if I were you. Or Hecate, for that matter. Prometheus is indeed your enemy, and as soon as you find him, you need to pray to Zeus, so he can protect you from harm. Do you understand, children?"

Hermie glanced at his sister, not sure whom to trust. Hecate would never lie to them, would she? On the other hand, Hestia had saved their lives. Surely, she could be trusted.

"Do you understand?" Hestia repeated.

"Yes," Hestie said.

Hermie swallowed hard. "Yes, of course."

CHAPTER TEN

The Captain and His Crew

After two days of hunkering down in the lavish palace Hestia had created for them, Hermie was anxious to run to the docks and look for *The Marcella*.

In all that time, they had heard nothing from the gods—not even from Morpheus.

According to the ferry station, the yacht was expected to arrive at noon, but Hermie convinced Hestie to go to the harbor right after breakfast and wait for it. He wanted to make sure they were the first to proposition the captain for a ride. Having the gold coins from Hestia in his front jean pocket made him feel more confident that they'd get to Beijing, but he still had no idea how he and his sister would travel from Beijing to Seoul without the gods noticing. In fact, Hermie still hadn't told his sister that Seoul, and not Beijing, was their final destination.

Hermie sat on the dock with his feet hanging over the edge. His sister sat beside him, swinging her legs anxiously, reminding him of when they were small, when he used to push her on the park swings. They didn't have a care in the world back then. As long as they blended in with the other children, there were no worries. He hadn't minded that he wasn't allowed to play soccer, or baseball, or football. He enjoyed video games, watching anime, and reading comic books. He taught himself every computer language in existence and enjoyed solving puzzles. And even though his sister sometimes got on his nerves, she'd been his best friend.

As he watched the ships coming in and out of the harbor and read the names of every vessel, he hoped his family still had a future. He hadn't been joking when he'd told Hestie and Morpheus that the nature of their destiny was unclear. There was no mention of whether they would live or die as they fulfilled it.

And Hermie badly wanted to live.

He wished he had worn a cap. His cheeks were getting sunburnt. A glance at his sister showed that she had the same problem. They had no hats, no sunscreen, no change of clothes. As each minute passed, Hermie became more aware of how ill-prepared he and his sister were for this journey.

Just before high noon, his stomach growled, and he wondered if he went back to the abandoned factory, if the magical palace would still be there with food on the table for him to eat. Hestie had wanted to wait. It had been his idea to get out here early, and now he regretted it. What a waste of time.

As he was about to suggest that one of them run back to see if there was food, another yacht pulled up to the harbor, and the words painted on it read *The Marcella.*

It wasn't the biggest boat in the harbor, but it was fancier than Hermie had expected, having three levels, including the hull and the captain's helm up top, enclosed on three sides by glass. It also had three large sails, which members of the crew were pulling down and fastening with ropes.

Hestia saw it, too, and climbed to her feet. He stood up beside her, using his hand as a visor and squinting against the sun to better make out the crew as the ship approached them. So far, they consisted of one man and three teens. The captain sat up top at the helm. Through the clear glass, Hermie made out the captain's features—dark curly hair beneath his white captain's hat and a long, impressive beard. It was hard to tell beneath his sunglasses, but the man appeared to be his parents' age or a little older. A pale-faced sandy-haired boy and two Asians—a boy and a girl—were fastening the sails on the deck. When the boat reached the dock, the Asian boy, who was at the back of the ship, tied on.

The captain climbed down from the helm to the front deck, which was higher than the one at the back of the ship. He was a tall, bulky man with a burly beard that nearly reached the center of his chest.

"Patras, at last!" he cried cheerfully.

The sandy-haired boy followed, to whom the captain said, "Poros, help our guests with their luggage." Then he added, "You, too, Jinsoo. Mina, you and I will tidy up the place before heading into port."

Hermie stood watching, waiting for the captain to notice him and his sister, and not sure if he should speak up.

Meanwhile, the sandy-haired boy, whom the captain had called Poros, and the Asian boy, Jinsoo, carried luggage up from the hull of the ship to the back deck, which was lower and level with the pier. Four passengers followed—two middle-aged Asian couples. One of the men thanked the captain as he stepped onto the dock.

The captain waved from the upper front deck of the ship and called out, "Happy life, my friends!" Then he and the Asian girl, Mina, disappeared into the hull.

As the passengers walked past, followed by the two boys carrying their luggage, Hestie stopped the Asian kid, who was about her height and age.

"Would it be possible for us to book passage to Beijing on your boat?" she asked him.

The boy smiled back at her. "Hello. You ask Captain. Okay?"

Hestie nodded and thanked him, and the boy went on his way.

The sandy-haired boy, Poros, who was nearly at the end of the dock behind the two couples with their bags, called back, "Feel free to go aboard and see what Captain says."

Hermie turned to his sister. "Should we go? Or wait here?"

"Won't the captain get mad if we just pop in?" Hestie said. "I don't know, though. The guy said to go ahead."

"Let's go then," Hermie said, then, changing his mind, added, "or not."

"Hermie! Make up your mind."

"I just don't want to get off on the wrong foot."

"The guy said to go aboard, so let's go."

"But that guy's not the captain."

Before he and his sister had gone anywhere, the two boys had returned. The sandy-haired boy called Poros was almost as tall as the captain and a head above the boy named Jinsoo—maybe an inch taller than Hermie. He had wide shoulders, big hands, and a thick neck. But more remarkable than his build were his gray eyes. They reminded Hermie of Athena's eyes.

"When you need to leave?" Jinsoo asked them.

"Today," Hermie said.

Poros laughed. "That's not possible. We won't be ready to ship out until tomorrow."

"That's for Captain to decide," Jinsoo said.

Poros shook his head. "He'll want to stay."

"Let's talk to Captain." Jinsoo held out a hand to Hestie and helped her onto the back deck of the ship. Then he offered his hand to Hermie, and Hermie, who had no pride, took it. The last thing he needed was to trip and break his neck before ever leaving shore.

Hermie and Hestie followed the two boys to the upper deck, where they waited for the captain after the boys disappeared below. In a few minutes, the captain emerged from the hull with a smile on his face.

He extended his hand to Hermie. "Hello, there." Then to Hestie. "Welcome aboard *The Marcella*. What can I do for you?"

"We'd like to book passage to Beijing," Hermie said.

"Beijing?" the captain repeated. "Are you visiting relatives or running away?"

"Visiting relatives," Hestie said. "Or, looking for one."

"I see." The captain rubbed his beard. "We'll, I might be able to help you, if you can afford it. It'll cost you one thousand euros one way, and that doesn't include all of your meals—only some."

"One thousand each?" Hermie asked.

"No, for the both of you," the captain clarified.

Hermie dug ten of the twelve gold coins from his pocket. The banker down the road from the abandoned factory had told him that each coin was worth one hundred euros and had offered to exchange them, but Hermie didn't know what currency the captain would want. "Will you accept these, or should I go to the bank and exchange them?"

The captain took the coins and looked them over in his hands. He whistled. "Where did you get these beauties?"

"Our great aunt gave them to us," Hestie said.

"You must have a very rich aunt. These are rare coins." The captain handed five of them back. "I won't rob you blind. Each is worth at least two hundred euros."

Hermie couldn't believe the banker had lied to him—or maybe he didn't know the true value and had only guessed.

Hestie smiled. "Great. When do we leave?"

"And how soon will we get there?" Hermie asked.

"We leave first thing in the morning," the captain said. "We arrive to Beijing in three weeks, give or take a few days."

"Is there any chance we could leave today?" Hestie asked.

"I need to go into port and buy more supplies," the captain said. "And my crew needs a good night's rest before heading out again. The waters have been rough lately."

"What if we pay you more?" Hermie asked.

"You are in a hurry to find this relative, huh?" the captain asked.

"Yes, sir," Hermie said.

"Well, let me speak with my crew, young man, and I'll see what we can do."

The captain disappeared below deck, leaving Hermie and Hestie alone.

***

As Hypnos flew behind Selene on the dark side of the earth, bringing sleep to those mortals who needed it, he also spoke with Helios on the bright side of the earth. Helios invited Hip to have a seat in his golden cup and offered him a glass of amber wine.

"You're a good god, Hypnos," the sun Titan said. "I've watched you closely these many years, and I feel I can trust you."

"Thank you. That means a lot to me."

Helios leaned forward. "I know what you and your father are up to."

Hip felt the hair on the back of his neck come to attention.

Helios laughed. "Don't look so horrified. I'm on your side."

"Can we not be overheard up here?" Hypnos didn't like talking in the high skies where Zeus reigned.

"My cup is heavily warded. Our privacy is protected."

Hip studied Helios, wondering if he could be trusted.

"I know of many others who want the same thing."

"Who?" Hip asked, still unsure.

"My sisters, for example."

"Both? Selene and Eos?" Hip had suspected Selene to be sympathetic.

"Yes. And Asteria and her daughter, Hecate, as you know. Poor, poor Hecate. Such a brave soul."

"Anyone else?" Hip asked before taking a sip of the wine. It was good. Fruity.

"Oh, heavens, yes. Most of the free Titans I know are pulling for Metis and your father—especially my beloved Clymene."

Clymene was Prometheus's mother—and the mother of Atlas, Menoetius, and Epimetheus. Her husband, Iapetus, was sentenced with the other Titan rebels to the pit. An Oceanid and the goddess of fame,

Clymene spent her time in the eastern oceans watching over Asia and its many sea vessels. Some even called her *Asia*.

Legend had it that before rising each morning, Helios dipped his cup down into the eastern seas to kiss his lover, Clymene.

Helios and Clymene had had four children together, but they had all met tragic fates. Phaeton had once taken over Helios's cup and had lost control of it. The burning cup-like chariot had destroyed much of the African continent before Zeus struck Phaeton down with a lightning bolt, paralyzing him. Zeus condemned Phaeton to remain in the bottom of the Po River in Italy. His three sisters—the Heliades, who were the daughters of Helios and Clymene—sobbed uncontrollably for days and days, until Zeus turned them into poplar trees along the bank of the Po River.

"Do those in the pit know?" Hip asked, feeling more secure with Helios's trust.

"I doubt it, unless Hecate informs them. I doubt she would. I wouldn't trust them not to try to take over the world themselves, you see."

Hip agreed. He especially disliked Uranus, Cronos, Atlas, and Menoetius. Their strength would guarantee a victory, but they were wild cards, loose cannons, selfish and untrustworthy. "Do you know if any of the *Olympians* are willing to go against Zeus?"

"The only ones I can say with certainty are the twins—Artemis and Apollo."

"I think Athena and Poseidon might be recruited."

"I would think Athena would be very sympathetic to her mother and brother."

"It's hard to know what to expect," Hip admitted, "or what move Zeus will make. He's called a meeting on Mount Olympus. I'm headed that way now. Before I go, I was wondering if you'd seen my brother's twins."

"Indeed, I have. They are just below us at that port in Patras with the most able seaman I know."

Hypnos squinted as he searched the harbor. Then he saw them on the deck of a yacht.

"You think that seaman will get Hermie and Hestie closer to finding Prometheus?" Hip asked.

Helios laughed. Hip studied the sun Titan's face. What was so funny?

"Even better," Helios said.

"How so?"

"You see, Hypnos," Helios began. "That able seaman *is* Prometheus."

"But…how…" Hip was speechless.

Helios laughed even harder. "Gaia and Clymene arranged it."

Hip squinted against the brilliance of Helios and his chariot as he peered over the side of the cup at the captain of *The Marcella*.

"Are you sure that's him?" Hip asked. "It's hard to recognize him with the hat, sunglasses, and overgrown beard."

"I assure you, it is."

Hip studied the captain a moment longer and then asked, "Have you known where he was all this time?"

"Indeed. Clymene rarely strays far from her son's side. He's the only offspring of hers not imprisoned in one way or another."

"Did Hecate know?" Hip asked, wondering why she wouldn't have told him.

"No," Helios said. "We weren't sure of her loyalty, or of the loyalty of any of the Underworld gods, to our cause, until we heard about Hecate's treason and punishment."

"Have you been in contact with my father?" Hip asked.

"No," Helios said.

"Does Prometheus know that Hermie and Hestie are Than's twins?"

"Indeed, he does."

Hip frowned, worried for his nephew and niece. They were at the center of a dangerous game, and Hip had little power to protect them. "If Zeus and his allies discover Prometheus's identity…"

"We have to make sure that doesn't happen," Helios said.

"What about the son of Metis?" Hypnos asked. "Do you know his whereabouts, too?"

"Indeed. He's been at the side of Prometheus since he became a young man."

Hypnos jumped to his feet. "He's aboard the same vessel?"

Helios smiled. "The time for change is drawing near, my friend."

"How soon?"

"We're still gathering up our forces, are we not?" Helios said. "You continue to recruit Olympians in the Dreamworld, and, when the time is right, we'll make our move. Not before. Don't you agree?"

Hip scratched his beard. "Hermie and Hestie, their quest to find Prometheus—that's a distraction, to keep Zeus preoccupied while we get ready."

"I wouldn't share this information with anyone, Hypnos—except with your father. And only then in a safely warded space."

"Of course. I agree." Although he was still processing everything he'd been told, he needed to focus his attention on the meeting at Mount Olympus. "Thank you, Helios. I hope I can visit with you again soon."

"I hope so, too. Good luck."

"The same to you," Hip said. "We're all going to need it."

***

Hestie couldn't be more grateful when the crew returned to the upper deck and the captain said they'd leave today.

"Thank you!" she cried.

"Yeah, thanks," her brother added. "How much more do you want me to pay you?"

"Nothing more is necessary," the captain said. "Go get your luggage while my crew and I pick up more supplies, and we'll meet you back here in a couple of hours."

"We don't have any luggage," Hermie said.

The captain peered at them over his sunglasses, exposing dark brown eyes. "Surely you don't expect to wear the same clothes every day for the duration of our voyage?"

Hestie felt the heat rise to her cheeks. "We didn't have a chance to pack. It's kind of a long story."

"You have enough money to buy some," the captain pointed out. "Mina, why don't you take them with you to the department store?"

"Okay, no problem," Mina said. "But we can go to Mr. Burger first?"

The captain laughed. "Of course. I forgot. You and your brother have been looking forward to that, eh?"

"Yes, Captain," Mina said. She turned to Hestie and Hermie. "That okay with you? You come eat, too?"

"I'm starving," Hermie said to Hestie. "What about you?"

"Mr. Burger it is," Hestie agreed.

Mina turned to her brother. "Ready to go now?"

"Ready," Jinsoo said. "Follow me."

Hestie tried to hide her excitement when Jinsoo glanced back at her with a smile. He was super cute and just her type. But what was she doing? She shouldn't be thinking about boys. She had a destiny to fulfill, a Titan to find, and parents to save.

Too bad life couldn't be a little simpler, she thought with a sigh.

She jumped with surprise when Poros came up beside her along the dock and asked, "Have you ever eaten at Mr. Burger?"

"No. Is it good?" she asked.

"It's all the twins talked about for the past sixteen hours, so it must be."

"Oh, you're twins?" Hermie asked Mina.

She and Jinsoo nodded. Hestie recognized the likeness. They had the same almond eyes, thin brows, thin lips, and dimples. Their bowl-shaped black hair was slightly grown out. Jinsoo was a few inches taller than his sister and had the beginnings of a mustache—more like a shadow—over his upper lip.

"We are, too," Hestie said. "How old?"

"Fourteen," Jinsoo said.

"We're sixteen," Hestie said. "I'm Hestie, by the way. And this is Hermie."

"I'm fifteen," Poros said. "And the name's Poros."

"Now that we've got that settled…" Hermie laughed and so did the others.

"Hestie and Hermie," the captain repeated. "Those are unusual names."

"Nicknames. We were named after Hestia and Hermes, the Olympians," Hermie explained.

"Ah, yes," the captain said as they reached the end of the docks and crossed a set of railroad tracks. "Both very noble Olympians, too. You were named well."

"You believe in the gods?" Hestie asked as they walked a block into the town and took a left.

"Oh, yes," the captain said. He towered over all of them, though Hermie and Poros were only a head shorter, and Hestie was only a few inches shorter than they.

"Not many do these days," Hermie pointed out.

"It's hard to blame them," the captain said. "The gods seem more removed from humankind than ever. Fewer and fewer prayers seemed to be answered."

"Wait!" Mina said, stopping in her tracks. She turned to Hestie. "I know you! *Hestie's Style*, right? That *you*?"

That was the name of her channel—*Hestie's Style*. And she called her fans Hestie's Besties. "Yes!" She was elated that someone in the real world recognized her. "Oh, my gods, yes! That's me!"

"I love you!" Mina said. "So funny!"

"Me, too!" Jinsoo said.

"Thank you," Hestie said.

"How exciting to have a celebrity among us," the captain said.

"I wouldn't go *that* far," Hestie said, feeling the blood rush to her cheeks. It was easy to be carefree in front of a camera, but talking to people face-to-face was a different thing altogether.

They walked another block before they reached Mr. Burger. The captain opened the door for them and told the kids to get whatever they wanted.

"Don't spend your coins here," he said to Hermie as he swept his sunglasses to the top of his head, revealing his dark brown eyes. "I'll pay, and you can cash one of your coins in for euros before you go shopping. You can pay me back later. Capisce?"

"Don't you mean *capisci*?" Hestie asked.

"You speak Italian?" the captain asked.

"Si, signore."

"Si, Capitano, no?" the captain corrected with a grin.

"Si. Scusami, Capitano."

"But you're American, yes?" he asked.

"Yes."

When they reached the counter, the woman behind the cash register asked, "Ti boró na sas exypiretísei?"

Hestie turned to Mina. "What are you getting?"

"Ginger orange salad," Mina said. "And Jinsoo like bacon swiss burger and cheese fry."

Jinsoo smiled. "Oh, my God. I'm so hungry."

"The bacon swiss sounds good to me," Hermie said in Greek to the woman at the register.

The captain's eyes widened. "Your sister speaks Italian, and you speak Greek?"

"We both know a lot of languages," Hermie explained. "It's sort of our thing."

"Hestie speak Korean, too," Mina said.

"Ye. Naega joh-ahaneun nolaeneun hangug-eolodoeeoissda," Hestie said, which meant her favorite songs were in Korean.

"You like K-pop?" Jinsoo asked.

Hestie grinned.

"That's an understatement," Hermie said with what Hestie was sure was a twinkle in his blue eyes. "She's obsessed."

"It's true," Hestie admitted.

"She speak Japanese, and Chinese, and, what else?" Mina asked.

"Almost every language," Hestie replied.

"That's impressive," Poros said.

"Indeed," The captain said.

"Thank you," Hestie said again.

"We need to order, young people," the captain said. "Hestie? Poros?"

Hestie noticed a couple sharing a big platter of nachos at a corner booth. "Mmm. Those nachos look good."

Poros came up beside her. "I was thinking the same thing. Want to share?"

Hestie knew she couldn't eat an entire platter by herself. "Sure. Why not?"

Once they had all ordered and had been served their food, they sat around a table for six and got to know each other a little as they ate.

Hestie sat between Poros and her brother. Mina, Jinsoo, and the Captain sat across from them. While they ate, Hestie asked the kids how they ended up working on a yacht. Mina and Jinsoo said they were orphans, and their orphanage had helped them to find the job. Poros said the captain was his uncle.

"What about your parents?" Hestie asked Poros.

"My father wants nothing to do with me, and my mother, well, she encouraged me to travel. She doesn't believe in a traditional education."

"Our parents are like that, too," Hermie said. "We don't attend a regular school, either."

"Where are *your* parents?" the captain asked.

Hestie gave Hermie a worried glance, and when he didn't say anything, she said, "They're both in prison, but they're innocent."

"Is that why you are looking for the relative in Beijing?" the captain asked.

"Yes," Hestie said. "We're hoping he can help us get our parents out."

It wasn't exactly a lie, she thought.

***

Hip arrived on Mount Olympus just as Poseidon was leaving the garage, where he'd parked his chariot.

"Hello, Hypnos," Poseidon said as they walked together from the plaza toward the rainbow steps of the palace. "I had a dream about you. It ended rather abruptly."

"Zeus summoned me for questioning."

"As I predicted," Poseidon said, stopping just outside the palace doors. "And yet, you're free."

"Apollo vouched for me," Hip said.

Poseidon's turquoise eyes brightened, along with his expression. "That's wonderful news."

Since then, Hip had arranged a meeting with Apollo in his father's palace, where he had shared all that Helios had told him. He'd also told Apollo that he was in the process of recruiting Athena and Poseidon. Apollo had said that Artemis was with them, too, and that he'd also met with Metis and Poros.

"What of Hermes?" his father had asked Apollo.

Apollo had shaken his head.

Now, Hip and Poseidon entered to find Hades just inside the doors. Poseidon strolled over to his throne in the main hall without saying anything to anyone. Hip greeted his father, and followed him in, where most of the other gods had already gathered.

Cupid stood beside his mother with Psyche on one side of him and Therese and Than—still in their cuffs—on the other. Than met Hip's eyes, but Hip quickly looked away, unable to bear his brother's worried gaze.

Jen rushed through the great hall toward him and took his hand, standing at his side.

"You okay?" she whispered.

Telepathically, he replied, "As well as can be expected."

"Where's Morpheus?" she asked.

Hip looked around the room but did not see his son among the faces there. "Hopefully, on the way."

More soon arrived—Aphrodite's Graces, the Muses, and, to Hip's surprise, Dionysus. Ariadne and her brother, Asterion the Minotaur, soon joined him. Asterion, obviously unaware of the gravity of the meeting, gave a friendly wave to Hip and Jen before he noticed Than and Therese in cuffs. Then the half-man, half-beast frowned and turned a perplexed face to Hip. Hip avoided it, just as he had his brother's.

After several more minutes of idle chatter among them had passed, Zeus stood on the dais before his throne and lifted his arms in the air.

"Thank you for gathering here with me today," he said. "We have a sensitive matter to discuss."

The great hall became quiet, and all eyes turned to their leader.

"As you have heard by now, our great pantheon is in jeopardy," Zeus continued. "Metis disguised herself as my beloved Hera and deceived me into lying with her. She used dark magic to become pregnant, and it's been confirmed that she bore a son, who is now of age."

A cacophony of whispers erupted, but Zeus raised his arms again and quieted the room.

"A prophecy was first told by Prometheus while he was still chained to the mountain and serving his punishment for treason. The son of Metis would overthrow me."

More whispers erupted, so Zeus lifted his arms.

"As you know, only the Fates know with certainty what the future brings," he said. "Our way of life is not doomed. We can fight."

Now applause broke out, and the expressions of many present transformed into hopeful smiles.

"Hear, hear!" Aphrodite shouted.

"Defend Olympus!" Ares yelled.

"Hooray!" others cried out.

Zeus basked in the cheers for many moments before lifting his hands again for silence.

"I have no doubt that we can defend our way of life, but only if we are vigilant and prepared," Zeus said. "Right now, I have spies working night and day, collecting information for our cause. For example, I'm sorry to report that we now know Gaia is against us."

Shouts of reproach resounded throughout the hall.

"How could she?" Demeter cried.

"Our own Mother Earth, a traitor?" Hermes asked, incredulously.

Zeus raised his hands and continued. "Unfortunately, the intelligence collected by my spies has cast a shadow of suspicion over this court as well. Signs indicate that there may be traitors among us, in this very room."

From the crowd came sounds of disbelief and confusion, of smacks, of hisses, and of groans. Gods and goddesses glanced suspiciously at their neighbors. Hip once again met his brother's worried gaze and looked away.

Jen noticed, and squeezed his hand.

"We knew this wasn't going to be easy," she said telepathically.

Zeus raised his hands to silence the room.

"So that we might put to rest those fears and doubts, I have asked you to come and swear your allegiance to me and to this court on the River Styx."

"Oh, no," Jen's telepathic prayer came.

Hip avoided making eye contact with anyone, but, with his peripheral vision, he sensed glances being stolen his way by his father, Poseidon, Athena, Apollo, and, unrelentingly, his brother. Zeus's demand for a public swearing could easily stifle any chances Hades had of building a strong alliance among other Olympians against Zeus. If those against Zeus swore their allegiance on the River Styx, they would be sentencing themselves to an eternity of visits from the vicious Maenads. On the other hand, if they told the truth and revealed their intentions to work with Metis's son, they would be thrown into the Titan Pit immediately and rendered useless in what was, in Hip's opinion, the most important war of all time.

Worst of all, if any Underworld god admitted dissent, Than and Therese would be killed on the spot.

CHAPTER ELEVEN

A Curious Meeting

Hestie wasn't too thrilled with the clothing selections in the department store. Everything was generic—not at all what she'd expected to find in Europe.

"Is there another store we can go to?" she asked Mina with a frown. "I don't see anything I like."

"It cheaper here," Mina said. "Other store expensive."

"I'm fine with this," Hermie said.

Of course, he was. He wore the same thing every day: a funny graphic t-shirt with blue jeans. The shirt he'd been wearing for the past few days was a string of math symbols that read: $\sqrt{-1}\ 2^3\ \Sigma\ \pi$

The symbols meant, "i 8 sum pi." Below the symbols were the words, "and it was delicious." Maybe graphic tees helped Hermie express himself; but, in her case, her clothes needed to have a certain flare.

She went up to her brother. "Give me some money. I saw a boutique across the street."

He handed over several euros—she had no idea what they were worth—and then she left the department store and went alone to a shop on the corner of the block. She had liked what she'd seen when they'd passed by the window, and when she walked inside, she wasn't disappointed.

She had a passion for prints from India and was happy to find three sets of adorable shorts made of Indian patterns—a black and gray pair with little elephants, a green pair with kaleidoscope designs, and an indigo pair with a cool geometric pattern. She found cute crop tops to match each pair—all solid colors with adorable lace-up necklines that complemented the shorts. She picked out two pairs of trousers and two long-sleeved tops, in case it got cold. The boutique also had nice bras, panties, sandals, purses, and hair accessories, so she added some of them to the bundle in her arms.

And makeup! She *lived* for makeup! It was a splurge to buy some, but what the heck?

She wished her phone wasn't dead. She could do a vlog in this boutique and upload it to her channel. Her viewers were probably wondering why she hadn't posted anything lately.

She held one of the tops against her and studied her reflection in a mirror. Without realizing it, she had begun to think of Poros and whether he would like the way she looked in her new clothes. Jinsoo was much more her type, but at lunch he'd shown little interest in her, seeming to have relegated her to the friend zone. On the other hand, Poros hadn't taken his eyes off her—his gorgeous eyes, to boot. And she had to admit, she hadn't minded.

She wasn't sure if she had enough money for all the items she'd gathered, so she flagged down an attendant to help her. On her way to the register, a cute pair of pajamas caught her eye, so she added them to the pile in her arms. Then she asked the attendant to help her determine if she had enough money.

They went to the counter to lay everything out.

The attendant nodded. "More than enough."

While the attendant rang up the merchandise, Hestie noticed Poros in the shop standing in front of a mirror, where he was trying on a hat and admiring himself. He really did have the most striking gray eyes, and they twinkled in the light of the shop window, near where he stood. He didn't seem to be aware of her watching him as he made a series of expressions in the mirror. She covered her mouth and giggled and couldn't stand how adorable he was, but just as she was about to call out to him, he took off the hat, dropped it back on the rack, and left the store.

Once her items were bagged and she'd been given her change, Hestie raced from the store, hoping to catch up to him. She stood on the corner, looking in all directions, and spotted him just as he was rounding a corner a block away. She ran fast, but not too fast, because she didn't want to call attention to herself from people walking up and down the street.

When she reached the end of the block, she stopped and glanced around for him again but couldn't find him. As she was about to give up and return to the department store to meet Mina and Hermie, she saw Poros cross the street into an alley.

Wondering what he was doing walking the streets of Patras alone (wasn't he supposed to be getting supplies with the captain and Jinsoo?), she followed.

***

Morpheus and Iris lay side by side facing one another in the soft glow of the rainbow arch. They gently fanned one another—she with her left wing and he with his right. They didn't have much time before the meeting on Mount Olympus. They never had much time.

A few years ago, when she'd still thought of him as a child and a playmate, he'd convinced her to leave her pitcher and duties behind for three days, and they'd both received a scolding from Hera when they'd returned. The goddess queen wasn't so much concerned with drought—which was the real threat if Iris neglected her duties—as she was with not having her servant handy at her every beck and call.

Iris always corrected him when he said *servant*. She said *attendant*. He supposed it made her feel better about herself, and that was okay with him.

"What are you thinking about?" he asked after he'd kissed her for a long, lovely while.

"My sister."

"I didn't know you had a sister."

"She was my most beloved. Her name was Arke."

"Was?"

"She's all but destroyed—condemned to the Titan Pit."

Morpheus stroked Iris's soft, curly hair.

"We were both recruited by Zeus when he went to war against Cronos, and he offered to make us messengers to Mount Olympus. Since Cronos was cruel to us, we accepted, and together we made the most beautiful double rainbow arcs between the gods and mortals, and between Mount Olympus and the Underworld, to send messages between them."

"What happened to her?" Morpheus asked.

Iris flicked a tear from her cheek. "She betrayed us. She became the messenger of our enemies."

"Did she ever say why?"

"No, but I knew my sister. She did it for love. Another Titan had stolen her heart, and she loved him more than she loved me."

Morpheus used his thumb to wipe away another of her tears and then gently kissed her cheek. "What made you think of her today?"

"Before he threw her into the Titan Pit, Zeus ripped her beautiful iridescent wings from her body."

Morpheus choked on his own spit. He couldn't imagine the pain and the indignity of having his wings stripped from him. He coughed and cleared his throat and said, "Just wow."

"It was as horrible as you might imagine," she said. "To add insult to injury, Zeus gave the wings to another as a gift—to Thetis, mother to Achilles. And then she later gave them to her son. It nearly killed me to see them with anyone other than my sister. I still love her, even though she broke my heart."

Morpheus took her in his arms as she continued, "I can't ever risk going against Zeus and Hera, because I couldn't bear to be treated in such a cruel and barbaric way—to have my precious, golden wings ripped from my back and given to another!"

"That won't ever happen, my love," he said to her. "You'd never betray your king and queen."

She pulled back and studied his face. "Would you?"

"Never."

***

Hestie hid on the side of a building as she watched Poros make his way down an alley to the back of one of the businesses. The sun had moved to the west, and the alley was in shadows, but Hestie had excellent eyesight and she knew what she saw: Poros had taken a gold coin from his pocket—one that Hermie had given to the captain.

Had Poros stolen it?

Hestie was further horrified when a woman joined Poros in the alley and gave him a full paper sack in exchange for the coin. The woman, who looked twice his age but was still pretty—black hair in a ponytail and equally black eyes—winked at him and kissed his cheek, which sent a wave of jealousy down Hestie's back.

What did she care if this woman was flirting with Poros?

Just as she was wondering what could be in the sack, Poros lifted a small item—a plastic medicine bottle—and studied its label.

Was Poros buying drugs?

He spoke for a few more minutes with the woman, then he turned back in Hestie's direction. She quickly darted behind the building, hoping she hadn't been seen. Then, without waiting a moment longer, she ran at full speed to the department store, nearly running into Hermie and Mina as they were stepping out.

"Slow down," Hermie complained.

"You so fast!" Mina cried.

Hermie gave Hestie a disapproving frown.

All she could think to say was, "Wanna see what I bought?"

***

Morpheus and Iris arrived late to the meeting on Mount Olympus, but no one seemed to notice as they fluttered in from the rainbow arch above the great hall and landed at the foot of Hera's throne. Morpheus held tightly to Iris's hands, unafraid of what the other gods would think of his public display of affection. They probably had all thought of them as playmates. Morpheus would show them with his body language that the goddess was his.

His expectations of getting the notice of the gods as Iris's lover were thwarted when he soon realized the seriousness of the mood in the room. Many of those present were frowning, and others seemed outright frightened. What had happened here?

He prayed to his father, who replied telepathically, "We've been asked to swear allegiance to Zeus on the River Styx."

"Oh, that's easy," Morpheus said in a return prayer to his father. "Then why is everybody freaking out?"

"Kiddo, there are things I haven't had the chance to tell you," Hip began.

Morpheus looked from his father to Iris and back again. "What things?"

Zeus had begun to address Apollo, but Morpheus didn't hear what the king said, because he was too busy listening to his father's telepathic reply.

"Whatever happens, follow my lead," his father said. "Trust me, okay?"

"You got it, Pops."

From the corner of his eye, Morpheus saw his grandfather, Hades, disappear. Had he returned to the Underworld? Or had he slipped on his helm? Regardless, why would Hades choose to disappear as the other gods were preparing to swear their allegiance?

CHAPTER TWELVE

The Marcella

Hermie offered to help unload the wagon the captain had pulled along the dock to the boat. It contained boxes and sacks of supplies—canned and dry goods, meats, fruits, vegetables, jugs of fresh water, paper products, and medical supplies, from what Hermie could see. Hestie carried his shopping bag of clothes for him while he picked up a heavy box, and they followed the others aboard.

Little did the others know that Hestie was just as capable of carrying heavy boxes, but Hermie wouldn't rat her out.

Once the wagon was unloaded, Poros left to return it to whichever shopkeeper they'd borrowed it from while the captain put away the goods. Hermie was glad when the captain told Jinsoo and Mina to show Hermie and Hestie to their rooms and to give them a tour of the boat. He liked talking with the other twins—especially with Mina.

He liked her short, wispy dark hair, and her shiny, dark eyes. Her thin lips were always stretched into a bright smile, that created dimples in her cheeks. She was pretty without makeup or fancy clothes. She was simple, practical, and very cute. More importantly to Hermie, she seemed to like *him*.

They started at the very top of the ship. Hermie, Hestie, and Mina carried their shopping bags with them.

"This flybridge," Jinsoo said. "Great cockpit, yes?"

"Yes," Hermie agreed.

He touched one of the two leather captain's chairs and discovered it swiveled. The controls on the dashboard were computerized. He wished he could study the systems. Maybe the captain would allow him to observe during the trip.

Beneath two built-in flat-screen monitors was the steering wheel, ignition, and a horn. Above, in the corner of the three-sided enclosure, was a silver bell.

He glanced back at Mina, who was watching him with a smile as he took everything in. It was all so impressive, and she seemed pleased that he was pleased.

Behind the two captain's chairs was an L- shaped couch angled around a small table—both bolted to the deck. Although the three-sided enclosure reached the L-shaped couch, the upper deck extended past it to the back of the boat. The extended deck was separated from the cockpit by three descending steps. One of three masts shot up from the center of it.

"Such a great view," Hestie said with her hand on the metal rail at the back of the ship.

"Yes. Very nice," Mina agreed. "We spend most time up here."

"Come on," Jinsoo said.

Jinsoo led them down a series of steps to the wrap-around deck that connected to the front deck of the ship.

"This port side," Jinsoo explained, pointing to their left. "That starboard side." He pointed to their right.

They entered the interior of the yacht from the port side.

"Galley," Mina said of what resembled a kitchen.

Hermie was impressed with the u-shaped countertops, built-in sink, three gas-burner stove-top, oven, microwave, and refrigerator. "It has everything."

"It great," Jinsoo said. "Get fresh water here." He opened the refrigerator to show stocked bottles of water. "Recycle bottles there." He pointed to a bin built into the lower cupboard. "Trash there." He pointed to another bin beside it.

In the very front part of the interior of the yacht, built in against the front windows, there was a u-shaped bench around a table, reminding Hermie of the largest booth in their local diner. It was directly across from the kitchen counters. The captain was putting some of the supplies in cabinets beneath the bench and in cupboards in the kitchen.

"This ship is incredible," Hestie said to him.

"Have you had the full tour already?" he asked.

"Not yet," she said.

Then Jinsoo pointed to the front of the boat. "Bow." He pointed to the back of the boat. "Stern."

Mina repeated, "Left port, right starboard, okay? Front bow, back stern. Got it?"

"Got it," Hestie replied.

"But aren't right and left relative?" Hermie pointed out.

"Face front always," Jinsoo explained. "Port left when facing front and starboard right."

"Okay?" Mina asked him.

"Okay," Hermie said.

"There will be a test later," the captain said with a teasing smile.

Hermie laughed and followed Mina down three steps into another large room.

"Salon," Jinsoo said.

Another full-length couch stretched across the starboard side. It had a long coffee table in front of it, bolted to the floor. On the port side were two large armchairs. There were cabinets and storage bins in every nook and cranny, but over the armchairs and the couch stretched windows down the length of the room.

"In here, we play games," Mina said. "You play cards?"

"Yes," Hermie said. "Magic the Gathering? Yugioh?"

"You play Yugioh?" Mina asked with an even bigger smile. She turned to her brother. "We need more cards!"

Hermie had an awesome deck at home. He wished he had it with him.

"You like anime?" Jinsoo asked him and Hestie.

Hestie frowned but Hermie nodded.

"She only likes *Death Note*," he said of his sister. "But I like a lot of anime. I've watched all 220 episodes of *Naruto* and over four hundred episodes of the sequel. I'm about halfway through *Berserk* on Netflix."

"I like *Death Note*, too!" Mina said to Hestie.

"I love L!" Hestie said.

"But *Naruto* my favorite," Mina said to Hermie. "We watch together on Captain's phone, okay?"

"Okay," Hermie said, trying not to blush.

"Me, too!" Jinsoo said.

Since he attended school and played video games online, Hermie had never had so many friends in person. It felt nice.

"Come on," Mina said.

She beckoned them toward the back of the salon, *toward the stern*, Hermie mentally noted, through a door leading to the lowest deck, where they had first boarded the ship. One of the three masts protruded from the decking. There was another couch and table and a stepladder leading down into the sea.

Hermie followed the others down a narrow hatch on the starboard side that lead to the hull.

The steps led down to the center of the hull—*amidships*, according to Jinsoo. Mina explained that there were three cabins in the bow and two in the stern. A laundry room and engine room were amidships.

"A laundry room?" Hestie said with disbelief. "Awesome!"

"You sleep here," Jinsoo said to Hestie.

Hermie followed them into the bow of the boat. The cabin on the starboard side had a queen-size bed and private bathroom with a walk-in shower.

"You sleep here," Jinsoo said to Hermie.

The cabin directly across from Hestie's, on the port side, was identical to hers.

"Nice," Hermie said, dropping his shopping bag on the bed.

"The head," Jinsoo pointed. "Bathroom on a ship called the head."

"Got it." Hermie pointed to the cabin door between his and his sister's leading to a room in the very front of the hull—*in the bow*, he reminded himself. "Who sleeps in that one?"

"Captain, but he not use much," Jinsoo said. "He like sleeping in cockpit."

"Sometime we use it for customers," Mina said.

"What about you and Jinsoo?" Hestie asked. "Where do you sleep?"

"In other cabin," Mina said. "Come on. We show you."

They followed Mina to the stern of the ship, to a cabin with two twin beds.

"We sleep here," Mina said. "Poros there." She pointed to the cabin directly across from hers and Jinsoo's, to the port side.

"If we have more customers, we sleep in salon," Jinsoo said.

"The chair and couch make bed," Mina added.

Hermie looked inside Poros's room and saw something that surprised him. Hanging on the wall over the bed was an exact replica of Athena's shield.

***

Hip looked up as Cybele, whom they also called Rhea, lifted her manly hands toward Zeus. "Please do not make the same mistake as your father."

"Which one, Mother?" Zeus asked warily. "He made more than even a god can count."

"The mistake of putting his crown before his family," she said.

Zeus's mouth dropped open. "Do you expect me to hand over my throne to my son?"

"If it better serves your family to do so, yes," she said.

"If it better serves my family?" he repeated angrily. "How could that possibly better serve my family?" His voice became enraged. "I saved my family from *your husband*! I overthrew that wicked Titan. And I have ruled in all ways opposite to him, have I not? I even agreed to a more democratic system in what was once a traditional monarchy! What king gives up some of his power if not a good one?"

Hip wanted to point out that Zeus had been forced by the Athena Alliance to create a democracy, but he kept his mouth shut.

Before Cybele could say more, Zeus continued. "I will not roll over and play dead like an old dog so that my inexperienced son can steal the leadership of this council from me." He grabbed a lightning bolt from behind his throne. As he shouted, "I refuse!", he thrust it into the sky over Mount Olympus.

The bolt exploded into a thunderous burst of light, shaking the palace walls.

***

Hestie glanced inside Poros's cabin, looking for the sack she'd seen him get from the alley in Patras. Was Poros a thief and a druggie? What else could he have been doing with the gold coin and the pill bottles? The sack was too full to merely be medical supplies for the yacht. There must have been dozens of bottles in there. Was he a drug dealer? Maybe the captain was, too. Maybe they bought and sold drugs all along the coastline.

She gasped when she turned to find Poros standing behind her.

"Like what you see?" he asked, full of double entendre.

As suspicious as she was of him, she couldn't stop from giggling. He was too cute.

"Where did you get that shield?" Hermie asked.

Hestie hadn't noticed it, because she'd been too busy looking for drugs. Now that she studied it, where it hung on the wall over the bed, she gasped. It looked exactly like photos she'd seen of Athena's.

"My mother gave it to me," Poros said. "It once belonged to my sister."

"You have a sister?" Hestie asked.

"Yeah, but I've never met her. She's much older and was already out and on her own by the time I was born."

"What's her name?" Hermie asked.

"A..." Poros stammered. "Anna." Then he added, "It's just for decoration. It's not a real shield."

Poros acted as though he was hiding something. Is that where he hid his drugs, behind the shield?

As they all headed back up the stairs—she took the rear—she glared at the back of Poros and, in her mind, asked, "Are you a drug dealer?"

He stopped and turned to face her. "What?"

She flinched and looked up at him with surprise. "I didn't say anything."

"Oh. I thought you did." He turned and continued up the steps.

As she followed, she questioned herself. *Had* she spoken out loud?

***

Morpheus and Iris clung to one another as Zeus raged at Cybele—too close to Morpheus for comfort. Why would the goddess even suggest that the king step down for his family?

After shooting lightning over them and throwing a hissy fit, the lord calmed down, and Morpheus immediately felt less tense.

"I want to know who's loyal to me," Zeus said less angrily. "That is the sole purpose of this meeting. Is it too much to ask each of you to swear your allegiance on the River Styx? Would anyone here deny me that?"

"I don't think it's too much to ask, Lord Zeus," Morpheus said. He couldn't believe he'd spoken out loud. His cheeks burned with embarrassment as everyone in the hall stared at him.

"You, there, Morpheus," Zeus said with what looked like a twinkle in his eye. "You haven't disappointed me once since we brought you into the fold. The newest god among us is prepared to swear his allegiance! Let him be an example to the rest of you!"

A huge prideful grin spread across Morpheus's face. Iris kissed his cheek. He glanced at his father, but his father didn't return his gaze.

At least his mother smiled back at him, though it wasn't as bright as Iris's smile.

"Look at me, Pops," Morpheus prayed.

Slowly, his father's eyes met his. Morpheus was baffled. He saw neither pride nor approval in his father's expression—only fear.

Poseidon stood before his throne. "Dear brother," he said to Zeus. "The problem with ordering everyone to swear their allegiance on the River Styx is this: They could lie. They could be willing to suffer the consequences of the Maenads as an oath breaker, like Thanatos once did, to hide their guilt. You'll be no more the wiser. So why command actions that will serve no worthwhile purpose?"

"Ah, Poseidon," Zeus said narrowing his eyes at the god of the sea. "You bring up an interesting point. But, you see, this is where Apollo comes in. No one can lie before Apollo."

Morpheus continued to study his father's face and to wonder where Hades had gone. Were they enemies to Zeus? And if they were, did that make Morpheus an enemy of Zeus, too, and of Iris?

***

After they left the harbor and set out for the open sea, and while the crew hoisted the sails, Hermie and Hestie took showers and dressed in their new clothes before meeting Mina in the galley to watch Jinsoo make kimchi for their supper. He had ten heads of green nappa cabbage, which he chopped expertly and soaked in the sink with salt.

"That's going to make too much food, isn't it?" Hermie asked from where he sat in the booth between Mina and his sister.

"It last long time," Mina said.

"We eat this all month," Jinsoo added.

"You like squid?" Mina asked him.

Hermie glanced at Hestie, who laughed.

"We've never tasted it," Hestie said.

"Jinsoo, let them try your squid kimchi," Mina said.

Jinsoo took a sealed container from the refrigerator, opened it, and put some on a small plate. He handed Hestie and Hermie each a pair of chopsticks. "Taste."

The dish was bright red, mushy, and full of juice. The squid looked like it might be alive and swimming in it.

"Try it," Mina said.

Hermie didn't want to, but he didn't want to disappoint his new friends.

He watched as Hestie took a bite.

"Not bad," Hestie said.

Hermie dipped chopsticks into the soupy veggies and, avoiding the squid, scooped a bite into his mouth.

He hadn't been expecting the combination of flavors he encountered: sour, sweet, and spicy all in one bite. It wasn't what he'd call *delicious*, but it wasn't awful either. He nodded as he chewed and then said, "Yeah. Not bad."

But he hoped he wasn't going to have to eat it every day of the voyage.

"It better with fresh rice and sesame seeds," Jinsoo said. "I make rice next."

"Where did you learn to cook, Jinsoo?" Hestie asked.

"Orphanage," he said.

"How long did you live there?" Hermie asked.

"Twelve year," Mina replied. "We still have friends there. Jinsoo's boyfriend."

"He want to come with us," Jinsoo said. "But he only thirteen. You have to be fourteen to get job on ship."

"How long have you been working for the captain?" Hestie asked.

"Six month," Jinsoo said. "In six more month, my boyfriend can join."

"But we get new job," Mina said. "Captain get new orphans, train, and help them get better job. New orphans each year."

"That's great that the captain does that," Hestie said. "Maybe your boyfriend can get a job on the same ship as you, after the captain trains him, so you can be together."

Hermie wasn't sure if they were using the term boyfriend correctly. "By boyfriend, do you mean friend or…"

"They love each other," Mina said. "Not just friend."

"Cool," Hestie said.

"What's his name?" Hermie asked.

"Hanjae," Jinsoo said.

Hermie imagined it must be hard to be so far away from someone you cared about. This got him thinking about his parents. He'd never been away from them for this many days. "Can you visit him?"

"Yes," Mina said. "We see him after we drop you at Beijing. We visit all our old friends once a month. Captain takes food and medicine."

Hermie lifted his brows. "What city?"

"Seoul," Mina said.

Hermie smiled. "I've always wanted to see that city."

"Shut the truck up, Hermie!" Hestie teased. "You don't care about Seoul. Now, *me*, on the other hand, I'm *dying* to go!"

"You so funny!" Mina said. "Like on show!"

"Maybe we go to Seoul before Beijing?" Jinsoo said.

"That would be awesome," Hestie said. "But we're in a hurry to find our relative."

"Maybe we can make time for one day," Hermie said.

Hestie bent her brows as she glanced his way, but Hermie only smiled. He began to feel more hopeful about finding Prometheus without the notice of the gods.

CHAPTER THIRTEEN

Confrontations

Therese held tightly to her husband's hand where they were both being held prisoner in the great hall of Mount Olympus. Cupid and Psyche stood on either side of them near Aphrodite's throne. They weren't far from Hip and Jen. She could take five steps through the Graces and be beside them. But she couldn't get them to look at her. Couldn't they hear her prayers?

Unable to control the panic building inside her, Therese wanted to scream. She had a horrible, horrible feeling that Hades, who had just disappeared, was planning to undermine Zeus. If so, she and Than didn't have much longer to live.

She would be okay with that, she thought, if she could just see her kids one more time.

"Please look at me, Hip! Jen, what's going on?" she prayed again to each of them.

Suddenly, she felt someone beside her—someone invisible. Since neither Psyche nor the Graces seemed to notice, this person must also be invisible to them. That could only mean the helm was involved. What was Hades up to?

She felt pressure on her wrists, and then again on her ankles. Was he trying to free her? That seemed awfully risky, to attempt a rescue mission with nearly every god and goddess in the same room.

Than must have felt it too, because he gave her a worried look. Hopefully no one else noticed it.

"Whatever happens," she prayed to Hades and to Hip and to Jen—hoping they could hear her. "Whatever happens, please take care of Hermie and Hestie. Please tell them I love them."

"Apollo," Zeus said again. "I need you."

***

Hip flinched when his father reappeared at his side.

"Where have you been?" Hip prayed telepathically, just as Apollo had been called on by Zeus.

"Trying to free your brother and his wife, to no avail," he replied.

"Should I put everyone into the deep boon of sleep?" Hip asked.

"Save that as a last resort. If you do, they'll know you're a rebel."

Hip was ready to make the sacrifice if it was the only way to get Than and Therese out of Mount Olympus safely. Zeus had made it clear that if any Underworld god went against him, he wouldn't hesitate to kill them.

Apollo stepped down from his throne and walked to the center of the court, where he faced his father. "I have something to say."

"Is it another vision?" Zeus asked eagerly.

"No," Apollo said. "It's a confession."

To Hip's surprise, Apollo began to sing, and since his voice was the most beautiful of all the gods and mortals ever in existence, everyone in the great hall was happy to listen.

The last-born son of Cronos is the mightiest of all.
When he wields his thunderous lightning bolt,
And thrusts it into the heavens,
Any god or mortal in its wake is sure to fall.

Father to many and leader of all,
When he rules from his throne on Olympus,
His eagle soars the heavens,

And every god and mortal looks up to Zeus in awe.

His enemies fear him, as do those who follow him,
For he is the most powerful deity above;
Yet, he is my father, and, more than his might,
I want his love…

Familial love has escaped us for these many centuries.
Every god for himself or for herself,
Each one of us self-serving.
Today I will put an end to those miseries.

I choose love…

I choose love over power…

I choose love.

When Apollo had finished, Zeus looked down at him from where he stood on his throne and asked. "What are you saying, Apollo?"

Apollo glanced around at all present in the room, and it was then that Hip noticed the tears falling down the healing god's cheeks.

Apollo cleared his throat. "I can no longer serve you, Father."

"What? This is an outrage!" Hera cried.

"You can't be serious!" Ares shouted.

Hermes stepped from his throne toward Apollo. "Brother, think this through."

"I have," Apollo said, his face twisted in agony. "And I *am* serious. We need a pantheon that puts the needs of others first, that listens to the prayers of mortals and acts on them when possible."

Demeter stood on her throne. "How dare you? I answer prayers all the time."

"For half the year, you listen to no one," Apollo pointed out.

Demeter gaped. Then she cried, "Who are you to stand there and judge?"

"I am just as guilty," Apollo said. "I don't deny it. But I'm ready to change. I hope others among you are also ready. This needn't go to war."

"I will not step aside," Zeus said through gritted teeth.

"I will not serve you," Apollo repeated. "You are not the right leader for the change. You're too impulsive, selfish, disloyal…"

"Stop!" Hera demanded.

"Apollo, please!" Aphrodite cried.

Zeus's face turned pale white, and then, just as quickly, red as fresh blood. "You choose to turn your back on me, your own father? How can you do such a thing?"

"Like you did to Melinoe, your daughter, and to Poros, your son?" Apollo asked, through tears.

"Poros?" Zeus repeated. To himself, he muttered, "So that's his name." Aloud to Apollo, he asked, "You've seen him? What's he like?"

"Just and wise, like his sister," Apollo said.

Athena gasped and covered her mouth with a trembling hand.

Apollo continued, "He isn't self-serving—far from it. He doesn't want to rule."

"What does he want?" Zeus asked.

"To replace you with another," Apollo said.

"With whom?" Zeus demanded, still red-faced.

"He wants the council to vote," Apollo said.

"Please don't do this!" Hestia cried.

"You could run for the position, Father," Apollo added. "We needn't go to war."

"I will not step aside," Zeus said again.

"I will not serve you without the vote." Then Apollo shouted to the others, "You wanted democracy! Many of you joined the Athena Alliance and…"

Zeus shouted, "Put him in the trick chair and silence him!"

"This is our chance!" Apollo shouted again. "For true democracy!"

Ares and his sons overtook Apollo, who did not resist. They gagged him and threw him into the trick chair. Hermes helped.

Hip wondered what Zeus planned to do now. With Apollo's betrayal, Zeus had no way of discovering with certainty who was with him and who was against him.

Hip prayed to Apollo, "Thank you for your sacrifice."

Apollo replied, "I'm counting on you and your father to see this through."

***

Hestie stood on the extended upper deck beside her brother, with Mina and Jinsoo on the other side of him, watching the brilliant colors of the setting sun. Hestie could imagine Helios sitting in his cup, steering the brilliant chariot to the other side of the earth. The yacht was moving in the opposite direction across the Mediterranean Sea. Hestie waved, just in case Helios could see her.

"Who are you waving to?" Poros asked, coming up beside her. And then, before she could answer, he added, "Mmm. You smell good."

She blushed and couldn't quite meet his eyes. She looked down at her new shorts—the pair with the tiny elephants on them. "No one. Well, Helios. Do you believe in him?"

"Yes. I do," he said before lifting his hand to wave.

Hestie laughed. "I think he waved back."

"I'm sure he did," Poros said with a grin. "We're old friends."

"You're funny." Hestie giggled.

"It's nice to see you smile," he said. "I'd begun to worry I had somehow made a bad impression."

Hestie felt the blood leave her face. "No. Well, it's just…"

"Go on."

She decided to be straight with him. "I saw you in the alley in Patras." She lowered her voice. "You had one of the coins we gave the captain. What were you doing with all those pills?"

"Buying medicine for the poor," he said.

Hestie narrowed her eyes. "Seriously?"

"It's what we do, my uncle and I," he continued. "We buy medicine and food in the wealthier areas and deliver them to the villages along the coast that have nothing."

"You make enough money from passengers to afford that?" she asked, still not sure she believed him.

"No." Then he added, "We dive for buried treasure. My uncle is an expert at finding it."

Hermie overheard and repeated, "Buried treasure?"

"Seriously?" She thought he must be joking.

"True," Mina said. "We dive each month. Captain teach us."

Poros added, "Captain had one planned on this return trip to Seoul, but I think he'll postpone it."

She hoped not. "I've always wanted to learn how to deep-sea dive. I bet it's magical."

"Captain and I have been doing it together since I was ten years old," he said. "And it *is* magical." His brilliant gray eyes gleamed.

She was beginning to piece things together. He and his uncle trained orphans, to help them find jobs on ships, and they delivered food and medicine to the impoverished. They helped fund the operation by diving for treasure. "So, you aren't part of an offshore drug cartel?" she teased.

"Hestie!" Hermie reprimanded her. "Why would you say that?"

"I don't even know what that means," Poros said, laughing. "But I don't think so."

She laughed, too.

***

Hypnos stood between Jen and his father in the main chamber of the Underworld. Pete, Tizzie, Alecto, and Meg were with them. Hades had just informed the other members of their family of his secret rendezvous with Metis and Gaia and their plans to help Poros dethrone Zeus. They'd decided to leave Morpheus out of the meeting, because they were worried about his ties to Iris.

The Furies had questions, as was to be expected—such as who would lead in Zeus's place. Hades told them their plan to put it to a vote once the new council was formed. Until then, Hades would lead them.

Next, they discussed the Olympians they planned to recruit. Hip shared what Helios had told him about Apollo and Artemis—which was further enforced by Apollo's sacrifice earlier that day. This put Artemis at the top of their list. Hades also shared what Hip had told him from Helios about Prometheus, his mother Clymene, and Poros.

"Hermie and Hestie don't know that they are already on board with Prometheus?" Meg asked.

"No," Hip said. "But they're safe."

"Unless the identities of Poros and Prometheus are discovered by one of the loyalists," Alecto pointed out, as she stroked the snake around her neck.

"As a precaution, we will not share this information with the others," Hades said. "Agreed?"

Everyone nodded their consent.

"But isn't Prometheus recognizable?" Meg asked.

Her falcon squawked, as if in echo.

"I couldn't tell who he was," Hip said. "He wears a white captain's hat, dark sunglasses, and a burly man's beard—and I mean *burly*! He looks nothing like himself."

"But what about Poros?" Tizzie asked, her wolf sitting beside her on its haunches. "Apollo revealed his name. Won't the spies suspect that the son of Metis is on the same ship as the twins?"

"There must be hundreds of Greek boys named Poros," Hades said. "It's a common name."

"What about Than and Therese?" Pete asked. "Where are they?"

"They're still being held prisoner on Mount Olympus," Hades said. "Which leads me to our next order of business."

"Rescue?" Jen asked.

"Precisely," Hades said. "Before we can risk approaching any new recruits, we have to get Than and Therese out of there."

"We need to bring them here, for safe keeping," Hip added. "I would think at least until the war is over."

"Who else is on the list of recruits besides Artemis?" Tizzie asked.

"Poseidon and Athena," Hades said. "Hip approached them in their dreams."

"Poseidon has dropped several hints in the waking world, too," Hip said.

"He could be a spy," Alecto said. "He could be setting us up."

"The same could be true of Athena," Tizzie said.

Meg sighed as she pushed a strand of her blonde hair from her face. "That would break my heart."

Her falcon cawed.

"Which is why we must be very careful," Hades said.

"If we do get Poseidon," Hip said, "we can free Hecate from the pit."

"That will be our third objective," Hades said. "One: rescue Than and Therese. Two: recruit Artemis, Athena, and Poseidon. Three: free Hecate from the pit."

"And after that?" Jen asked.

"Don't worry," Hades said. "I have a plan."

"Won't rescuing Than and Therese put the twins in danger?" Pete asked.

"It might," Hades replied. "We must hope that Zeus's desire to use them to find Prometheus will outweigh his desire to exact his revenge on us."

"The twins are destined to restore humanity's faith in the gods and in one another," Meg pointed out. "Surely that means they're safe?"

"Unless they're destiny is fulfilled by their deaths," Pete said.

Hip frowned. "Let's try to be positive here."

"Sorry," Pete said.

CHAPTER FOURTEEN

A Ship in the Night

When the sky and sea became dark, the world seemed much smaller to Hermie where he stood beside Mina on the extended upper deck. He felt as if invisible walls had encased the ship.

But sometime after they'd passed the island of Crete, the dark clouds overhead dispersed, the night sky became bright with luminous stars and a brilliant moon, and the world was large again.

The captain sat in his swivel chair at the helm with Poros beside him. Hestie and Jinsoo sat across from them on the bolted-down couch behind the table. Only Mina and Hermie stood in the open air, away from the glass enclosure of the cockpit, to gaze at the stars.

"You see Big Dipper?" Mina asked, pointing straight above them.

Hermie had always been interested in stars and space, so he knew the constellations well. He also knew that now, in the springtime, the northern sky afforded the best view of the Big Dipper from their vantage point.

"Yes, and I can also see Big Bear," he said. "Can you?"

Mina wrinkled her nose in that cute way of hers when she wanted to show she didn't know something.

Hermie was glad for the chance to show off his knowledge to her.

He told her about Artemis, and her lover, Callisto, and how they used to run and hunt together with the nymphs of the woods.

"Artemis loved Callisto above all others, and Callisto loved Artemis," he said. "They even swore their loyalty to one another."

"Beautiful," Mina said with a gleam in her eye.

Hermie wanted to kiss her, but instead, he continued. "One day, Zeus disguised himself as Artemis and lay with Callisto."

Hermie noticed that he had drawn the attention of the captain and the others.

"Please continue," the captain said.

Hermie would rather tell the story to Mina, so it could be *their* moment, but he didn't want to be rude. He turned his back to the supporting rail to face the others and spoke a little more loudly.

"Callisto became pregnant," Hermie said. "And Artemis took this as a sign of infidelity."

"Oh, no," Mina said. "What happen?"

"Artemis told Callisto to leave, and while the nymph was running away with her broken heart, Hera, who'd heard of what had happened, turned Callisto into a bear."

"This is the part of the story where our mom always gets mad and says Hera shouldn't have punished the victim," Hestie said.

"I agree," Jinsoo said.

"Then what happen?" Mina asked.

"Years later, Callisto's son, who was born human, was out hunting and was about to unknowingly kill his own mom," Hermie said.

"Did he?" Mina asked.

"No." Hermie smiled at the expression of concern on her face. She was the cutest girl he'd ever met—not that there'd been many. "Zeus turned the son into a bear and threw them both into the sky, and they became Big Bear and Little Bear, or Ursa Major and Ursa Minor."

Hermie pointed to the stars and helped Mina see the constellations. He wanted to continue the story with how his mother had rescued Callisto and had helped her to reunite with Artemis, but he knew that would be saying too much.

"Very good, Hermie," the captain said. "I should tell that story to everyone I train. I teach them about the northern star and the big and little dipper, but that story makes a good impression. They'll remember it better."

"Thanks," Hermie said.

"Want to go watch *Naruto* on Captain's phone?" Mina asked him.

"We can watch it on my phone. I bought a charger and plugged it in earlier. It should be fully charged in my cabin by now. Are you sure we'll get a signal, though?"

"I subscribe to Maritime Internet Services," the captain said. "The customers seem to like it, and it's good to have for emergencies."

"Oh, can you text Lynn and let her know we're still okay?" Hestie asked him.

"If we get a signal," Hermie said.

"Come on," Mina said, leading the way.

He followed her to his cabin, where she opened the door and plopped on his bed, making herself comfortable with one of his pillows. He unplugged his phone from his charger and sat on the edge of the bed, trying to connect to the internet. He was surprised by how good the signal was.

"Four bars," he said. "Awesome."

"Yes."

First, he texted Lynn. She answered right away with one word: Cool.

Well, she didn't seem too worried.

"Which episode?" he asked Mina.

"*Shippuden*, one. Okay?"

Shippuden was the name of the second part of *Naruto*. "You want to start at the beginning of Part Two?" he asked, to be sure he understood her.

"Yes. Okay?"

"Sure." He liked the second part much better than the first, anyway, and it had just become available on Netflix. "I like to watch it in Japanese. Do you mind reading subtitles?"

"Sure. Okay."

He sat yoga-style on the bed next to where she lay. She moved the pillow to his lap and lay her head there, presumably to get a better view of the phone. He'd never been this close to a girl before—other than Hestie or Lynn. It felt strangely exhilarating, causing his hands to tremble.

He rested his hand on his knee to keep the phone from shaking, and, after a while, the episode distracted him enough that he began to feel more comfortable. He loved when Mina laughed or cried, "Oh, no!" in her dramatic way at something in the show. She'd look up at him, to see his expression, and he'd try to mirror hers.

As much as he loved his sister and his family, he couldn't recall ever enjoying someone's company quite as much as this.

***

Hestie could tell that Jinsoo was disappointed that he hadn't been invited to watch *Naruto* with Hermie and Mina but that he respected his sister's space enough not to invite himself. So she asked him about his favorite K-pop bands. After discovering that they shared some favorite singers and songs, they danced together on the extended deck—both knowing all the moves to a popular song by a group called BTS. Hestie felt a little silly and crazy dancing in front of Poros and the captain, but Jinsoo was just as crazy, and very enthusiastic, so she went with it. The captain and Poros clapped and asked for more.

They did two more dances, singing out loud in the otherwise quiet night, and then they collapsed together on the L-shaped couch, laughing and panting.

"We're so crazy," Hestie said. "I don't know what got into us!"

"That was fun!" Jinsoo said. "You got moves!"

"*You* got moves!" she said.

"We should make video!" he said, laughing.

"We should!" Hestie said. "I could post it to my channel. Would you like that? Half a million viewers would see your moves."

"No way."

After a while, the conversation ebbed again, and Poros and the captain seemed quiet and contemplative, so, once Hestie turned to the captain and said, "Poros told me that you deliver food and medicine to the less fortunate. That's really cool of you."

"There's a South Sudanese village I'm anxious to get back to," the captain said. "We should reach it in two days, if the weather cooperates."

Poros leaned forward, putting his elbows on his knees. "An epidemic has caused hundreds of people in the area to get deathly sick. A doctor from Alaska took a crew there to build a clinic, and people from miles away flock to it for medicine."

"The doctor wasn't prepared for the massive numbers of infected," the captain said. "They have to be given a treatment daily, you see, or they'll die."

"Some have died already," Poros said.

"How terrible," Hestie said. "I wish there was something I can do."

"Not unless you also speak Nuer," the captain said with a laugh.

"I do!" Hestie leaned forward. "I can speak every language."

"Really?" Jinsoo asked.

"*Every* language?" Poros asked.

"If it's one I haven't heard before, I need to hear it first," she explained. "But then I pick it right up."

When they each gave her a dubious look, she added, "It's a strange gift. I was born with it. Hermie, too."

"That's fantastic!" The captain slapped his thigh with glee. "Poros and I can speak the language, too, but the more, the better."

Poros leaned toward her, sitting on the edge of his seat. His brilliant gray eyes sparkled in the moonlight. "You and Hermie should come with us."

"The people need as much comfort and hope as we can give them," the captain added.

"We'd be happy to help however we can," Hestie said.

"The treatment is very painful," Poros said. "We try to comfort them with candy."

Hestie had never met such kind and generous people before. "That's so sweet."

Poros laughed, and then she realized her pun.

"Very sweet," the captain said, also laughing.

As the conversation ebbed again, she didn't mind the silence. She looked up into the night sky at the large moon. Once again, she had the feeling it was following her. She decided to send a silent prayer to Selene, "I don't know if you know me, but I feel like you're watching over me. Thank you."

And, again, she could have sworn she saw the moon wink at her.

"Selene looks beautiful tonight, does she not?" the captain remarked.

"She seems close," Hestie said.

"She is," Poros said. "You can almost reach out and touch her."

"Can I watch *Naruto* on your phone, Captain?" Jinsoo asked.

"You know where it is. Help yourself."

Hestie was surprised that the captain didn't keep his phone with him. Maybe he only used it in emergencies. Maybe he never expected anyone to call.

Jinsoo got up. "See you in morning."

"See you," Hestie said.

After a few more minutes of enjoying the night sky from the cockpit, Hestie said, "I guess I'll turn in, too. It's been a long day."

"'I'll walk down with you," Poros said.

She said goodnight to the captain as she climbed to her feet.

"Good night," he said. "If the weather cooperates, we'll be out of the Mediterranean Sea and well into the Suez Canal before you wake up."

"What about you, Captain? Don't you need to sleep?" she asked.

"Poros and I take turns on watch. You don't need to worry about that."

"Well, thank you," she said.

A nervous shiver shot up her spine as she led Poros down the hatch. She could feel those brilliant gray eyes on her. She wondered if he was assessing her. *Do you like what you see?*

When they reached the hull, Poros stopped her in front of the laundry room. "I'm curious, Hestie."

"About what?"

"About you."

Her brows lifted. So, she'd been right to think there was a spark between them.

"And your brother," he added.

She tried not to frown. "What about us?"

"Your gift with languages…I was wondering, were you born with any other special gifts?"

"You mean aside from beauty and brains?" she teased. She hadn't said it to sound cocky.

He smiled at her. "Yes, apart from those obvious gifts."

She laughed at his charm. Those eyes of his were mesmerizing. As much as she wanted to be honest with him, though, she couldn't very well tell him the truth. It would freak him out. "Like what?"

"I don't know…like extra strength, super speed."

Was this guy serious? "Why would you ask me that? I'm just a normal teenage girl."

"I don't think you are." He moved closer. "I don't think there's anything normal about you."

"I hope you meant that as a compliment."

"Absolutely."

His face was uncomfortably close to hers. She could even feel his breath on her mouth, which she opened as if to speak, only no words came out.

How awkward, she thought. *What are you trying to do to me, Poros?*

Suddenly he threw his head back and laughed, as though he could read her mind.

"What's so funny?"

"Do you play chess?" he asked—out of the blue, it seemed to Hestie.

"A little." Her father had taught her. They used to play all the time when she was younger, but she hadn't played in years.

"I have a handmade set in my room. Care to try your luck against me?"

It was her turn to laugh. "There's no luck in the game of chess, and it won't be luck when I beat you."

"Challenge accepted." He motioned toward his cabin. "After you."

***

Hypnos drove his father's chariot across the dark sky over the Aegean Sea toward Mount Olympus. Beside him, his father hid beneath the helm of invisibility. They were on a quest to find a weak spot in Zeus's fortress that might later be exploited in a rescue mission to save Than and Therese.

Hip glanced over his shoulder, and, with his godly sight, could just make out Prometheus's vessel sailing in the opposite direction toward the Red Sea. Selene flew close above it. Though she was miles away, he could see her perched in her chariot. He smiled at her, as he often did while bringing slumber to the dark side of the earth; and, as she often did, she smiled back.

Then she did something he'd never seen her do before. She jumped from her chariot and spread her luminous wings. In all these centuries, he'd never even seen her wings. They reminded him of Morpheus's, except that his were silver and opaque, whereas hers were transparent and surrounded by a halo of light.

Her chariot continued its usual route toward the west, in his direction; but Selene gave him a wave and turned away to follow *The Marcella* to the east.

Highly unusual.

When they reached the gates, Hip shouted, "Fall, Summer, Winter, Spring, open the gates of Mount Olympus so that I, Hypnos, may enter."

The clouds parted and the great gates opened, and they were enveloped in sunshine, since the sun always shone here. Hip drove the chariot into the garage and parked it beside the others. Usually Cupid appeared to attend to the horses, but, tonight, it was Psyche.

"Thanks," Hip said.

"My pleasure," she replied as she unbridled Swift and Sure and fed them some hay.

When he entered the palace, only Zeus and Hera were in the main hall on their thrones. The other gods were either in their rooms or away from Mount Olympus.

Zeus climbed to his feet. "Hypnos! It's a pleasure to see you. What brings you here?"

"Two things, Lord Zeus," he said. "First, I want to report that the twins are still headed in the direction of Beijing in their search for Prometheus."

"Yes, we know," Hera said. "There was no need for you to come all this way."

"And the second reason, my queen, is to visit Than and Therese," Hip said. "We wouldn't want them to die of boredom and render themselves useless, now would we?" he added with a wink.

"Are you suggesting that we lack the powers to entertain?" Zeus asked in a light and teasing tone.

"Of course not, my lord," Hip replied. "But I know you're far too busy with more important matters."

Zeus laughed. "Well, go on then. You know where they are."

As Hip crossed the great hall to Demeter's rooms, he wondered if his father was still beside him. It was eerie how undetectable one was when beneath the helm.

When Hip entered the room, Therese, who'd been seated beside Than on Demeter's couch, stood up. "Are Hermie and Hestie okay?"

"Yes," Hip said. "Relax. Selene is with them."

Near the door, Cupid asked, "What do you mean, Selene is with them?"

Hip inwardly berated himself for not keeping his mouth shut. "I just mean that she happens to be above them right now. I saw her on my trip over."

"Ares and Hermes are watching the twins," Cupid said under his breath. "There's no reason for Selene to keep an eye on them, too, unless…"

Hip watched in horror as a shadow of suspicion crossed Cupid's features.

"Unless what?" Hip asked, innocently. "You know the moon goddess has always remained neutral in these matters. I wouldn't worry about it. I was just trying to comfort my sister-in-law."

Now Hip felt as though he had protested too much. His defensive stance probably made him suspicious along with Selene. Maybe he should stop talking, he thought.

"Come and join us," Than said. "Tell us how everyone is doing back home."

By "back home," Hip knew his brother meant the Underworld. It had been his home for centuries before he moved to Colorado. Colorado would never be "home."

Hip sat down in a chair across from Than and Therese. Persephone came in from a back room and kissed his cheek. Cubie and Galin followed and said their hellos.

"Oh, I'm so happy to see you, my darling!" his mother sat on the couch beside Than. "I've been worried sick about everyone, with all that's going on."

"We're all fine," Hip said.

"Except for my poor, sweet Hecate." Persephone frowned and wiped a tear from her cheek.

Cubie whined until Persephone stroked her fur and quieted her down.

"Hopefully the crisis will pass soon," Hip said, not wanting to give anything away.

"Any more news on Prometheus's whereabouts?" Than asked.

"The belief is that he's still in Beijing," Hip lied. "Hecate's location spell was performed several days ago, so we can't be certain he hasn't moved."

"Have you had a chance to check on our animals?" Therese asked. "Has Lynn been managing alright?"

"Oh, I forgot," Hip said. "I've just disintegrated and am looking through the house now. They look fed—though since my arrival, they've all fallen asleep."

"Let them sleep," Therese said. "They'll have less time to worry."

"Perhaps Morpheus can send them good dreams," Persephone suggested.

"I'll mention it to him," Hip said.

Galin curled up in a ball. "I pray you do the same for me."

Hip granted her wish.

"What about Carol and Richard and Therese's parents?" Than asked.

"Everyone seems fine. The birds look worried, but Carol and Richard don't seem to be." Then Hip added, "Enjoy your nappy-nap. Sorry, that was meant for *them*, not *you*."

Persephone laughed. "You've always been such a delight to me, son."

Hip was happy to see his mother smile. Very few people were smiling these days.

After a few minutes of catching up, Hip found himself struggling to come up with safe conversation. He had to keep it going, so Cupid wouldn't suspect anything as his father searched for a way to free Than and Therese. He hoped the plan would include bringing his mother home as well—if that was even possible before summer's end.

At least his mother could defend herself. Than and Therese were like sitting ducks.

C H A P T E R   F I F T E E N

Rescue Missions

Two days of eating nothing but kimchi had Hermie eager to try something new. The captain had promised to take them to the best restaurant in Port Sudan when they returned from the village in South Sudan.

What Hermie hadn't realized, since geography wasn't his best subject, was that they would be chartering a small plane.

"Doesn't someone need to stay with the ship, so no one steals it?" Hermie asked as they unloaded the supplies onto the dock.

"It's locked up," Poros said. "No worries."

As soon as he could, Hermie pulled his sister aside. "Gaia said to avoid flight, remember?"

"I know, but these people need our help."

"Mom and Dad need our help."

"I already said I would go, to speak with the locals," she said. "If you want to stay behind, that's up to you."

He sighed and followed her and the others with his boxes to the end of the dock.

They took a twenty-minute shuttle from the harbor to the airport, to a private hangar, where they met with their pilot. The whole time they loaded the cargo area of the plane with their sacks and boxes, Hermie's stomach churned. It was an awfully small plane.

The six of them barely fit with the pilot. Even having Mina squeezed up against him didn't make him feel better when they took off. She noticed his expression—there was no way to hide it because he was utterly terrified—and took his hand. He didn't feel her hand squeezing his until they had finally landed in what seemed like the middle of nowhere. He took two puffs from his inhaler, but it didn't help.

The South Sudanese village was a mile hike from the tiny airstrip, and there were a lot of sacks and boxes to carry without the help of a cart. Hermie was just glad to be alive and on land again, and he was also glad for his super strength as he plodded along behind Mina beneath the hot sun on the dirt road. But he felt sorry for the others and found himself asking, "Everyone still doing okay?" every few minutes.

There weren't shuttles, buses, subways, or even mules here. People had to be their own mules.

"I can carry more, if you need me to, Captain," Hermie said again.

"Thank you, Hermie," the captain said from the front of the group. "I think we're all still doing okay."

Poros and Hestie laughed.

"Sorry," Hermie said, feeling indignant. "Just trying to be helpful."

Mina slowed to walk beside him. "Can you take this?"

Jinsoo passed them as Hermie stopped to take one of Mina's sacks.

"Thank you," she said.

Hermie wished they could walk faster, but he kept himself at Mina's pace. She was breathing hard, and he could see she was tired.

"I think we're almost there," he said, though he had no clue how much farther they had to go.

It turned out that he'd been right. Within five minutes of his prediction, a settlement came into view. It consisted of a squat metal building and a half-dozen tents.

"That's the doctor's camp," Poros said. "See all those people? They come each morning for their injections."

"There must be at least five hundred people!" Hestie said, taking out her phone.

"Nine hundred," Jinsoo said. "Many babies. Cute. But sick."

"Is it okay if I record some of this?" Hestie asked.

"It would be helpful if you posted it," Poros said. "If more people knew about this, maybe more would help."

"I agree," the captain said.

Many of the locals wore fine, colorful clothing and jewelry. Hermie hadn't expected them to look like regular people. He'd been expecting them to look like the bloated-bellied and half-naked victims on the Feed the Children commercials.

The people stood or sat on the ground in a long line. Healthier-looking kids played along the perimeter. When the healthier kids noticed Hermie and his group, they started clapping and making a high-pitched sound, like birds.

The patients in the line turned to see what was happening, and their faces lit up when they saw that more medicine was coming. They joined the clapping and the chirping.

It made Hermie very glad he'd come. He would have hated to have missed this.

As they got closer to the line, Hermie noticed that many of the patients did *not* look normal. Now he could clearly see the malnourished and the dying. He could see their pain and despair. Some patients were much worse off than others.

"What causes their illness?" Hestie asked.

"A parasite," Poros said. "Carried by a fly."

"Can we get the parasite, too?" Hermie asked.

"It's possible, but not likely," the captain replied.

One of the South Sudanese leaders and an American greeted them and showed them where to put the supplies. Once his hands were free, Hermie gave the people in line a wave. A little boy waved back.

If he could hear their language spoken, Hermie could pick it up and speak it back to them, but he needed to hear it first.

That opportunity came quickly when a doctor announced that they would now begin the injections. To speed things up, syringes were given to everyone in line. Hermie followed one of the South Sudanese doctors carrying the box of syringes, so the doctor could more easily hand them out. The others in the captain's crew went to different parts of the very long line to do the same.

In their language, Hermie told each of them, "I hope you feel better soon." And he was told in reply, "Thank you."

Hermie thought that once the supplies were delivered and the syringes handed out, that it would be time to leave, but Hestie told him that they were going to stay and comfort the patients with candy after each of them received a shot.

Although his belly was starving for something other than kimchi, Hermie was glad to be there to help. It was difficult to watch the patients suffer through the painful injections, especially the children. Many of them screamed, and all of them shed tears, but Hermie gave each person a lollipop and said the gods were watching over them—even though he doubted that they were.

After they had given the last patient her candy, Hermie was surprised when Mina came up beside him and kissed him on the cheek.

Two little boys standing nearby chirped like birds.

***

Hestie was pleased when, on the plane ride back to Port Sudan, she ended up sitting beside Poros. On the way down, she'd sat between Mina and Jinsoo.

The ride back was far more exciting than the ride there.

And she felt better now, in the plane. While they'd been at the medical camp, the pain and agony of the patients and the despair of their loved ones was overwhelming. Hestie had put on a brave face as she spoke with the people in line, helping to hand out syringes and then, after, candy. She'd asked them to wave to the camera and to say hello, which many had done cheerfully, in spite of how ill they'd felt.

But as soon as it was all over and it was time to hike back to the airplane, Hestie had broken down in tears. She wept for the ones that had already died, the ones that looked like they would be next, and for those still struggling. She was especially sad for the relatives who had to watch their loved ones fight for their lives.

Poros had come and had put an arm around her as they'd walked, but, instead of taking comfort, she'd turned and asked, "Why don't the gods help them? Instead of fighting amongst themselves, why can't they intervene on behalf of those people?"

"Hestie," Hermie had warned from behind. "Don't."

Hestie had clamped her mouth shut, though she'd wanted to say more.

Poros had calmed her down by saying, "Maybe if we pray hard enough, the gods will answer our prayers."

She'd looked up at his brilliant gray eyes twinkling in the afternoon sun. "I hope so." Then she'd closed her eyes and prayed, "To any god or goddess who can hear me, I beg you to help the dying people in South Sudan and those in need everywhere."

Beside him in the plane, she looked up again at his brilliant gray eyes, and even though she knew everyone would hear it, she whispered, "Has anyone ever told you how beautiful your eyes are?"

Poros laughed. "Only my mother."

Everyone else in the plane laughed too, including the pilot.

***

Hip glanced across the main room of the Underworld palace at his father, who'd been sitting with his head in his hands for many moments, while Hip and his sisters, along with Jen and Pete, waited in silence.

Then Jen did something unusual. She walked up to Hades and put a hand on his arm. "There must be something we can do."

At last, Hades looked up—first at Jen, and then at the others. "There is. But it's very dangerous, and I'm not sure we should attempt it."

Jen returned to Hip's side.

"Tell us," Hip said.

His father sat back, crossed his arms, and sighed like a tired old man. "I searched long and hard for any possible weakness and found none."

"You found nothing?" Tizzie repeated. Her wolf, beside her, whined. "No way in or out?"

"There is one way," he said. "We've used it before."

Hip's stomach tightened. He didn't like where this was going.

"Those cuffs on Than and Therese are impenetrable," Hades continued. "The only way to break their bond is through death."

"I don't like the sound of this," Pete said.

"What do you have in mind?" Alecto asked, stroking the snake around her neck.

"Persephone is prepared to give Than and Therese ambrosia," Hades said. "Since they're mortal, it will kill them instantly."

Hip felt his mouth go dry. "Would our mother agree to such a thing?"

"It was her idea," Hades said. "All of this—praying to Metis, the rebellion—all of it was her idea. She's hated Zeus ever since we discovered what he did to Melinoe."

"What will happen once Mother gives Than and Therese the ambrosia?" Tizzie asked.

"Pete will collect their souls while I follow beneath the helm," Hades said. "I'll gather the bodies and follow Pete back through the gates. We'll take the chariot, just to be safe, so as not to be intercepted."

"Will our mother come, too?" Hip asked.

Hades pulled at his beard. "Unfortunately, no. Her stay on Mount Olympus is an ancient deal that even I can't break. Who knows what Demeter would do? It's unthinkable."

Alecto's hands rushed to her fire-red hair. "What if Zeus swallows her?"

"I intend to pass her my helm at the gate," Hades said. "She'll remain on Mount Olympus, hidden. Safe."

Hip wasn't so sure about that. Being invisible didn't necessarily make her safe.

"Then what will you do with Than and Therese?" Meg asked. "Will you resurrect them here?"

"The Fates may not allow that," Pete pointed out.

"I want to do more than resurrect them," Hades said.

Hip glanced at Jen before turning back to his father. "What do you mean?"

"I want to make them into gods again."

"You can't do that!" Tizzie cried, and her wolf howled. "Jen will become a mortal again! And Pete…Pete will die!"

Hades climbed down from his throne and put his hands on Tizzie's shoulders. "I wouldn't have them trade fates again, my dear. Your husband and his sister are safe."

"Then what?" Meg asked.

Hades turned. He now stood in the center of their gathering, and Hip could see the fear and the worry on his father. It had aged him.

"Than and Therese will have to undergo apotheosis again," Hades said. "The same way Therese was transformed the first time."

All of them looked at one another with shock on their faces.

Jen was the one who asked, "You're going to burn them alive?"

Hades took a long, deep, sad breath. "It's the only way."

CHAPTER SIXTEEN

Diving into Trouble

Over the next few days, *The Marcella* delivered food and medical supplies to ports in Ethiopia and Somalia. Trucks met them at the docks and carted off the boxes and sacks, so Hermie didn't have the satisfaction of meeting the end users like he had experienced in South Sudan. He still felt good, however, knowing that he was helping people, and he had secretly hidden notes in the supplies with his drawings of some of his favorite anime and comic book characters, hoping children would find them and enjoy the surprise.

He'd also hoped that the captain would take them to a restaurant, like he had in Port Sudan, where Hermie had feasted on the most delicious seafood platter of his life. Unfortunately, the last few days had been kimchi days.

He swore to himself that if he ever got off this ship, he would never eat kimchi again.

On the other hand, as anxious as he was to find Prometheus and free his parents, and as much as he was growing to despise kimchi, he was still enjoying his time on the ship, mainly because of the pleasure he took in his new friends—especially Mina.

Jinsoo had a decent collection of Yugioh cards that he was given at the orphanage, and they created two strong decks from them. It was fun to have a tournament together with Mina and Jinsoo in the salon. Alongside them, Poros and Hestie had a chess tournament with the captain. When it was the captain's turn to play, Poros manned the ship and vice versa; and when the captain and Poros played one another, either Mina or Jinsoo took the helm.

Tonight, they were all gathered in the cockpit—the captain and Poros in the leather swivel seats and the rest of them on the L-shaped couch. Hermie and Mina had been playing dominoes against Hestie and Jinsoo, until there was no longer enough light to see by. Now, they just sat together and visited, enjoying each other's company. This was the part that Hermie would miss the most.

Then Poros asked, "Will we be diving in the Arabian Sea this month, Captain?"

"Please?" Hestie blurted out. "I've always wanted to do that."

"I'm afraid I can't allow you to dive without proper instruction," the captain said to her. "It's not something you can just pick up in a few days."

Hestie frowned.

"But you could snorkel while some of us dive," he said. "Would you like that, Hestie?"

"Yes, I would!" she said.

"So that means we're diving?" Poros asked.

Jinsoo clapped his hands. "When?"

The captain chuckled at everyone's enthusiasm—except for Hermie's, because he had no desire to get in the water. "Tomorrow. We should reach the Arabian Sea tomorrow."

"Why the Arabian Sea?" Hermie asked.

"If I tell you, you must swear on the River Styx to tell no one," the captain said.

Hermie was surprised to hear a regular mortal require an oath on the Styx. "I swear."

"Me, too," Hestie said.

"Everyone else has already heard this story," the captain said. "Back in the seventies, a wealthy diplomat to the Shah of Iran was afraid his very valuable Persian family heirlooms would be taken by the revolutionaries, so he secretly commissioned a cargo ship to carry his treasure from Bandar Abbas all the way to France."

"What kind of treasure?" Hermie asked.

"Jewels, coins, paintings, sculptures, golden chests and urns—I don't even know the extent of it," the captain said. "These were very fine, and many dated back to the old Persian Empire."

"That's incredible!" Hestie said. "But why a ship? Why not a plane?"

"This diplomat was afraid that if he tried to smuggle his treasures through the airport, they would be confiscated, and that he would be detained as an obvious defector."

"That makes sense," Hermie said. "So, was the ship attacked?"

"No," Poros said. "If it had been, others would know of the sunken treasure."

"Exactly," the captain said. "We've been fortunate that very few other divers seem to have come upon any of it, as it's spread throughout the Arabian Sea, and probably beyond. We've already uncovered coins and jewels worth millions."

"What happened to the ship?" Hermie asked. "Does anyone know?"

The captain crossed one leg over the other. "Sometime in the dark of night, as it entered the Arabian Sea from the Gulf of Oman, the ship went down."

"Does anyone know why?" Hestie asked.

"The survivors said it cracked in half," Poros said.

"Cracked in half?" Hestie repeated. "How?"

The captain ran his fingers though his impressive beard. "They believed it was caused by a design flaw. The treasures weren't on the official cargo record, so the diplomat received no compensation and had no grounds for suing the manufacturer of the ship. He lost everything."

"Did he ever look for it?" Hestie asked.

"He was killed in France by the revolutionaries before he ever had the chance," the captain said.

"How terrible," Hestie said.

"How do you know about it, if you don't mind my asking?" Hermie said.

"He was a friend of mine, and I was the captain of the ship that went down. I was helping him and others like him to relocate, but the revolutionaries got wind of his whereabouts. He and his wife and two young girls were murdered in their sleep."

Hermie studied the captain's face. If he was old enough to have captained a ship in the seventies, he had to be in his sixties, but he looked half that age.

"How awful," Hestie said. "Why is there so much evil in the world?"

The captain sighed. "I ask myself that every day."

***

"Let me go with you," Hip said to his father as he prepared to rescue Than and Therese with Pete.

Pete was already sitting in the chariot, waiting, while Hades gave Swift and Sure an apple each before the drive.

"It will put you at risk unnecessarily," Hades said. "You stay here and guard the Underworld."

"Jen and my sisters can handle that," Hip said. "I want to drive the chariot."

"Pete can do it," Hades said. "You do recall that he can be at more than one place at a time? It's called disintegration."

Pete smirked.

"I'm aware," Hip said. "But if something happens to Pete…"

"Nothing's going to happen to Pete."

"I hope you're right. I'm almost sure you're right. But if something *does* happen to Pete, the chariot will be vulnerable. Let me go with you."

Maybe because he was tired of arguing, or maybe because he was in a hurry—for whatever reason—Hades relented, and Hip drove the chariot toward Mount Olympus.

"Do you feel their souls calling to you yet?" Hip asked Pete once they were in the air above the Ionian Sea.

"Not yet."

"What if my mother doesn't go through with it?" Hip asked.

"She will," Hades said from beneath the helm. "Now stop talking and drive."

***

Thanatos looked up from Demeter's couch at his mother as she handed him and Therese a goblet each, filled with ambrosia.

"Have a drink," she said nonchalantly, putting herself between them and Cupid, who stood guard at the door.

Than narrowed his eyes. "But…"

"Trust me," she said, in light-hearted speech. She lifted her brows up and down, beseeching him to drink.

Silently he prayed, "How do I know you're my mother?"

Aloud, and in the same casual tone, she said, "I can still recall when you were a baby, when your brother was being born. Remember? Hera sent those horrible Harpies, and you helped fight them off as I gave birth to Hip."

"Doesn't everyone know that story?" he prayed silently.

"We don't have a lot of time…before your dinner." Again, her eyes pleaded with him. "Trust me. You'll like it."

Than looked at Therese. The blood had left her cheeks, and tears had formed in her eyes. She sat beside him very, very still—as if she'd stopped breathing. He wished he could read her thoughts. As if in answer, she nodded and put the cup to her lips.

Perhaps Hermie and Hestie were in danger, and the only way for his father to save them was to kill Zeus's prisoners.

"What's going on over there?" Cupid asked. "Is something wrong?"

Persephone turned, blocking Cupid's view of Than and Therese on the couch. "No, my dear."

If the goddess before him wasn't his mother, she wouldn't need to trick Cupid, right? It must be her.

Then he recalled a song she used to sing to him when he was a baby. No one else knew it.

"Sing me the song you used to sing when I was a baby," he prayed to her.

Aloud, the goddess sang:

Sweet little cherub, don't you cry.
Sleep will be coming, and soon you'll fly
Up to the stars and into the night.
A kiss for Selene and all is bright.

That was it. This must, indeed, be his mother. Therese looked at him, wide-eyed, as he put the cup to his lips. This was the end. He'd never know how it all turned out, if his children fulfilled their destiny. He held Therese's hand and sent a prayer to everyone in his family, telling them he loved them and that he hoped he was doing the right thing. Tears flooded his eyes as Therese drank, too.

***

Hestie hadn't thought to buy a bathing suit at the boutique in Patras, but Mina had one she could borrow—though it was a tiny bikini that barely fit. Hestie had at first refused to wear it, but Mina, who had followed Hestie into her cabin, and who was wearing one herself that was even tinier, had insisted.

"You look good," Mina said. "Very good. Okay?"

"Thanks." Hestie checked herself out in the small mirror over her bathroom sink. She felt very self-conscious, but she really wanted to snorkel. "Should I put on a pair of shorts? I think I should."

"No shorts. Just go. Captain waiting."

Mina shooed Hestie from the cabin. At the bottom of the steps, near the laundry room, Poros emerged from his cabin in a pair of trunks. Without a shirt, his chiseled chest made him look much older than fifteen.

"Wow." He gave Hestie a once over.

"Good. Right?" Mina asked.

"Right," Poros said with a grin.

Hestie rushed up the steps and through the hatch, trying to hide her embarrassment. She found the captain on the lower deck, at the stern. Jinsoo was already in his gear and in the water, holding onto the ladder at the rear of the ship. The captain was suited up, too, and fell back into the water with a splash just as Hestie and the others had arrived.

"Ready?" Poros asked her, handing her a mask and snorkel.

"Aren't you going to suit up first?" she asked.

"Nah. I'm going to snorkel with you." He handed her a pair of flippers. "Besides, I can hold my breath for a very long time."

"True," Mina said.

"What about you, Mina?" Hestie asked. "Aren't you coming?"

"No. I stay with Hermie."

Hestie wasn't surprised that Hermie wasn't going. "Okay. See you."

"See you," Mina said.

"Before you get in, I need to go over some rules with you," the captain said from where he was treading water near the boat.

After he had given her his spiel, she jumped in, feet first, unable to believe how utterly cold the water was. It was much, much, much colder than Lemon Reservoir back home.

She sprang back up to the surface and squealed, "Oh my gods!!"

Poros, who had jumped in behind her, laughed. "You'll get used to it." Then he added, "I wonder if you're as competitive in the water as you are on the chess board."

"You better believe it!"

As she treaded water, she fitted the mask and snorkel to her face and mouth, pressing the mask against her to get a good seal. She knew what she was doing, because she grew up snorkeling and kayaking in the reservoir across from her house. Hermie used to go when they were little, too, but once a water moccasin surprised him, and he never went into the water again.

She pulled the snorkel from her mouth and asked Poros—since Jinsoo and the captain had already gone under, "Are there any sharks or octopi, or any other big sea creatures around here?"

"Don't worry," he said. "They never bother us."

"So, you're saying yes?"

"Yes." He moved closer to her. "But I promise to protect you."

She smiled sweetly, wishing she could reveal the truth: if they *did* get attacked, *she* would have to protect *him*. *She* was the one with the super strength. And she hadn't asked because she was *afraid* of sea creatures. She'd asked, because she was hoping to see some.

She slipped the snorkel into her mouth, took a deep breath, and dove.

***

It's time," Pete said to Hip.

Hip gripped the reins and prayed to his father. Pete stayed with him in the chariot, even as he entered the gates of Mount Olympus. Hopefully Hades would have no problem sneaking in behind him.

Hip hated that all he could do was wait. He wanted to go in there and defend his brother and Therese. He wanted to protect his mother. He wanted to do anything but sit here.

But sit he did.

In the next moment, he heard shouts coming from inside the palace walls. Now was the moment of truth. He disintegrated into the hundreds to form a barrier around the chariot just as Nike flew from her post at the gates on golden wings.

Pete was behind her, also disintegrated into many, and he carried the souls of Than and Therese. But Nike's arrow penetrated his side, and Pete integrated into the one injured. Hip rushed to his aide and helped him and the souls into the chariot as more arrows flew.

Artemis appeared and shouted at Nike to stand down.

A lightning bolt shot from the palace and barely missed the chariot.

Hades appeared, without his helm, holding the bodies of Than and Therese. He shouted to Hip to drive as Artemis shot Nike down.

"You better come with us," Hades said to Artemis as another lightning bolt illuminated the sky.

"I won't leave my brother," she said.

Zeus and Hera were visible, just inside the open gate, from where the Graces, followed by Phobos and Deimos, emerged, armed.

"Get in. We have a plan. Trust me," Hades insisted.

Hip drove the chariot down, down toward the depths of the Underworld as more lightning bolts shot at them. If anyone were to get hit, they could be paralyzed forever.

Through gritted teeth, Hades muttered, "Damn that Artemis for not trusting me. Now we're going to have to save her hide, too."

"Don't curse me, Uncle," Artemis said, appearing beside them in the chariot.

"Good!" Hades said, clapping her back. "Smart move. I'll explain the plan when we get home. Meanwhile, tell Callisto to hide."

***

Hermie stood on the upper extended deck beside Mina, watching Hestie and Poros snorkeling in the sea below. The captain and Jinsoo hadn't surfaced for over twenty minutes. He hoped, for their sakes, they wouldn't come up empty-handed. He'd hate for them to be disappointed, especially considering all they did for others.

Mina laughed beside him. "Look how cute!" she pointed to Poros and Hestie, who seemed to be racing from the surface. "You think he love her?"

"It's too soon for that," Hermie said.

"I mean *like*. He like her, yes?"

"I think so."

"I like *you*," Mina added, her cheeks flushed pink.

Hermie felt color rising to his own cheeks. "Thanks. I like you as well."

He had tried to speak to her in Korean, but she had insisted that they speak English, because the captain said it was important to learn.

But sometimes he wasn't sure if he was understanding her completely. When she said she *liked* him, what exactly did she mean? He had the feeling she meant as someone more than a friend. He hoped so, because he felt that, even though it was too soon to *love* her, he was falling for her. He wasn't sure what he was going to do when it was time to leave the ship to hunt for Prometheus.

"I really hope we'll keep in touch," he added.

"Me, too."

Suddenly the sky to the west cracked in half, and lightning exploded. Shortly after, thunder roared, and a chilling wind burst past them, flattening their hair in all directions.

"That storm blew in fast," Hermie said.

The water where they were anchored was still smooth, but in the distance, swells were forming.

"It getting rough," Mina said. "I tell Poros to tell Captain."

Mina disappeared through the hatch and reappeared on the lower deck. She cupped her hands around her mouth and shouted, "Poros! Poros!"

Suddenly, the ship pitched back, and Mina fell overboard. Hermie held tightly to the rail. "Mina!"

He was relieved when she popped up to the surface and looked up at him. But her face held an expression of horror. She pointed and screamed.

Hermie looked up in time to see a sky full of Harpies.

"Hermie!" Mina screamed. "Jump!"

Before Hermie could react, one of the Harpies swooped down with her giant wings and snatched him from the ship.

"Hermie!" Mina screamed.

He kicked and flailed and grabbed at the talons clutching his left arm, but nothing succeeded in setting him free. He was soaring through the sky over the wide sea, to where, he did not know.

CHAPTER SEVENTEEN

Carried Away

As Hestie swam beside Poros toward the bottom of the sea, she refrained from going full speed, but every time she pulled ahead of him, he pulled ahead of her, until they were both swimming much faster than was expected of mortals.

Was Poros a demigod, too?

She studied his face, only to find him smiling back at her. He didn't seem surprised by her speed. Since she needed air, she headed back toward the surface. She swam more slowly going up than she'd swam going down, so as not to put her body through the change in pressure too quickly again. She was already feeling light-headed.

She tried to distract herself by admiring the colorful school of fish only a few yards away. It was too dark for her to see the ocean floor, but there were plenty of things to see on the way up—no sharks, though.

But she couldn't shake the feeling that there was more to Poros than she had realized.

When she reached the surface, she heard Mina screaming over by the ship, about thirty feet away. Mina was looking up and pointing toward the sky. Hestie looked up, too.

Harpies swarmed the sky, and one of them was flying off with her brother.

***

Hip helped his father lay Than and Therese's bodies on the big golden banquet table of the Underworld palace. Then he pulled the arrow from Pete's side, so he could heal and disintegrate again.

Pete had smuggled the souls in through a back entrance, near the Hydra's sink hole, because, if he had taken them to Charon, they would have had to pass through judgment and be sentenced to Erebus, Tartarus, or the Elysian Fields. Then the Fates would have been made aware of the deaths. And, if that had happened, the only way to bring Than and Therese back to the world of the living would have been through a trade.

Two people would have had to die.

Than and Therese could not undergo apotheosis unless their souls inhabited their bodies.

Even now, they were in danger of being caught. Pete needed to make the souls malleable, so they could re-enter their bodies again; however, mortal souls weren't meant to do so. It was unnatural. Once they left their bodies, mortal souls became indifferent to them and quickly lost their will to live.

Hip watched helplessly as Pete tried, again and again, to coax the souls, but it was if Than and Therese were dream-walking, or stoned, or…dead.

"What's wrong?" Artemis asked. "Why isn't it working?"

"Is it your wound?" Hip asked. "Is that's what's preventing…"

"No," Pete said. "I'm already healed."

"Something is interfering," Hades said in a desperate voice Hip wasn't used to hearing. "Something is wrong. I can sense it."

"How much time do we have before the bodies will completely reject the souls?" Hip asked.

"We need to put them on ice," Hades replied. "It's already been an hour, and they've grown cold." Then he muttered, "Dear gods, what have we done?"

Hip disintegrated to gather two basins of ice. He knew it was risky to god-travel, but Therese and Than's lives were on the line. He went to two different ranches for troughs that were long enough, and then he filled them with chiseled ice from a mountaintop in Canada.

"I don't understand," Pete said in frustration. "It's like some force is blocking them from entering."

"Funny you should say that," Clotho, the spinner, said, as she appeared at the end of the long table wearing her pink velvet pantsuit. Half of her gray hair sat in a bun on the crown of her head, and the other half lay in straight lines along her back and shoulders.

"I didn't realize we had come to this part already," said Atropos, the cutter, as she appeared, holding her blue shawl tightly across her plump shoulders. "Ever since you put in that roulette wheel, time flies."

"You could show more gratitude," Hades said.

"And you call yourself the god of justice." Lachesis, the measurer, appeared and glared at Hades over her black-rimmed spectacles. "You know the rules, and yet you chose to break them."

"If only my brother were here," Artemis said. "Maybe he could save them."

"These threads have been cut," Atropos said. "It's too late, even for Apollo."

"These souls can't leave here without a trade," Clotho added.

Hip disintegrated into the dozens and created a wall around the souls. "You can't have them."

The three Fates laughed.

"He thinks he can stop fate!" Lachesis screeched.

"You're hilarious!" Clotho said. "And rather easy on the eyes, if you don't mind my saying."

Hip wanted to spit, but he refrained. How could the Fates make light of life and death? This was his *brother*—his *best friend*. He couldn't lose him.

His fragmented selves arrived with the basins of ice.

"Better be quick with those," Lachesis warned. "Their time is running out."

Pete and Artemis helped Hip slide the basins under each body on the table.

"You said they can't leave the Underworld," Hades said. "So be it. But let them inhabit their bodies while they remain here forever."

Hip opened his mouth in shock. Than and Therese wouldn't want to spend eternity imprisoned. What was his father doing?

"Would they want such a thing?" Artemis asked.

"We need a trade," Atropos insisted. "Two souls for two souls."

"I know of many who are on the verge of death," Pete said. "I'll trade you two of them."

"That won't work," Clotho said. "You can't trade souls who are practically ours already."

"We need fresh souls," Lachesis said. "Or Than and Therese stay dead."

"You have twenty-four hours to decide," Atropos said before the Fates disappeared.

Hip's face twisted in despair. His father would never murder anyone, even for his own son. How had his plan gone so terribly wrong?

"What are we going to do?" Artemis asked.

***

Hestie climbed aboard the ship and ran as fast as she could toward the upper deck, where she could just make out her brother being towed away by a Harpy.

Then Mina screamed, "Watch out! Behind you!"

Hestie turned in time to see another Harpy, and it was coming for her. She flattened against the floor of the deck, but the half-bird, half-woman snatched her in its talons and lifted her into the air.

Poros was suddenly in the sky, flying beside them.

Poros could fly?

From out of nowhere, he conjured a sword and attacked the Harpy. Two other Harpies circled around from above and flew down to attack. Poros expertly used his sword and wounded one of them, frightening the other so that it retreated up into the skies.

Then Poros caught up to the Harpy carrying her and whacked off the Harpy's leg. Blood spilled everywhere as Hestie dropped through the air toward the sea below. The Harpy screamed in pain and flew away. Poros swooped down toward the sea and caught Hestie in his arms.

"Are you okay?" he asked her.

"What the hell is happening?" she mumbled.

"Let's get you to safety first," he said. "Then I'll explain, I promise."

He flew down to the ship and carried Hestie into the salon. Mina had come aboard and was waiting for them.

"Poros?" Mina asked. "Who are you?"

"I'm a god," he said.

"A god?" Hestie repeated.

"What about Hermie?" Mina asked, her face red and her eyes full of tears. "You save him too?"

"I will, Mina," Poros said. "I promise. Okay?"

"Okay." Mina fell on the couch, shivering and sobbing.

Poros set Hestie down in one of the armchairs and grabbed a towel, which he used to wipe the Harpy's blood from her and then from himself.

Then he found two clean towels and gave one to Mina and the other to Hestie. "Try to get warm."

Hestie was shivering, but not from cold. She was terrified for her brother and still in shock over what had happened. She couldn't think. She wrapped the towel around her, trying to comprehend everything, trying to regain her composure.

If Poros was a god, she thought, was the captain one, too?

At that moment, the captain and Jinsoo appeared in the salon. The captain put down the chest he was carrying.

"Which way was he taken?" he asked Poros.

Mina pointed to the west.

How did the captain know Hermie had been taken? Had Poros communicated with him telepathically?

"Help me bring up the anchor," the captain said to Poros. "Jinsoo, keep an eye on the girls."

"Yes, Captain." Jinsoo rushed to his sister's side. Then he asked, "What happen, Mina? Where Hermie?"

Mina leaned into her brother's chest and cried.

Hestie climbed to her feet and rushed to the bow of the ship, where the captain and Poros were bringing up the anchor. The sky was free of Harpies, but the clouds were dark, and there were enormous swells in the distance. They appeared to be coming their way.

"Who are you?" she demanded of the captain. "What's going on?"

"My name is Prometheus," he said as he secured the anchor and headed for the helm. "I suppose it's no secret to Zeus any longer."

Poros followed, so Hestie did, too.

"Prometheus?" she asked. "*The* Prometheus who created human-kind?"

"That's the one," the captain said. "It looks like the storm is headed this way."

"But I'm supposed to be *looking* for you," she said.

"We know," Poros said. "I'm sorry, but we couldn't say anything without risking everything."

"And who are *you*?" she asked him. "Is your name even Poros?"

"It is," he said. "I'm the son of Metis and Zeus."

***

Hermie's head was spinning, and he thought he was going to be sick. He squeezed his eyes shut and stopped flailing. Maybe it was his time to die. *Just let it be quick.*

Suddenly he found himself hitting the ground hard and rolling several feet until he crashed into something. With tears filling his eyes, he sat up and assessed the situation. None of his bones were broken, but he was badly bruised. The Harpy had tossed him into a cave and then vanished. Coming toward him were two older women and a goat.

"He isn't much, is he?" one said to the other.

"Don't be fooled by appearances, Ida," the other said.

"Where's the girl?" the one called Ida asked. "Wasn't there supposed to be a girl?"

"How am *I* supposed to know?" the other said. "Really? Exactly *how* am I supposed to know?"

"Don't get all worked up, Andy," the one called Ida said. "I was just wondering out loud, not asking *you.*"

The two of them finally stopped bickering and stared at Hermie.

"Who are you? Where am I?" Hermie asked, rubbing the shoulder that had taken the brunt of his fall.

"Now wouldn't you like to know that?" the one called Andy said. "You just sit there quietly, or we'll tell our goat he can eat your hair."

Hermie's hand flew to the top of his head. He clamped his mouth shut and began to pray. He only hoped Hestie, Mina, and the others were alright.

Please let them be alright, he prayed.

He was startled by the appearance of two others. He turned to see Hermes and Ares standing near the mouth of the cave.

Hermie climbed to his feet. "Thank the gods! Hermes! Ares!" He stepped past the two older ladies and their goat to embrace each god. "I've never been happier to see you! Get me out of here. Please!"

"I'm sorry, buddy," Hermes said. "I'm afraid we can't do that just yet."

"What? Why?" he asked.

"Hades has betrayed Zeus," Ares said. "And he did it by killing your parents."

Hermie's mouth fell open. That couldn't possibly be true. He looked from one god to the other, hoping he hadn't heard right. "What? Why would you lie to me?"

"I swear on the River Styx," Ares said.

Hermie fell to his knees and covered his face with his hands.

"You didn't have to come out and say it like that," Hermes complained to Ares.

"It's better that he knows," Ares said.

Hermie looked up at them through his tears. "Why would Hades do that?"

"They were Zeus's only leverage," Ares said. "So, Hades got rid of them."

***

Hip glanced at his father's face when they heard Apollo calling from above. "Let me in! And hurry!"

Hades conjured his sword and cut a mark across one of the wards, and Apollo fell into the room beside his sister.

Hades quickly re-drew the ward and asked, "Were you followed?"

"I don't know."

Artemis took his hands, her face beaming. "How did you escape?"

"I'm not sure," he said. "The trick chair stopped working."

"It was Persephone," Hades explained. "She has my helm. She stole the key from Zeus and set you free."

Apollo noticed the bodies on ice. "What's happened?"

Pete had already taken the souls to Tartarus for safe keeping.

"It was the only way we could free them from the cuffs," Hades said. "I'd hoped to resurrect them as soon as we arrived, but the Fates won't allow it."

"They require a trade," Artemis said.

"How unfortunate," Apollo said sadly. "Do you know of anyone willing?"

Hades cocked his head to one side. "In all the centuries I've ruled this kingdom, I've only known of two types of people who are ever willing to sacrifice themselves for others."

Hip knew the answer. "Parents and lovers."

"Precisely," Hades said to Hip. "You know what you must do."

Hip disintegrated and dispatched to Colorado, looking for two red birds.

At the same moment, they heard Poseidon above them. "I've come to help! Allow me to enter!"

"He speaks the truth," Apollo said when Hades sought his advice.

Hades made a mark on the wall with his sword, and Poseidon dropped inside. Hades quickly redrew his ward.

"I've come to join the rebellion," Poseidon said. "You won't believe the chaos you've already caused."

***

An enormous wave was headed for *The Marcella*.

"Hestie, go to the salon with Mina and Jinsoo and tell them to put on life vests," the captain said. "You do the same. It looks like we're going to be taking on a lot of water."

"What about the two of you?" Hestie asked. "Will you be okay?"

"We'll be fine," Poros reassured her. "We've handled storms like this before."

Hestie climbed down the hatch toward the salon, noticing the wave only yards from the ship. It was as tall as the highest mast.

"Where are the life vests?" she asked the twins. "Captain says to put them on."

Jinsoo jumped up and opened the seats of the armchairs and pulled out orange vests for each of them.

As Hestie fastened hers on, she prayed to Poseidon, "Please help and protect us, Lord of the Sea."

She'd barely uttered the words when the bow of the ship pitched into the air, and she and the twins fell, stern side, against the salon door. Water rushed in beneath the door and filled the floor of the salon.

Hestie and the twins climbed to their feet as the ship leveled out again.

Then Mina pointed and screamed.

Hestie followed Mina's finger to the starboard window. A giant monster—part man, part crab, and part fish—flung itself from the surface of the water and struck its claws against the ship.

CHAPTER EIGHTEEN

Betrayal

Hip flew in his father's chariot over the familiar Colorado skies, but it wasn't comfort he felt when he pulled up beside the Melnor Cabin; it was dread.

The red birds immediately spotted him from the trees outside Than and Therese's kitchen window, and they leapt from the branches on fluttering wings toward him.

Landing on the rim of the chariot, Therese's mother chirped, "Are Therese and Than safe?"

"What can you tell us?" the father asked. "We've been worried sick."

"I'm afraid I have some bad news," Hip said solemnly.

***

Hermie sat at the back of the cave where Hermes and Ares had abandoned him. He'd sobbed for many minutes over his parents' deaths, but now he was angry.

This shouldn't have happened. And he needed to do something to avenge them.

The old women—nymphs, he now knew, because he remembered the stories his parents had told him about this cave on Mount Ida—bickered by a stream that ran through the cavern. They were positioned between Hermie and the exit. The nymphs might look old, but their hearing was excellent, as he'd discovered when he'd tried to make a run for it earlier. The goat had brayed during the excitement, which had caused the nymphs' obvious concern. Apparently, they loved their goat more than each other and didn't like to see it upset. So, they'd scolded Hermie and made him sit at the very back of the cavern in the darkness and had sworn that if he tried anything else, the goat would feast on his hair.

But Hermie couldn't just sit there. He had to do something.

What?

It occurred to him that he'd have to use the goat. The innocent animal was sleeping soundly near the edge of the stream, about ten feet from the old nymphs. There were plenty of loose rocks in the cave. Maybe Hermie could bash in the goat's head, which would distract and impair the nymphs, so that Hermie could get away?

No. He couldn't bash in the goat's head. He just couldn't.

But perhaps he could frighten the goat enough to make it run away. Would the nymphs chase after it? Or would they remain in the cave, preventing Hermie's escape?

Hermie thought long and hard for many more minutes and could think of no better plan. So, he reached for a rock, about the size of a golf ball, and aimed to hit the floor of the cave near where the goat was sleeping.

He threw the rock. It hit perfectly—only a foot from the goat. But the animal merely lifted its head and looked at Hermie sleepily. The nymphs didn't even notice.

Hermie grabbed another rock and another, throwing at very high speeds, even allowing the last few to hit the goat's leg—though not hard enough to hurt it.

The nymphs noticed and shouted at Hermie to stop.

Finally, the goat jumped to its feet and high-tailed it out of the cave.

The one called Ida followed, but Andy stayed behind. Hermie decided it was now or never. Maybe he had a chance against one nymph, but certainly not two. He jumped up and pushed the old lady into the stream—which seemed so wrong! It went against every fiber in his being to push a little old lady over like that. As he ran from the mouth of the cave, he reminded himself that she was a nymph and would be alright.

Outside of the cave, he climbed toward the top, praying to Morpheus to come and get him.

"I'm at Mount Ida, I think," he prayed. "My parents were…they're…dead. I'm next, if you don't save me."

***

Morpheus stood in his room in the Underworld, took a deep breath, and blew the painting dry. The moonflower shone bright against the black canvas. He hoped the silver highlights along the fragile-looking petals would make Iris think of him and his silver wings.

He god-traveled with the painting into the sky and searched for rainbows. He found one over the Aegean Sea. The sky appeared ominous, with lightning and thunder crackling overhead. He hastened inside the rainbow arch, before the rain began to fall.

"Iris?"

He didn't see her anywhere inside the colorful arch. Surely, she wasn't filling the clouds before they were even empty.

He set the painting down and flew toward the black clouds against the cold drops that were pelting his skin.

"Iris?"

"Morpheus?" she asked as she flew with her empty pitcher toward him. "What are you doing here?"

"I brought you a present. It's there, in the rainbow."

At that moment, he heard a distressful prayer from Hermie.

"Oh, man," Morpheus said to Iris. "I'll be right back."

He god-traveled to Mount Ida, where he and his parents often went to play night Frisbee with Ariadne and Asterion. Clinging to a ledge in the darkening sky was a small figure that must be Hermie. Morpheus flew down, grabbed him, and god-traveled back to Iris's rainbow, in the shelter of the colorful arch, where Iris was admiring his painting.

She had tears in her eyes. "I love it. No one has ever done anything like this for me before." Then she turned toward him and noticed Hermie.

Hermie was drenched and shivering, so Morpheus blew on him until he was dry.

"Why did you bring him here?" Iris asked.

"Thanks for saving my life," Hermie said to him. "Ares said that Hades killed my parents. I was captured by Harpies. I don't know what to do."

Tears filled Hermie's eyes.

"You were captured by Harpies?" Morpheus repeated. "Why?"

"I don't know," Hermie said. "I don't know why all this is happening."

"It's because he's a prisoner of war," Iris said angrily. "You shouldn't have brought him here, Morpheus. You need to take him to Mount Olympus, right away, before we get in trouble. Zeus will rip out our wings for this. Come on!"

"No, wait!" Hermie pleaded.

"My dad will know what to do," Morpheus said.

"Your dad's a traitor," Iris said. "Come on, before Zeus suspects us, too."

Morpheus god traveled with Hermie and Iris to the gates of Mount Olympus. The storm was fierce down below.

"What's going on?" he asked Iris.

"Hades betrayed our king," Iris said. "And your father helped him."

Morpheus prayed to his father, asking him what he should do. "I'm at the gates of Mount Olympus with Hermie," he prayed.

Within minutes, Swift and Sure appeared, pulling his father behind them in Hades's chariot. Two red birds barked shrill notes at him, warning him to get in.

"Come on, sonny!" his father cried.

The gates of Mount Olympus opened, and Zeus stood, towering over him.

"Morpheus, bring the prisoner to me!" Zeus bellowed.

"Morpheus!" Iris pleaded. "Don't betray our king!"

"Please," Hermie begged. "Don't throw me to the wolves."

Morpheus looked from his father to his cousin to his girlfriend, and then at his father again.

"Trust me!" Iris wailed.

She'd been his best friend and constant companion since he was four years old. He knew her and she knew him better than anyone. How could he turn his back on her, let alone their king?

"Why are you doing this, Pops?" he asked. "This is treason. I can't be a part of that!"

Morpheus followed Iris through the gates, with Hermie in tow, trying to ignore his father's pleas and his cousin's shouts. He wiped the tears from his cheeks and fought the urge to be sick. He couldn't believe he'd just turned his back on his own father.

As soon as they crossed into the great hall of the palace, Hermie was taken by Ares and put on Hephaestus's old trick chair.

"I'm sorry, Hermie," Morpheus said. "I can't go against my king. I hope you understand."

Hermie glared at him with eyes full of tears but said nothing. Morpheus turned away. Before he reached Iris's side, a golden bird cage dropped around him, enveloping him and trapping him inside of it. He grabbed the bars and called out to Iris, who was imprisoned in a similar cage beside him.

His jaw dropped open as he turned to Zeus and Hera. "But, why? I don't understand? We're on your side!"

"I know," Zeus said. "And I appreciate your loyalty. It hasn't gone unnoticed. You see, I need leverage to coerce Hades back into submission. Since Thanatos is already dead, I'm afraid his son won't be enough.

But Hypnos and Jen will do anything for you, even sabotage their father."

Morpheus couldn't believe it. Why didn't he listen to his father and jump beside him in the chariot?

"And Iris?" he asked. "Why imprison her?"

"I'm afraid her affection for you might weaken her loyalty to me, now that you're my prisoner," Zeus replied.

Morpheus sank to the floor in despair. What had he done?

***

Hestie screamed right alongside Mina as the salon window shattered and one of the monster's pinchers barely missed snapping Jinsoo in half. She couldn't believe this was happening. Unlike other mortals, she knew monsters were real, but she'd never been attacked by one. It took her a minute to comprehend the enormity of the moment.

"Run!" Hestie shouted, and when neither of them moved, she grabbed each of their hands and led them toward the upper deck, looking for the captain and Poros.

But when they reached the cockpit, they found it empty.

She couldn't think as she looked around, gulping at air.

Then the bow pitched again, throwing them toward the stern. Hestie grabbed onto the railing of the extended deck as a giant wave washed over her. The water was cold and forceful, knocking the air from her lungs, but she clung on to the railing. Once the ship leveled and the wave had passed, Hestie looked around and found herself alone on the ship.

"Mina! Jinsoo!" she screamed as she searched the turbulent waters for signs of her friends. "Oh, my gods! Help them!"

Please don't let my friends be dead, she prayed.

Then she saw the captain and Poros. They were flying above the sea with swords and shields, battling the monster that had attacked the ship. She realized now it was Phorcys, the Old Man of the Sea.

She heard the captain shout to him, "Why are you attacking us? You're no friend to Zeus!"

The Old Man of the Sea reared his ugly head and shouted, "He promised me the sea when Poseidon betrayed him."

From the depths, another monster appeared right before Hestie, snapping its ugly snakehead at her. It had three heads—a lion, a goat, and a snake.

"Chimera!" Hestie shouted.

As much as her parents had trained her, she hadn't been prepared for this. How could she fulfill her destiny if the sight of these monsters had her weak and trembling like a dead leaf in the wind?

Just as the snakehead lashed at her again, Poros lopped it off with his sword, and blood spewed across the deck as the beast wailed and returned to the sea.

"Hang on!" he shouted down at Hestie before the ship began to pitch.

She grabbed the railing as another wave washed over her, nearly ripping her from the deck. If it weren't for her super strength, she would have fallen into the sea.

Once the wave had passed, she shouted to Poros, "Save Mina and Jinsoo! They fell in!"

A beautiful mermaid with hateful eyes leapt into the air. She held Mina tucked in one arm like a football. Mina flailed her arms and legs and screamed at the top of her lungs as the mermaid plunged back into the ocean, taking Hestie's friend with her.

Hestie shouted at Prometheus, who was now facing a creature that was a woman from the waist up and a snake from the waist down.

It was Echidna!

Since Prometheus couldn't help her, Hestie turned to Poros, but he was slicing his sword through the air, trying to cut off Phorcys's claws.

There was no one else to help Mina, so Hestie dove into the water after her friend.

Hestie swam as fast she could in the direction of the mermaid, who she now realized must be Keto, Phorcys's wife, and the mother of monsters. Hestie could barely make out the mermaid's tail flapping against the current ahead of her. Keto was too fast. Every time Hestie thought she might be gaining on her, the mermaid plowed ahead.

Suddenly Hestie became aware of something silver swimming beside her. It was a beautiful goddess. She was fully silver but wasn't a fish.

"I'm Dione," the goddess said. "I've come to help you and your friends."

"So have I," said another beautiful goddess—this one gold—who had swum up on Hestie's other side. "I'm Clymene, Dione's sister and Prometheus's mother."

Hestie couldn't speak underwater, nor could she breathe, and she was running out of air. She prayed to the goddesses to save her friends as she raced to the tumultuous surface to catch some air.

When she emerged from the water, she found Poros flying above her. He reached out a hand for her to grab.

"But Mina and Jinsoo!" Hestie cried.

Then something wrapped around her ankles and pulled her under, and she went down, down, down, faster than she could think. Above her, Poros swam toward her.

She looked down to see Echidna's enormous serpent tail had coiled around her ankles. Hestie kicked against the leathery coils, to no avail.

A cloud of red blood surrounded her in the sea, and the coiled serpent relaxed just enough that Hestie could escape. She swam at her top speed toward the surface. Poros was no longer in sight, and Hestie was dizzy and on the verge of passing out.

When she reached the surface, she bit the air hard, filling her lungs, gasping, choking. In the distance, something was coming toward her— something huge.

Poros lifted her into the air, and she screamed before she realized it was him. He swept her down into the huge thing that she now saw was

Poseidon's chariot, being pulled across the sea by three white mares—Seaquake, Crest, and Riptide. Poseidon stood at the reins, his sun-bleached hair and beard blowing in the wind, his turquoise eyes narrowed and focused. Inside the chariot, Mina and Jinsoo sat on the bench behind him. Hestie burst into tears.

"Oh, thank the gods!" she cried as she and Poros sat on the bench behind them, and Poseidon drove his chariot into the sky. "But where's Prometheus?"

"There." Poseidon pointed toward *The Marcella.*

Slowly, the ship rose from the tumultuous sea into the air, and beneath it, holding the bottom of the hull amidships with his bare hands was Prometheus. He lifted *The Marcella* at least fifty feet above the surface of the water. Clymene shot from the water to join him at the bow, and Dione flew up to hold the stern. Then Poseidon raised his mighty trident and pointed to the monsters in the sea below. A jolt of electricity shot from the three prongs, paralyzing all of them. Phorcys, Keto, Chimera, Echidna, and Charybdis floated stiffly near the surface before they began to submerge. Only their eyes were capable of movement, and they looked up at those in the chariot with hate.

Then Prometheus and his mother and aunt lowered *The Marcella* back into the sea, which had begun to calm. Except for the broken window in the salon, the ship appeared unscathed. Prometheus flew to the cockpit, where he was joined by the two goddesses—one silver and the other gold.

"Come, Prometheus!" Poseidon hollered from the chariot.

"A captain never abandons his ship!" Prometheus called back.

"The rebellion depends on it!" Poseidon shouted.

Prometheus turned to his mother and said something Hestie could not hear, and then he joined them in the chariot beside Poseidon.

"Where are we going?" Prometheus asked.

"To the Underworld," Poseidon replied just as a lightning bolt shot at them through the sky.

CHAPTER NINETEEN

Sacrifice

Hestie gripped the side of the chariot with one hand and Poros's arm with the other as Poseidon's chariot sped through a chasm into the depths of the Underworld. She'd never entered this way before; her parents had always god-traveled her in directly to the palace.

They passed Cerberus at the big iron gate and Charon and Pete on the raft, floating along the Acheron toward the House of Judgment. Then Poseidon brought the chariot to an abrupt halt at the garage and stables where Hades's chariot was usually parked—only now, it wasn't there.

Mina and Jinsoo wore expressions of disbelief on their faces—jaws dropped, eyes wide, mouths speechless.

Prometheus put a hand on each of their heads. "Are you kids okay?"

They looked up at him but said nothing.

"I'm sorry you had to endure that back there," he said to them. "But I promise to keep you safe from here on out, okay?"

They nodded, but not enthusiastically. They were still in shock.

As Poseidon led them down the dark passageway along the brightly flickering Phlegethon, Poros took Hestie's hand and whispered, "What about you? You okay?"

"I'm not sure yet," she whispered back. "I need to know if Hermie's okay. We need to find him."

"We will," he assured her.

She wished she felt as confident as he seemed.

When they reached the door to the palace, Poseidon turned to Hestie. "You're about to see something…troubling, my dear. I need you to be strong for the rebellion. Can you do that?"

Hestie felt her stomach drop. "Is Hermie dead?"

"That I don't know, I'm afraid," Poseidon replied.

"Take a deep breath, Hestie," Prometheus said, kindly. "You've got this."

Poseidon opened the great door and led them inside, where others were standing around a long banquet table. Meg and Alecto stood with their backs to them, each holding their familiars. Meg's falcon was perched on one shoulder, and Alecto's snake draped around her neck. They turned and gave her half-smiles. Across from them, on the other side of the long table, stood Apollo, Artemis, Hades, Hip and Pete, with Tizzie holding Pete's hand at the table's head. Tizzie's wolf sat on its haunches beside her. Hestie filled with happiness to see them, until her Aunt Jen burst into the room and shouted, "I can't find Morpheus!"

Then Jen stared at the table, her mouth and eyes wide. She took three long strides to Tizzie's side and said, "Oh, my gods! What's going on?"

Hestie moved past Meg and Alecto to look more closely at the table. What she saw made her fall to her knees. Her parents…they were…lying on beds of ice, with their mouths slightly open, their eyes closed, and their bodies…lifeless.

Hestie screamed.

***

Hip's heart was breaking for Hestie as he watched her take in what had happened to Than and Therese. He reminded Pete that he needed to leave while mortals were in the room, and then he put the mortals into the deep boon of sleep. Hestie was caught by Poros as slumber overtook her; the Asian kids were held by Prometheus. Back in the chariot with the two red birds, Hip rushed like mad to get home. He raced to the palace, to the banquet hall, the birds flying quickly behind him.

He pulled open the door and let them in, shouting, "I've found two willing souls! They agree to trade!"

"Where's Morpheus?" Jen asked, still in a panic.

"He…he's with Iris on Mount Olympus," he said. "He doesn't want to betray Zeus."

"What?" Hades shouted.

"Morpheus handed Hermie over to Zeus," Hip admitted, his heart breaking in two. He couldn't believe his own son had chosen Zeus and Iris over him.

The two red birds fluttered to their granddaughter, who was propped in a chair, and each landed on a different shoulder. Even though Hestie was sound asleep, the birds kissed her goodbye and told her they loved her and her parents and that they would do anything for them, including giving up their lives.

Hip was sorry she couldn't be awake to say goodbye. He decided to leave the room, so she could be. He flew to the next chamber and watched her from afar. First, she yawned. Then, she opened her eyes. The two Asian kids followed.

"What's going on?" Hestie asked drowsily.

The red birds repeated what they'd said before, and the girl began to cry again.

Hades asked the birds, "Are you sure you want to give your lives in exchange for Thanatos and Therese's souls?"

They tweeted their reply without hesitating.

Hades snapped his fingers, and the birds went still and began to drop toward the floor. Poros was the nearest to them, and he caught each bird in his palms.

Meg's falcon squawked.

The souls of Linda and Gerry Mills appeared, along with Pete, who held a hand on each of their shoulders.

Hip watched as Hestie stared at the souls in awe.

"You're a good, sweet, smart, beautiful girl," Linda said to her granddaughter.

"We're both so proud of you and your brother," Gerry added. "Please tell him goodbye for us, will you?"

Hestie bent her brows. "But…"

"Sshh," Linda said. "Please don't make this harder than it has to be. It's the only thing that can be done. Period."

Hestie slowly nodded as tears flowed down her cheeks.

"Please don't cry," Gerry said. "We're happy to do this for your parents. Our time was up a long time ago, anyway."

"We were lucky to have the chance to watch you grow up," Linda said.

"Take care of your parents for us, will you?" Gerry asked. "Tell your mother we love her."

Hestie nodded again, unable to speak. She rushed her hands to her throat. She couldn't breathe in Pete's presence.

Then Pete led the souls away and appeared again, disintegrated, on the other side of the room with two others—Than and Therese. He'd brought them up from Tartarus.

Hestie noticed them right away, and her jaw dropped open.

Pete quickly led the souls to their bodies, and this time, they transitioned back into them with ease. It seemed the Fates were satisfied and no longer blocked their reentry. Pete left, so as not to bring further harm to the mortals.

Jen prayed to Hip again and again that they must convince Morpheus to come home; and he assured her telepathically as best as he could that they would.

Then Therese's eyelids fluttered, and she looked around. Thanatos sat up.

Tizzie and Alecto brought blankets to them and helped them from the table.

"Hestie?" Therese said, shivering. "You're safe?"

"Where's Hermie?" her father asked through chattering teeth.

Hip rushed into the room and clapped a hand on Than's shoulder. "I'm so glad to see you, bro'." Tears filled his eyes, but he blinked them away, not wanting anyone to see them. Relief filled him. Aside from Jen and Morpheus, Than was the most important person to him in the world. "Zeus has Hermie, but I promise we'll get him back."

***

Hermie sat in the trick chair in the main hall of the palace on Mount Olympus between the thrones of Hermes and Poseidon, neither of which were home. Hera and Zeus sat, arguing, while Hestia served them food and wine. Athena paced back and forth near her parents, and Demeter sat on her throne frowning at the caged prisoners—Iris and Morpheus, who were still in the center of the room. No one else was there, except for Aphrodite's Graces, who were helping Hestia. Aphrodite had been there earlier but had left to find Ares.

As Hermie was wondering where his grandmother, Persephone, was, he felt something warm touch his hand, and he flinched. Then the tickle of breathing near his ear was followed by a whisper, "It's me, your grandmama."

Hermie tried not to react, coming to understand that she must be hidden beneath the helm of invisibility, since no one else in the room seemed to notice her speaking to him.

"I've come to say I'll protect you and not to worry, my darling," she whispered again.

Hera turned from her table of grapes and cheese and whatnot to study him, as though she had heard something. Hermie looked up at her, and then looked down at his shoes. Now that he knew his grandmother was watching over him, he could think about his parents again—not that he wanted to cry, but he couldn't help himself.

Why had his grandfather killed them? How could he do such a thing? He prayed to Persephone for answers, but, as he had expected, none were given.

After what must have been an hour's time, Aphrodite reappeared with Ares and Hermes. Hestia took away the table she'd put in front of Hera and Zeus and then fetched Hephaestus from the forge. Phobos and Deimos appeared, followed by Cupid, Psyche, and a handful of other gods Hermie had never met. Then Zeus stood up in front of his throne and thanked everyone for coming.

"And thank you, fellow members of the court, for your loyalty today," Zeus said. "Some of you may be worried about my ability to maintain the throne, but I assure you, I am still the most powerful god in existence. You're safe with me. Go against me, and you'll be sorely punished; stay with me, and enjoy the fruits of my reign for many more millennia to come."

Hermie wanted to point out that Zeus was lying. Morpheus had been loyal and look where it had gotten him.

"We know they are holed up in the Underworld. Poseidon, Artemis, and Apollo have joined the Underworld gods, and we believe Prometheus and Poros are there as well," Zeus said.

"Then Phorcys failed us," Hermes pointed out.

"Do you question my decision to solicit his help?" Zeus challenged.

"No, Father," Hermes replied, his face turning a bright hue of pink.

"As you can see," Zeus continued, "I have taken Iris and Morpheus as my prisoners, because it's a sure way to weaken the Underworld gods. Hypnos will do anything to rescue his son, even if he must undermine his father." Then he turned to Hermes again. "Notify Hades of our prisoners. Tell him that if he doesn't surrender within forty-eight hours, I will paralyze Morpheus and kill Hermie."

"Yes, my king," Hermes said just before he vanished.

Morpheus turned to Hermie from his cage and mouthed, "I'm so sorry."

Hermie nodded. He'd already forgiven his cousin, and there didn't seem to be a point to holding a grudge. Besides, his grudge against Hades for killing his parents was all the anger and hate one person could stand.

***

Hestie threw her arms around her mother's neck and hugged her hard. Then she did the same to her father. Her mother pushed Hestie's hair from her eyes and kissed her forehead.

"I'm so glad you're safe," she whispered to Hestie. "Tell me what happened."

Hades cleared his throat. "We have much to discuss, I'm afraid. Why don't you all have a seat?"

The chairs from the banquet table disappeared and then reappeared behind each person, so all they had to do was bend their knees and sit back, precisely where they were. The banquet table vanished, which left them in a sort of circle, with Hestie, Poros, and her parents in the center of it. Her Uncle Hip had left, so she and her parents wouldn't fall asleep. Jinsoo and Mina sat in silent shock beside Prometheus as they took in their surroundings and all the strange things they were witnessing.

Hades strolled over to the center to stand behind Poros. "First, I want to introduce you all to Poros, the son of Metis and Zeus. He's the one destined to help us bring about the change."

Hestie smiled at Poros when the room erupted into applause. "I guess they like you."

"Yeah, but they don't know me like you do, poor buggers," he whispered back.

"British idioms? Really?" she teased.

"Now, now. I thought we were international," he teased back.

The applause died down, and Hades walked across the room to Prometheus. "There are some things you need to know about our friend, Prometheus." Hades went on to tell the other gods about all the good things Prometheus had been doing for humankind since he went into hiding centuries ago. Some of them, Hestie already knew about, such as taking medicine and food to the sick and impoverished. But Prometheus hadn't always been a sailor. He began as a scientist, and he'd helped find cures for many of the diseases that would have otherwise wiped out all of humanity.

Some of the other Titans—such as Hecate, Helios, and Selene—had known this about their friend all along; because they feared that Zeus would feel threatened, or would want to continue his vendetta against Prometheus, they had kept his whereabouts a secret.

Hades now asked Prometheus to explain to the gods, from his point of view, how he came to find himself at the center of this rebellion.

Prometheus stood up in front of his chair and told his story. He said that when Metis—who was still in hiding—had first approached him when Poros was barely ten years old, the Titan had been apprehensive about taking over the raising of her son and was wary of the idea of a revolution. But as Metis recruited more gods to her way of thinking, Prometheus began to see an opportunity for improving the relationship between the gods and humanity.

And he couldn't turn down the opportunity to indoctrinate another god into his way of thinking, so he took Poros under his wing. When he got wind of Apollo's vision and of the prophecy surrounding Hermie and Hestie, he decided to accept his role in bringing about the fall of Zeus.

Wanting to minimize human casualties, Prometheus had asked Hades to recruit as many Olympians to the rebellion as possible without incurring Zeus's suspicion.

Done with his tale, Prometheus returned to his seat.

"I kept the core group small for many years," Hades said, "because I knew the first thing Zeus would do was threaten the mortals in our family, which is exactly what he did."

Hestie turned to her parents, and her mother kissed her forehead again.

"Our first objectives as a rebellion were to rescue Thanatos and Therese, recruit Poseidon and other Olympians, and free Hecate. And now we will add the goal of freeing Hermie," Hades said. "But before we continue with those objectives, I want to minimize Zeus's threat to my family by asking Thanatos and Therese to undergo apotheosis, like they did years ago at Demeter's winter cabin, when they became the oath breakers of Olympia."

"You want to do what?" Hermes appeared on the outskirts of their circle, near the door to the banquet hall.

Every god in attendance conjured and drew a sword, including Poros.

CHAPTER TWENTY

Hard Freedom

Hip panicked when he noticed Hermes in the banquet hall. Hades must have forgotten to ward against their most frequent visitor from Mount Olympus. Hip stood in the next room watching through the walls, ready to do whatever he needed to defend his family.

"You know I'm faster than any of you," Hermes said. "So, don't try to take me as your prisoner. I've come with a message from Zeus. Then I'll be on my way."

"I don't want you as my prisoner," Hades said. "I want you as my friend and ally."

"I'm your *friend*, Lord Hades," Hermes said. "But I'm afraid I can't be your *ally*. Not in this. I can't play a role in unseating my own father and king."

"We call him 'king,'" Hades said, "and yet we want a democracy. You were part of that, in the end. You helped the Athena Alliance. Help us again."

"He was going to swallow Therese and kill her twins," Hermes said. "I only intervened to save them."

Apollo frowned. "Another example of his tyranny."

"Join us," Artemis said.

Hermes shook his head. "I…"

"We gave Zeus plenty of chances to be a good leader," Poseidon said.

"When he imprisoned Than and Therese, he showed what kind of leader he is," Meg added.

"And now our Hermie!" Tizzie said.

Her wolf wailed.

Alecto stroked her snake. "It's time to give up on Zeus."

"Would you give up on *your* father?" Hermes challenged.

"If he was an ass, I would," Poseidon said. "My father was an ass, and, I'm sorry to say, yours is too."

Hip received a telepathic prayer from his mother on Mount Olympus asking him to meet her at the gate, so he disintegrated and left in his father's chariot. Meanwhile, he watched the other gods trying to persuade Hermes to join the rebellion, but his cousin was resistant.

"My father is the one who asked Prometheus to make humankind," Hermes said. "Have you forgotten?"

"He wanted humankind so he could harness the power of their faith and worship," Prometheus said. "It was self-serving, as always. Their faith gives the gods more strength."

"Like I said," Poseidon snorted. "An ass."

"I'm anxious to get Hecate from the pit," Hades said to Hermes. "Now deliver your message and go."

Hermes's eyes widened at the mention of Hecate. "Okay, then. Zeus says that if you don't submit to him as your king, he'll paralyze Morpheus and kill Hermie."

"What?" Jen cried. "He's threatening *Morpheus*? After Morpheus *obeyed* him?"

Hip thought he was going to be sick. Zeus had gone too far.

"He's imprisoned Morpheus in a golden bird cage," Hermes said. "Iris, too. And Hermie is stuck on the trick chair."

"He can't kill Hermie!" Hestie cried.

"It's not going to happen," Than reassured her.

"He'll only do it if you won't cooperate," Hermes insisted. "Don't make it so that he has no choice. Stop this nonsense! We've been a happy pantheon together for many centuries. Why ruin that? Why fix what isn't broken? You have forty-eight hours to surrender, or Zeus fulfills his promise."

To Hip's great surprise, Poros sheathed his sword, took the two dead red birds from his pocket and handed them to Hermes.

"What's this?" Hermes asked.

Therese gasped at the sight of the dead birds, not having known what her parents had done to restore her and Than's lives. She broke into tears as Hestie and Than comforted her.

"This is what parents are supposed to do for their children," Poros said. "Not threaten them. Not swallow them. They're supposed to be willing to die for them—or in our case, since we can't die, to suffer for them." Then Poros added, "We haven't been formally introduced. I'm Poros, your half-brother. Even though my father wants to swallow me, even though he has no love or tenderness for me, I don't hate him. I don't seek revenge, either, for what he did to my mother and sister. But people are suffering. Humanity needs their gods, and we need a leader who makes that a priority."

Than stood up and crossed the room toward Hermes. He had no sword, no powers, no defense whatsoever, and this made Hypnos nervous.

"You have a chance to be on the right side of history," Than said. "Don't let the love you feel for your father cloud your judgment on this. Do the right thing, cousin."

"I can't make any promises," Hermes said. "But I'll give it some thought."

Then Hermes disappeared.

Hypnos hoped Hermes would think fast because they didn't have much time.

Forty-eight hours.

When Hip arrived at the gates of Mount Olympus, he did not ask the four seasons to open it. Instead, he kept a watchful eye for defenders of the fortress who might attack him at any moment.

He sensed Nike around the bend, headed his way.

"Mother?" he prayed. "I'm here. Where are you?"

"I've opened the gate," she returned his prayer. "Disintegrate and enter. I'll find you. Then take the chariot home."

"Hypnos!" Nike shouted and took aim with her bow and arrow.

Hip couldn't afford to be injured, or his mother's plan would fail. He slapped the reins against Swift and Sure and raced away.

His disintegrated self barely made it through the gates of Mount Olympus and beneath the protection of the helm at his mother's side when sounds of alarm rang through the courtyard, warning everyone that Hypnos had been sighted outside the gates. Cyclopes marched from the outer buildings into the plaza and placed themselves around the walls.

Persephone took him by the hand and led him into the palace. Telepathically, she said, "Put everyone here into the deep boon of sleep, so we can save Hermie before it's too late."

It wouldn't be easy. The gods were never as easy to manipulate as mortals were, and the more of them present, the more difficult the task. Even more problematic was the warning they'd received that he'd been spotted. They would be on guard against him, for sure.

Hip called upon every ounce of power he possessed, until even his own mother yawned beneath the helm.

It might have worked had Hermes not returned in the middle of it.

"You won't believe what Hades is about to do!" Hermes shouted as he entered the great hall.

The sound of Hermes's loud and abrasive voice stirred all the gods from their drowsiness.

Hip froze beside his mother, asking her telepathically what he should do.

"Hypnos!" The king of the Olympians jumped from his throne and sniffed the air. "He must be wearing the helm. Secure the gates at once!"

"The gates have already been secured," Ares said. "Don't worry. We'll find him."

"That's not good enough," Hera said.

"We need to show the Underworld gods how serious we are," Zeus said. "I want Hypnos to have *no doubt* that I'll paralyze his son if he doesn't back down."

"What would you have us do?" Hephaestus asked—but not in a tone of obedience. It was more like a challenge.

"Kill Hermie," Zeus said. "It's the only way."

"No!' Morpheus shouted from his cage. "Please! Take me instead!"

Then, silently, Morpheus prayed to Hip, "Oh, Pops! This is all my fault. Will you ever forgive me?"

Hip's heart was breaking, and his chest felt tight. He had to do something, but what?

"Keep Hermie in the deep boon of sleep," his mother prayed to him. "I've got the key and am going to unlock the chair."

"How will I get him out of here?" Hip prayed back. "As soon as I touch him, the other gods will know our position."

"Just do it quickly," she prayed.

"He's an innocent boy, Father," Athena said. "Surely there's another way."

"Is my own beloved daughter turning against me now?" Zeus asked.

"They're bound to snag one of us, Mother," Hip prayed. "It's too dangerous."

"We have no choice," Persephone insisted.

"Please, Father," Athena said. "Let's sit down and talk about this."

"What will Zeus do to Morpheus if we do this?" Hip asked his mother.

"I promise to protect him," Persephone replied. "Besides, Morpheus is the only card Zeus has in his hand. He won't play it now."

"Bring me the son of Thanatos!" Zeus shouted.

"Where's the key?" Hera asked. "It's missing!"

"Hip," Hermes prayed silently as he approached the trick chair. "Release the boy from the chair, and I'll save him."

Now Hip's stomach churned, because he couldn't know for certain whether Hermes meant to help or to trick him.

Zeus stood from his throne and headed for the trick chair. "We don't need the key. I'll kill him where he sits."

"No!" Morpheus cried. "Please, Lord Zeus! I'll do anything!"

"I won't let the boy die," Hermes prayed to Hip. "Do it now."

Since Hip knew there would not be another chance to rescue Hermie, he made the split decision to take the key from his mother and unlock the chair. Then he led his mother a safe distance away.

"What are you doing?" she prayed.

"Taking a chance on Hermes," he replied. Then to Hermes, he prayed, "The boy is free."

In one swift motion, Hermes swept the sleeping boy into his arms and left, just as Zeus was raising his hand to strike.

Zeus pounded a fist into the air. "Hermes! Hermes, what have you done?"

Hip kissed his mother's cheek, hoping it wasn't for the last time, and reintegrated with the version of him who was parking the chariot in the Underworld and heading toward the banquet hall. He hoped with all his might that Hermes would be there waiting for him with the boy.

***

It was Hestie's turn to comfort her mother, whose face was pale—even for someone who'd been recently dead. Her mouth hung open. Her eyes stared off blankly as tears welled.

"Are they really gone?" Hestie's mother mumbled.

"The Elysian Fields," Hades said. "They gave their lives for yours."

"I didn't get to say goodbye," her mother said.

"I'm sorry," Hestie whispered as she stroked her mother's hair, her own eyes filling with tears. "Mom, I'm so very sorry."

"I don't mean to sound insensitive," Poseidon cut in, "but let's get on with this, so we can free Hecate from the pit. My realm is vulnerable, and Amphitrite needs all the help she can get."

"We can release Hecate now," Hades said. "Hip can handle this when he returns."

"Can I join you in the pit?" Prometheus asked Hades. "There are people imprisoned whom I haven't seen in a very long time."

"I'm not sure if that's a good idea," Artemis said. "If he goes, I want to go, too, in case things get out of hand."

"Apollo, too," Hades said.

"I want to go," Hermes said, as he arrived with Hermie.

Hestie blinked. Her brother was alive!

"Hermie!" Hestie's mom cried. "Oh, thank you, Hermes!"

"That's twice you've saved his life," her father said.

Hestie ran to Hermie and threw her arms around his neck. "I thought you were dead!"

"I thought *they* were dead!" Hermie said, his eyes wide. "Ares said that Hades killed our parents."

"He did," Hestie said. "It's a long story. I'll tell you all about it later."

"We're glad you're home safe," Hades said to Hermie. "And I forgive you for all the horrible things you've been praying to me."

Hermie's face turned red. "Sorry, I…"

"We're on our way to free Hecate and will talk to you again shortly," Hades said as he waved goodbye.

As most of the gods left the room, Hestie sought her mother's eyes. "Does this mean what I think it means? The story you told me about how…"

Her mother nodded. "I don't want you to be here, Sweetheart. Either of you. Give me another hug and then please go. I'll find you when it's over."

"Why?" Hermie asked. "What's happening?"

"Apotheosis," Poros said.

"Oh, gods," he said.

"At least they're alive," Hestie said. "We might not be able to live with them, but at least they're alive!"

"I'm okay with that," Hermie said.

"There might be a chance for all of us to live together forever," their father said.

"Hades needs our help in fighting this war," their mother explained. "Don't worry. We'll find a way for all of us to be together."

"We better go," Poros said.

Hestie didn't think she could bear to watch her parents be burned alive, anyway, so she nodded as Poros took her by the hand.

"Mina and Jinsoo, come with us," Hermie said.

When they left the banquet hall, Poros asked, "Where should we go? I've never been here before."

"I still can't believe Mom and Dad are alive," Hermie muttered. "I'm so happy."

"I so happy to see you," Mina said, taking his hand. "I was scared you dead."

"Yeah, man," Jinsoo said. "Me, too."

"Let's go to Hecate's room. She won't mind." Hestie led the way.

She half expected to find Galin and Cubie waiting on the big bed, as always, but she'd forgotten that they were still on Mount Olympus with Persephone and wouldn't be back until the fall. The room seemed lonely without them.

Hestie plopped on the bed, and the others each found a place to sit on, too. Poros sat close to her, as if he worried that she was going to fall apart again, and he'd have to put the pieces back together. But she wasn't going to fall apart. She was still scared, but she was glad her family was safe, and she was determined to help them win the war.

"Are you guys okay?" Poros asked Mina and Jinsoo.

"Are we really in Underworld?" Jinsoo asked. "Are we dead?"

"Yes, you're in the Underworld," Poros said. "But you're not dead. You and Mina are going to be fine. We'll get you out of here soon and working on a ship in no time."

"I did not believe in gods," Mina said. "Now I do. Now I pray real hard."

Hestie jumped to her feet. "That's it! Oh, my gosh! That's it! Mina, you're a genius!"

She hugged Mina, who only stared back at her with bent brows.

"What?" Hermie asked.

"Do you mind filling the rest of us in?" Poros asked with a smile. He was easily amused, it seemed.

"I figured out how Hermie and I can fulfill our destiny!" Hestie said.

***

Over twenty years ago, Therese had begged Than to do this very thing, this very thing they were about to do again. She'd wanted to be with him forever, and the only way she could was to become like him. Even now, when she looked at him, she felt no regret—not for going through with it once before to become a god, nor for giving it all up to be with her children.

But what if they went through with this today only to discover they would be unable to live with their children? What if gods and mortals couldn't coexist in the same household? And would Than become Death again? Or would he have to find some other purpose? Would the rule of finding a purpose within three months apply to him? And if so, if he found no purpose, would he lose his immortality, only to leave Therese a god without him?

So many things could go wrong.

Therese turned to Than. "Are we sure about this?"

"The rebellion needs you," Hip said.

"I'm ready," Than said. He met Therese's eyes. "You?"

"I don't know," Therese admitted, stifling a yawn.

"Isn't this what you've wanted?" Jen asked.

"Probably not like this," Hip said to her.

"That's not it," she said with hooded eyes. Hip's presence was putting her to sleep.

"I'll step out for a moment," Hip said. "Call me when you're ready."

Therese recalled that the anticipation of going up in flames was worse than the experience itself, because her body went into shock, and she lost consciousness and died shortly after. The anticipation was overwhelmingly frightening, and she noticed she was already trembling just thinking about it.

But that wasn't why she hesitated.

"Will you become Death?" she asked Than.

"I don't know. I hope so."

Therese lifted her brows. "Seriously? But then you can't be around our children."

"I believe they'll be gods, too," he said. "And I can't imagine being a god and not being Death. I miss bringing peace to the suffering. It was monotonous work, but it's who I am."

"What about Pete?' Jen asked.

"He would have to find a new purpose," Than said, "if I become Death. Or maybe *I'll* find a new purpose. I don't know. But either way, we need to do this, to help the rebellion."

Therese agreed that, for the change to happen, the rebellion needed as many allies as possible. As mortals, she and Than weren't much help to the cause; but, as gods, they could make a difference.

"I'm ready," she said through quivering lips.

Than turned to Jen. "I know you want to be here for us, to help in any way you can, but could Therese and I be alone? Having an audience makes it all so much more difficult."

"I get that," Jen said, squeezing Therese's hands. "Just call out if you change your minds."

Hip appeared and said, "It might help to have a bed to lie down on."

He snapped his fingers, and a bed appeared.

"And here's the ambrosia," Hip said, handing them each a bowl. "You can use the Phlegethon to…well. you know what to do."

"Good luck," Jen said.

Hip and Jen vanished.

"Take off your clothes," Than said with a smile.

Therese grinned. "I will if you will."

***

As Hip was saying goodbye to Than and Therese, he was also standing before the door to the Titan Pit. Hermes stood beside him.

"I'm so happy you're with us, cuz," he said to Hermes. "I've never been happier to see you."

"I still don't know if the rebellion is the right thing," Hermes admitted. "But I couldn't let my father kill Hermie. I just couldn't do it."

"You're not with us, then?" Hades asked with his back to the door of the Titan Pit.

"I'm undecided," Hermes said.

"What do you mean, 'undecided'?" Alecto, who stood in the very back of the group, asked.

Hermes turned to face her. "I can't go back to Mount Olympus. My father will probably never forgive me." Then he spoke to Poseidon. "But I'm not sure if I want to help you dethrone him. I just don't know."

"I appreciate your honesty," Poseidon said.

Apollo put a hand on Hermes's shoulder. "I can sense how conflicted you feel."

"Keep in mind that our father could still have a place in the new order," Artemis said. "He doesn't have to be out of the picture."

"That depends on how much more damage he does before we overtake him," Prometheus said.

Hip frowned. He knew what Prometheus meant: if Zeus were to paralyze Morpheus, or maim him in any way, the current king would *not* be welcome in the new order.

A shudder crept down Hip's spine.

"Ready then?" Hades asked.

Poseidon lifted his trident. "Ready."

The Furies stood behind him with their familiars.

"Ready," Tizzie said, and her wolf howled.

"I don't have the helm," Hades reminded them. "So, I need everyone to pay close attention to the prisoners. We can't afford an ambush."

"Got it," Artemis said.

"I'll dowse everyone with drowsiness as soon as I step inside," Hip offered.

"But not too much," Prometheus said. "I'd like to speak to them."

"What are your intentions?" Hades asked.

"Might we recruit a few to the rebellion?" Prometheus suggested. "We have Apollo to help us identify those who are true to their word."

"Just because they're true to their word today doesn't mean they won't turn on us in the future," Poseidon pointed out.

"That's true of every one of us," Prometheus said. "Is it not?"

"Perhaps we should allow one or two more admirable Titans the chance," Hades said. "Your father, for example?"

Prometheus nodded. "That would be my choice. And Hyperion as well."

"What would Helios have to say about his father's release?" Hip asked.

"He longs for it," Prometheus assured them.

"Iapetus and Hyperion," Hades said. "Only those two. Agreed?"

Everyone nodded their assent.

Hades unlocked the ten deadbolts and the adamantine chains before he shoved the heavy door open.

CHAPTER TWENTY-ONE

The Change

Than dipped his fingers into the bowl of ambrosia and rubbed more of it onto Therese's neck, shoulders, and arms. She lay on the bed smiling up at him, and he sat beside her, admiring her beauty. He didn't often get to look at her like this. Their lives had become so busy, so routine, so ordinary.

Ordinary was fine for a while, but Than was ready to embrace his old life, his old duties, his immortality.

He moved down to her lower body, smearing the heavenly liquid on her heavenly flesh. Her moans made him grin.

"We may not need the Phlegethon to catch fire," Therese said with hooded eyes.

Her skin was hot beneath his touch, and he felt his own heat rising.

She lifted her lips to his and gently caressed his mouth. He badly wished to show her just how much he loved her.

Once the ambrosia had been applied to every part of Therese's body, it was his turn to lie down and watch her spread the god's drink on his skin.

She began with his chest. At first, he sighed with pleasure. But those sighs soon turned to moans.

Gods, he wanted her.

"I love you, Therese," he whispered as he rubbed a lock of her vibrant red hair between his fingers.

"Oh, Than," she whispered back. "I can never be angry with the Fates, no matter how crazy things get, because I'll always be grateful that they brought you to me."

She leaned over and kissed him. He closed his eyes and relished the sensations of a mortal man for the very last time.

***

Hermie sat on Hecate's bed, where his sister had been sitting moments before. "I don't think it's that easy. You can't just think of a way for us to fulfill our destiny, all of a sudden, just like that." He snapped his fingers.

His sister put her hands on her hips in that way that had irritated him all his life. "You haven't even heard my idea yet, Hermie."

"Just listen, okay?" Mina asked him.

"Let's at least hear what she has to say," Poros said. "You never know."

"Okay. I'm listening."

Hestie began to pace. "Do you think it's a coincidence that you and I can speak every language imaginable?"

"Is that a rhetorical question?" Hermie asked. "Or do you want me to answer you?"

Hestie rolled her eyes. He hated it when she did that. She seemed to expect him to read her mind. He wanted her to be more specific, more direct. Was that too much to ask?

"I have over half a million followers on my Youtube channel," Hestie said. "And I get over a million views every time I post. These people live all over the world. They like how I speak in multiple languages on my show."

Hermie sighed. "And this is relevant because..."

"For someone so smart, you aren't so smart," Hestie complained.

Hermie tried not to get angry. That was another thing his sister did that he hated. Eye rolling was the number one pet peeve; saying he wasn't so smart for a smart person was the number two. He wished she'd just get on with it.

"When you play online video games, how many international gamers would you say you interact with on a regular basis?" she asked him.

Again, he wanted to ask if it was a rhetorical question, but he didn't want more eye rolling, so he said, "Unfortunately, there's a latency in the timing of actions in a game based on how far away the players are from one another, so they're set up regionally. I don't play with anyone internationally—only with other gamers in Colorado."

His sister frowned. "But you're always telling me what gamers from other countries are saying about different games."

"That's my subreddit," he said.

"Oh, yeah!" Jinsoo said. "I use Reddit a lot."

"What's a subreddit?" Poros asked.

"My subreddit is a place where gamers all over the world can review different video games and talk about strategies. I have like two million subscribers. I created a free app that translates each post into twenty-two different languages. I'm working to increase that number but haven't yet."

Hestie smiled. "You're such a nerd."

"Why does that sound like a compliment?" he asked.

"I like nerd," Mina said with a sweet smile.

"Don't you see?" Hestie spun around with her hands in the air, like a drama queen. He found this part of Hestie amusing and no longer felt irritated with her. "Prometheus said that gods get strength from the faith and prayers of humankind."

"I wasn't there to hear that, I don't think," Hermie said. "If I'd known that, everything you've been saying would have made more sense from the beginning."

The others laughed, and he did, too.

"So, you think our destiny will be fulfilled when we convince our subscribers and viewers all over the world to have faith in the gods and to pray to them," Hermie summarized.

"Not just any gods," she said. "We need them to pray for change." She snapped her fingers. "That could be our hashtag on Twitter and Instagram! We each have thousands of followers on those, too. We can make it #prayforchange."

"You might need to be more specific," Poros said. "You might need to tell them the truth about the current king—that he's selfish and needs to be replaced. Ask your followers to put their faith in Prometheus."

"We can say #prayforchange and #prayforPrometheus," Hermie said.

"And maybe even #prayforPoros," Hestie added, with a wink at Poros.

It was Hermie's turn to roll his eyes. His sister wasn't very good at hiding her crush.

"Good idea!" Mina said.

"What if people refuse to believe?" Hermie pointed out. "Just because we spread the message doesn't mean people will act on it. Maybe we should give them proof."

"I could demonstrate my powers on your video," Poros offered.

"People think it camera trick," Jinsoo said.

"But some might believe," Mina said. "You can try, okay?"

"The only problem is that we can't get a signal down here," Hermie said.

"We need to go home and do it," Hestie said.

"You mean back to Colorado?" Poros asked.

Hestie nodded.

"But it's not safe," Hermie insisted. "If we get killed, we won't be much help to anyone—not to mention that it will be a bummer to be dead."

"We can take the chariot," Hestie said. She turned to Poros. "Do you think you can fly it?"

***

Artemis and Apollo stationed themselves just inside the door to the pit as Hip followed his father and Prometheus inside. It smelled different today. Hip took another whiff.

It smelled like burning flesh.

As they worked their way further down the spiraling pathway, deeper and deeper into the shadows, where the Phlegethon didn't flow as much, Hip noticed something else was different. The Titans weren't lying around aimlessly picking their nails and staring at walls. They were gathered around like footballers in a huddle, and they were talking. Other than the one-hundred armed monsters that sulked near the Phlegethon, only a few remained on the perimeter, looking sullen and angry. Hyperion and Iapetus were among them. So was Epimetheus.

Hip studied the three Titans. They refused to meet his eyes.

Hades sent a telepathic message to the others to get ready to fight. Apollo and Artemis left the entryway and joined them where they stood on a precipice watching the huddle below.

"They've got Hecate," Hades said to them telepathically. "We may have to fight them to get her back."

Hip disintegrated into the dozens. Pete told them telepathically that he was with the Furies and had disintegrated into an army as well. Poseidon joined Hades with his trident, pointing it toward the huddle below.

"Show your faces!" Hades commanded.

The Titans looked up in surprise. They'd been so busy that they hadn't noticed the arrival of their enemies.

"Step away from her!" Hades shouted.

There were seven Titans with bloody fingers and gruesome smiles. Uranus was the bloodiest of all. Beside him stood his sons Cronos and Crius. Opposite them were Menoetius, Atlas, and Perses.

Lying on a flat rock in the center of their ring was poor, sweet Hecate—or what remained of her. The beasts had torn off her fingers and toes, pulled out most of her hair, burned her stomach and face, and appeared to be drinking her blood.

Hades flew down and swept her up in his arms. Hip followed, collecting her fingers and toes. Poseidon continued to point his trident as Hecate was taken by Hip and Apollo to Hecate's rooms. While Hip helped Apollo to heal poor Hecate, he also remained as an army inside the pit to help his family and allies in case they were attacked.

Prometheus turned to his father. "What happened here?"

"Hecate resisted for as long as she could," Iapetus said. "But she finally gave up and revealed your plot to unseat Zeus."

"We want to help!" Uranus shouted from down below. "Together we can make the change a reality!"

"Stay where you are!" Poseidon shouted. "You've done enough for one day."

Hades addressed the huddle below through gritted teeth. "Did you really think that we would accept you as our allies after you tortured one of our most beloved friends?"

"If she would have told us what was going on, we would have left her alone," Cronos said defensively.

"Stubborn one," Crius added.

"But tasty," Menoetius said with a laugh.

"I ought to have the Furies give you a taste of your own medicine," Hades mumbled.

"Just say the word, and I'll zap them," Poseidon said.

"What?" Crius cried. "No! Please don't do that!"

"Not the trident!" Cronos said.

The Titans fell to their knees and pleaded for mercy.

"Why didn't you participate, Father?" Prometheus asked Iapetus.

"We are fond of Hecate," he replied, referring to himself and Hyperion. "We hated to hear her screams, but we were overpowered."

"I don't care for her," Epimetheus said. "I just didn't want to get involved." Then, looking Prometheus up and down, he added, "You seem altered, brother."

"As do you," Prometheus said.

"We need to go," Hades said to Prometheus.

"But what about…" Prometheus began.

"You can count on our support if you want it," Hyperion said.

"We'll consider it," Hades said.

Then Poseidon added, "We'll be in touch."

The Olympians left the pit, and Hades restored the bolts and chains before joining Hip in Hecate's rooms where they worked together with Apollo to heal their friend.

***

As Hestie led the others down the winding path to the garage and stables, she was startled by blood-curdling screams. They were coming from the banquet hall of the palace. She covered her ears and ran, not wanting to think about her parents' pain. Tears rushed to her eyes, anyway, and she ran faster, not caring if the others kept up.

She waited for them in the chariot after bridling the stallions and giving them each an apple. Poros and Hermie had waited for Mina and Jinsoo. Hermie was also in tears, and the faces of the others were grave.

"I'm sorry," Poros said to her.

She nodded, not wanting to think about it. "Should I take the reins, or should you?"

"You know as much as I," he said. "Do you want to drive?"

Hestie just wanted to get away as fast as possible, so once everyone was seated, she took the reins and told the stallions to fly.

Hestie parked the chariot behind her house, nestled in the trees of the San Juan Mountains, and rushed inside through the back door, anxious to see her animal friends. Hermie called after her to wait, that there might be a trap, but she didn't hear him until she'd already entered the kitchen.

Clifford and Noodle noticed her right away and jumped from where they'd been lying on the couch to greet her. They lifted their paws onto her shins, barking excitedly. Chidori's tweets were soon added to the mix. Hestie could barely understand what the animals were saying, because they were speaking too quickly and over one another.

Kitty soon joined them from where she'd been perched on the television, and Jewels lifted her head over the side of her sandbox and winked.

Everyone seemed well fed. She ran up to her room to check on Prim and Katniss. Their cage reeked, but the animals were fine. "I'm so glad you're all okay." She let them out of their cage and had them perch on her shoulders. Then she met the others downstairs.

Not long after Mina, Jinsoo, and Poros had been introduced to the animals, including Katniss and Prim, Lynn surprised them by walking in through the back door.

"You're back?" she asked. "Yay! I've been worried."

"Not for good, I'm afraid," Hestie said.

"We just came home to do something," Hermie explained. "We have to return to the Underworld as soon as possible."

"I thought you were on Mount Olympus?" Lynn asked.

"I was," Hermie said. "And believe me, it wasn't pleasant. But then we were in the Underworld. That's where our parents are now, too."

"For how long?" Lynn asked.

"We're not sure," Hestie said.

"Are these demigods, too?" Lynn asked of their friends.

"Poros is a god," Hermie said. "But Mina and Jinsoo are regular mortals, like you."

"Hey," Mina said.

"Nice to meet you," Lynn said.

"Same," Poros said.

"So an actual god, huh?" Lynn said to Poros. "Like Athena and Aphrodite?"

"Yeah. They're my sisters. Well, Aphrodite is a half-sister."

"Cool," Lynn said.

Poros smiled. "Thanks."

"So how long will you be here?" Lynn asked.

"An hour tops," Hermie said. "But don't worry about feeding the animals today."

"Yeah. We got it," Hestie said. "And I promise to pay you my life savings when we get back."

"No worries," Lynn said. "I've got to go to practice, so I'll see you later."

After Lynn left, Hestie and Hermie filled the animals in on what was going on as they fed them and promised they'd return as soon as possible but explained that first they needed to create a video and post messages on their social media upstairs.

Clifford, Noodle, and Kitty followed the humans upstairs.

"Excuse the smell," Hestie said to their new friends. "I don't think Lynn has been cleaning the rat cage. In fact, Hermie, could you get the video camera ready while I do that?"

"Do you really want to take time for that?" Hermie asked.

"They've got to be miserable in there," she said. "I can do it fast."

"Can I help?" Poros asked.

This surprised Hestie, because the smell in her room was almost unbearable. "If you can stand it, sure."

While she and Poros cleaned, Hermie posted to his subreddit. He also posted from his and from Hestie's social media accounts, asking their followers to #prayforchange, to #unseatZeus, and to #prayforPoros and #prayforPrometheus. He even used #prayforHades for good measure and used his app to quickly translate and repost in twenty-two languages. Within fifteen minutes all five hashtags were trending on Twitter and Instagram.

Once the cage was clean, the messages posted, and the camera ready with the SD card inserted, the humans and two dogs went outside.

"Let me start solo, and then I'll introduce the three of you," Hestie said.

"Us too?" Jinsoo asked.

"We get to be on show, too?" Mina asked, clapping her hands.

Hestie laughed. "Sure!" Then she asked, "Ready, Hermie?"

He gave her a thumbs up from behind the camera, which he had on a tripod on the back deck.

"Hey, besties!" Hestie said into the camera. Then she said, "Hello good friends," in a dozen other languages. "I'm sorry I haven't posted a video in a while. I've been on an important quest, traveling the high seas! It's true. See this new outfit I'm wearing? You know how much I LOVE Indian prints, right, besties?" She translated that into twelve languages, before she said, "Aren't these shorts the cutest? I bought this outfit at the prettiest little boutique in Patras, Greece. From there, I sailed on a ship called *The Marvella*. Our first stop was South Sudan, where I helped the captain and his crew deliver important medicine to a village where a parasite is killing people every day." To Hermie, she said, this is where I'll insert some of the footage I captured. Then she said, "I made some amazing friends, and they're here with me today. First, I want to introduce you to Mina and her twin brother, Jinsoo."

Mina and Jinsoo stepped into the frame beside her while she described them in each of the twelve languages. Mina and Jinsoo smiled and waved at the camera. Jinsoo danced some of his Kpop moves. Then Hestie motioned them offscreen and replaced them with Poros.

"Poros is here with me today to give you an urgent message," she said thirteen different ways. "Not all of you will believe me, but I hope most of you will. The gods are real, and they are fighting. For so long, most of them have ignored us. Sickness, disease, poverty, and war plague us because most of the gods are more concerned with their own affairs. But I had a chance to meet Prometheus. This is his nephew, Poros. That's right. Poros is a god. And he's here with me to ask you to pray for change."

She looked at Poros, who nodded and said, "It's true. My father Zeus wants to destroy me, and since he's done very little to help any of you, I was hoping you would pray and have faith in me and in my uncle, Prometheus, and all the gods of the rebellion, such as Hades, Poseidon, Apollo, Artemis, Persephone, Hecate, and the Furies, along with some of the Titans, like Helios, Selene, and Gaia. Pray for change, because your prayers give us strength. And if we can dethrone my father, Zeus, we can create a new order that will better serve humankind."

At that moment, a lightning bolt shot from the sky. Hestie looked up and screamed as it struck Poros. She reached out to catch his limp body, electricity pulsed through her, and she lost consciousness.

CHAPTER TWENTY-TWO

The Rebellion

Therese opened her eyes and blinked. She scanned the room, trying to recall where she was and what she was doing here. Gradually, it dawned on her, and she recalled the ambrosia, the fire from the Phlegethon, and the searing, burning, and—strangely—freezing pain of her own flesh on fire.

She sat up and batted away the ashes of her old body, amazed by how good the new one felt. Her skin glowed, and, lying beside her, Than glowed, too. He opened his eyes and smiled at her.

She was dressed in a white tunic. She looked down and ran her fingertips along the smooth fabric.

"I did that," Jen said. "Didn't want you two naked as a jaybird when everyone else got here."

"Thanks," Therese said.

She noticed Hip and Pete on either side of her. But where was everyone else?

"Attending to Hecate," Pete said.

Therese hadn't realized she'd prayed her question to them.

"It may take a little getting used to again," Jen said.

"What's wrong with Hecate?" Than asked as he, too, sat up in the ashen bed beside Therese.

"Zeus sentenced her to the Titan Pit for treason," Hip explained.

"The secret message?" Therese asked.

Hip nodded. "While she was in there…"

Therese had never seen Hip get so choked up.

"The other Titans tortured her for information," Pete said.

"She's in pretty bad shape," Jen added. "But Apollo is helping her."

Therese felt something on her back and realized her old quiver and bow had returned. She leapt from the bed and into the air, delighting in her power of flight. She could already hear prayers coming to her from people worried about their pets.

"I'm back, baby!" she shouted with glee. "And it feels amazing!"

"Where are Hestie and Hermie?" Than asked.

Therese saw the three friends frowning.

"What's wrong?" she said, coming down from the ceiling to stand beside her friends. "Has something happened?"

"We're looking for them now," Hip said. "They went missing."

"Along with the chariot," Jen added.

"Check the house," Than said.

"I'm there now, searching the rooms," Hip said.

"No sign of them?" Therese asked.

"Oh, no," Hip's face fell. "I found them. They're outside."

"Spit it out," Than said, jumping to his feet.

Hermie is fine," Hip said.

"And Hestie?" Therese asked, her stomach twisting in knots.

"The other twins are saying that lighting struck Poros and Hestie," Hip said. "I'm bringing them home in the chariot now. Watch out! We're under attack!"

Therese grabbed Than and Hip by the hands. "Take us to them!"

"God travel isn't safe," Hip warned.

"Please," Than said.

***

Hermie laughed at his sister as he watched her on the video camera monitor. Her face lit up when she introduced Poros. But soon after, the sky lit up, too—literally. Directly above them, an electrical storm emerged out of nowhere, and…Hermie couldn't believe it when a bolt of lightning struck Poros directly on the shoulder. Hestie screamed and reached for him, and then she, too, collapsed beside Poros on the ground.

The twins screamed.

Hermie grabbed the video camera from the tripod and handed it to Jinsoo. "Get in the chariot!" He gave Mina the laptop. "Hold onto those!"

He used his super strength and speed to get Hestie and Poros into the backseat where Jinsoo and Mina could hold onto them while he took the reins. He didn't have time to be afraid. He had to get them to the Underworld and to Apollo. At least they were breathing.

Please let them be okay.

Before he commanded Swift and Sure to take off, his Uncle Hip appeared. Seeing that help had come made him weep. It was crazy. When no one else had been there to be the hero, he'd done it without thinking, but now that Hip was here, he allowed himself to feel what was happening to his sister and friend.

Then another lightning bolt shot toward them, and Hip took the reins and sped them up and away.

Hermie wiped his eyes and took the video camera from Jinsoo, removing the SD card. He gave the camera back and took the laptop from Mina. He had to get the video uploaded as soon as possible, because if people in the world prayed for change, the rebellion would become more powerful.

Hermie glanced once more at his sister and Poros.

Please let them be okay.

When he turned back to the laptop, he noticed he'd lost the wi-fi signal.

"Go lower, Uncle Hip," Hermie shouted. "We're too far away from the wireless routers below." He wouldn't be able to upload the video to Youtube without internet access.

Another lightning bolt shot toward them, and Hip swerved to miss.

"A little busy keeping you alive here!" Hip shouted back.

"This video is important," Hermie said, "and I won't be able to fight sleep much longer. This is how Hestie and I are going to fulfill our destiny."

Hip steered Swift and Sure down to the treetops and flew in zigzag along the southwestern states as lightning rained down on them, wreaking havoc on the earth below. Trees caught on fire, and some neighborhoods blacked out as they lost power.

Hermie desperately forced his eyelids open and searched for a hotspot, but the power outages were minimizing the router availability.

"This is no good!" Hip said. "We're putting too many mortals at risk!"

Hermie got an idea. "Drive us over the sea. I can hack into the maritime internet service."

Almost as fast as lightning, they sped over southern California toward the Pacific Ocean. Hermie found the maritime signal and gained access by finding a backdoor. Immediately, the video began to upload to Youtube.

Thank goodness, because he was about to give in to sleep.

Hip dodged another lightning bolt that nearly caught Swift on the front right hoof, but the entire chariot leaned left, and Hermie was thrown hard against one side. The laptop flew from his hands and over the edge. Without thinking, Hermie jumped from the chariot and caught the laptop mid-air. If the laptop got wet, how would he and his sister fulfill their destiny? As he fell through the air toward the see, he found himself unable to pray or to speak out loud. He felt numb, almost as if he had accepted that he was about to die, and everything was over.

Vaguely, he was aware of Mina and Jinsoo screaming his name.

Another chariot leapt up from the sea below and caught him. Poseidon steered his white mares up into the sky, in the direction of Zeus!

"Thank you," Hermie said as he found his breath. "But don't you want to go in the opposite direction?"

Ignoring his question, Poseidon pointed his trident toward the heavens and shot a blast of light toward the dark clouds above them. Zeus and Hera emerged from the clouds in a chariot, unscathed.

Hermie decided to focus on uploading the video. He was pleased and surprised to see it was already fifty percent complete.

"Come on! Come on!" he muttered.

All around him, more gods appeared in the sky to fight the battle. Artemis shot arrows at Zeus and Hera. Ares and Aphrodite appeared in another chariot and rained spears down on Artemis. She dodged them just as another archer appeared by her side. It was his mother!

"Go, Mom!" Hermie shouted, cheering her on.

He checked the laptop screen to see the video was eighty-eight percent complete.

"Almost done!" he muttered.

Then a spear pierced though his chest, shocking him beyond understanding. When he tried to breathe, his chest burned, as if he was on fire, and no air came.

The last thing he saw before losing consciousness was that the video upload was 100 percent complete. He gave up the fight and fell to the bottom of the chariot at Poseidon's feet.

***

Than saw Ares's spear fly through the storming sky and hit Hermie's chest. Than gasped at the sight of the spearhead emerging, bloody, from his son's back, nearly jolting the boy from the fast-moving chariot.

He fled to his son's side, fearing that the god who had once saved Hermie's life had taken it. To his utter despair, his suspicion was proved true when Pete appeared to take Hermie's soul.

"Back away!" Than cried through gritted teeth. "You can't have him!"

How many times had Thanatos been told those very words? How many times had he been forced to take a soul from a screaming parent, wanting to fight him for the soul?

But Than wasn't just any parent. Not anymore. Now he was a god, and he didn't care about the rules. He would do whatever it took to save his son.

"You know I can't," Pete said solemnly. "I'm so sorry."

"Duck!" Poseidon shouted as they dodged another spear.

"If you take him, the Fates will demand another trade," Than said to Pete, once the chariot had stabilized. Than would do anything to save his son except take another life.

"His soul is calling to me," Pete said. "You know how irresistible that is."

"Trade with me," Than said. "Let me be Death once again."

Pete arched a brow. "Seriously? You *want* this job?"

"I've never been more serious."

The chariot plummeted toward the sea. Than held his son with one hand and clung to the chariot with the other. Pete held on, too, as water splashed up and onto them and they skidded across the surface.

"I'm heading back into the thick of it, boys!" Poseidon shouted. "You better take the mortal child to safety."

"If I trade with you, don't expect me to trade back," Pete said. "Understood?"

"I swear on the River Styx," Than said.

Pete took his hand, and the duties of Death were transferred to him. Once again, he was literally Thanatos. He kissed his son goodbye and flew as far away from him as he could. If his dreams of seeing his children turned to gods never came true, he would never be able to be in their company.

He prayed to Hip to take his children to safety as he flew toward the battlefront, disintegrating into the hundreds.

***

Hip heard his brother's prayer and disintegrated, taking Poros, Hestie, and Hermie with him to the Underworld even as he continued to fly his father's chariot.

He was shocked by Hermie's state. He had lost a lot of blood, and it seemed impossible that he should still be alive. He prayed to Apollo to be ready. Hip did not want to risk god-travel, so he flew through the sky to the east until he found a chasm to the Underworld.

As he flew into the chasm, he also noticed from his father's chariot that the Olympians were retreating. The members of the rebellion turned around and began to fly back to the Underworld, full of the taste of victory.

Hip flew directly to the banquet hall, where he got rid of the ashen bed and replaced it with three new ones. He laid Poros, Hestie, and Hermie down on each one.

The Asian kids sat together on a chair. The girl couldn't stop crying. The boy did his best to console her. For some reason, they were fighting sleep. Perhaps they were determined to know the fates of their friends.

Apollo met up with Hip, and soon Therese was beside him, her eyes full of tears.

Hades and Poseidon arrived at the same time, followed by Artemis and the Furies. Prometheus had stayed with Hecate. A disintegrated version of Hip was with Prometheus as well, holding Hecate's hand.

Then Thanatos appeared beside Therese in the banquet hall. Tears streamed down his pale cheeks. "I can't hold back much longer. Hermie's soul is calling to me. Please do something, Apollo."

Therese put herself between her husband and her son, realizing who Thanatos had become. "Leave, Than. Please! I beg you. Leave!"

"Don't you think I've tried? I traded with Pete to hold off Death. I'm running out of strength."

"He needs blood," Apollo said.

"Use mine!" Therese cried.

"Yours won't work," Apollo said. "He needs Hestie's."

"But she's so weak," Jen pointed out.

"Her soul's not far from death, either," Than insisted.

"If I don't give Hermie some of his sister's blood, he *will* die," Apollo said.

"But doing so could kill her," Pete said.

"If we use her blood, they could both die, or they could both live," Apollo said. "Or the girl may die to save the boy."

"But if we do nothing, Hermie is sure to die?" Jen asked.

"And the girl is sure to live," Artemis said.

"Yes," Apollo said.

"Oh, gods! What should we do?" Therese's expression was frantic.

"If it's the only way to save them both, I think we should take the chance," Hades said. "And I don't say that lightly. I say it because something is happening to me. My power is stronger than it's ever been."

The Asian girl jumped to her feet. "The video working!"

The gods turned to look at her.

The boy said, "Hermie and Hestie made video asking pray for change, pray for Poros, and pray for Hades."

"For all you!" the girl added.

"On Reddit, Twitter, and Instagram, too!" the boy said.

The gods looked from one to the other. Hip could tell that none of them understood quite what the mortals were saying.

"They're talking about social media," Therese explained. "My twins must have used their language skills and social media presence to solicit prayers for the rebellion."

"Exactly!" the girl shouted.

"I feel it, too," Apollo said.

"As do I," said Poseidon.

"The faith of humanity is strengthening us," Artemis said.

"That means our twins…" Than began but seemed too choked up to finish.

"They fulfilled their destiny," Hades finished for him. "They restored humanity's faith in themselves and in us, at least for now."

"It's time to act," Poseidon said. "We can use this power to storm Mount Olympus!"

"First things first," Hades said. "Apollo?"

"Hermie is accepting his sister's blood, and she's stabilized," Apollo replied.

Hip's attention was suddenly drawn from his niece and nephew to the body of Poros, which had begun to glow almost as brightly as Helios.

"What's happening?" Therese asked.

Poros opened his eyes and jumped into the air as electricity pulsed from his body. Then his eyes fell on Hestie and Hermie. He flew to Hestie's side, put his hand on her forehead and closed his eyes. She, too, began to glow.

"What did you just do?" Therese asked him.

"I'm not sure, but I think…" Poros began.

"He turned her into one of us," Hades said beneath his breath.

Quickly, Poros moved to Hermie and did the same. Hermie's wound closed and his skin began to glow.

"Is he one of us, too?" Than asked.

"I think so," Poros said.

"Somehow you have gained your father's power of apotheosis," Hades said to Poros, with a look of astonishment.

"That can only mean one thing," Artemis said.

"Poros is stronger than Zeus," Poseidon said.

CHAPTER TWENTY-THREE

No Way Out

Morpheus gripped the golden bars of his cage. The other Olympians hadn't been gone long when Persephone showed herself to him beneath the helm and told him she would do everything in her power to free him. She conjured various weapons and tried to pry the bars apart, but they wouldn't bend. She said she was going to perform a spell she had learned from Hecate, but it only created a useless puff of smoke. She even recruited Hephaestus to hide with her beneath the helm and use his forge to melt the golden bars, but to no avail. Now, she assured Morpheus she would search every square inch of Mount Olympus for the key.

She had to be careful, Morpheus knew, because Hestia and the Graces were still at home, and they were in and out of the main palace throughout the day. Demeter was there, too, but she'd refused to leave her rooms, saying she couldn't go against her brother or her daughter and so would do nothing. Everyone else had gone to fight—except Hephaestus, who was supposed to be forging more weapons.

If Persephone didn't have the power of the helm, they'd have no hope. As it was, even with the helm, they had very little of it.

Persephone tried various keys she discovered, but none were the *right* key, until she returned later that day and whispered, "I think I've found it! It was with the key to the trick chair all along. This must be it!"

"Will you save Iris, too?" Morpheus asked.

Suddenly, Hestia was upon his grandmother. Persephone shoved the key into the lock before she was overtaken, and the helm seized.

"Please, Hestia," Persephone begged. "Please help us. Don't let your brother destroy our family."

"It's *your* family that threatens to destroy *mine*," Hestia said.

Morpheus turned the key and unlocked his cage. He sprang free and flew to Persephone's aid when suddenly Zeus and Hera appeared and quickly forced him back into his prison and shoved Persephone onto the trick chair.

Hera held up the key and said to Persephone in a taunting voice, "Now what are you going to do? No helm, no key? Poor Persephone. I'm afraid you're stuck, aren't you, dear?"

Ares and Aphrodite appeared. With a red face and raging voice, Zeus filled them in on what had transpired. Demeter emerged from her rooms to hear what had happened.

Then Zeus went on to say that he was done playing nice. "It's time to teach the dissenters a lesson and remind them who's king."

Morpheus exchanged worried glances with Iris, who was trembling with fear. He, too, was terrified of what Zeus would do next.

"Unlock the trick chair," Zeus said to Hera.

As soon as the key clicked in the lock, Zeus opened his mouth wide—as wide as a horse. Morpheus shrank back and Demeter screamed as Zeus took Persephone into his great mouth and swallowed her whole.

Demeter's cries rang throughout the great hall. They were awful earsplitting shrieks of the most profound despair.

"How could you, brother?" Demeter cried. "How could you!"

Morpheus hadn't had time to recover from the awful thing he'd just witnessed, when Zeus ordered Hera to unlock his cage. Was he to be swallowed, too?

"I love you," he told Iris telepathically, in case it was his last chance to ever speak with her again.

"Morpheus!" she cried out loud. "Please, my lord! Spare him!"

The other gods watched on with shock on their faces. Morpheus could tell they did not approve of what Zeus had done and was about to do, but would no one stand up and say so? Would no one stop this tyrannical king from consuming him?

"Father?" Hermes said.

Zeus took a lightning bolt from behind his throne and threw it at Hermes—threw to miss. Then he flew to Morpheus and said, "Get down on your knees and bow before your lord and king!"

Quivering like a freezing animal in the snow, Morpheus knelt on the palace floor.

To Hera and Ares, Zeus said, "Throw Demeter into the cage and lock her inside."

Demeter tried to flee, but she was unsuccessful and was thrust into the birdcage and locked inside.

"Bow to me, Morpheus! Bow so low that you kiss the floor!" Zeus commanded.

Morpheus did as he was asked, trying not to throw up on Zeus's sandaled feet.

He cried out in agony as the deepest, purist pain he'd ever felt made its way down his back. Then warm blood covered him from head to foot. The sound of paper shredding permeated the air, and that's when Morpheus realized what was happening to him: Zeus was ripping away Morpheus's beloved silver wings.

Over his own wails and moans, Morpheus heard Iris scream, and hearing that made him fight to be strong. He had to be strong for her. He couldn't let her see his pain, his agony, and his despair, because it hurt her more than it hurt him. He knew that would be true if their situations were reversed, and this thought made him beg in prayer to Zeus: "Please spare Iris. Do whatever you will with me, but I beg you to please spare her. She's been a loyal servant to you."

"Look at me," Zeus commanded him.

Morpheus lifted his head to see his dear wings dripping with blood in Zeus's hands. "I will spare Iris and give you back your wings if, and only if, you do something for me."

Morpheus was afraid to ask what it was the king wanted of him.

"I want you to go back to the Underworld and tell those dissenters that your grandmother helped you to escape, but not before you lost your wings in the battle and Persephone was swallowed."

"I will, Lord Zeus," Morpheus said.

"That's not all," Zeus said harshly. "I want you to report back to me on everything you see and hear. You will use the helm of invisibility and Iris's rainbow to travel back and forth."

Morpheus's mouth dropped open. Zeus wanted Morpheus to betray his family?

"If you fail me," Zeus continued. "I promise I will take pleasure in ripping those pretty little wings from your pretty little girlfriend. Then I will defile her in ways you can't imagine before I paralyze her and hide her at the bottom of a river, where she will spend eternity, just like Phaeton. Do you understand?"

Morpheus said nothing. He could only stare dumbly up at Zeus.

"Do you understand?" Zeus shouted, causing the entire palace to quake.

Morpheus nodded. What else could he do? He sucked in his lips and fought the tears welling in his eyes as he glanced back at Iris.

"I want to hear you swear it," Zeus demanded. "You will report to me, and you will tell no one about our arrangement. Do you swear on the River Styx?"

"I swear," Morpheus muttered, and then he did get sick on Zeus's sandaled feet.

THE END

Thank you for reading my story. I hope you enjoyed it! If so, please consider leaving a review. Reviews help my books to get discovered by other readers, which helps me.

Please enjoy the first chapter of the next book, *Storming Olympus*.

Morpheus's Return

Still bleeding from where his silver wings had been ripped from his back, Morpheus stumbled across Iris's rainbow from Mount Olympus toward the depths of the Underworld. He could hardly see through his tears. He couldn't think. He wasn't even sure if he was breathing. The horrible vision kept playing over and over in his mind: Zeus opening his great mouth and swallowing Persephone before throwing Demeter into the bird cage that had been Morpheus's prison.

He could still hear Zeus's threat: "I will spare Iris and give you back your wings if, and only if, you do something for me."

Then the king had said: "I want you to report back to me on everything you see and hear. You will use the helm of invisibility and Iris's rainbow to travel back and forth."

But, worst of all, Zeus had said: "If you fail me, I promise I will take pleasure in ripping those pretty little wings from your pretty little girlfriend. Then I will defile her in ways you can't imagine before I paralyze her and hide her at the bottom of a river, where she will spend eternity, just like Phaeton. Do you understand?"

Then Zeus had forced Morpheus to swear on the River Styx that he would obey, and Morpheus, full of fear and dread, had sworn.

Had it really happened? Or had it been a horrible nightmare in the Dreamworld that had passed through the Gates of Ivory, and not through the Gates of Horn?

Morpheus's knees quivered as he walked beneath the helm of invisibility. He'd never flown without his wings. His beautiful wings. Were they really gone?

He strained to see his back. No wings. Only fresh blood. So much blood.

He wondered if he would ever see his wings again, or if he was doomed to suffer the same fate as Iris's sister, Arke.

Poor, sweet Iris. The memory of her lovely face twisted with fear and agony brought a new wave of tears to Morpheus's eyes. She'd been a faithful servant to Zeus, and the king couldn't care less. Morpheus had once believed that if you were a good and loyal subject, the king would always protect and reward you. But now he knew that wasn't true. Unlike her sister, Iris had done nothing to deserve the threats against her. Persephone may have taken her chances against her father, but what had Demeter done to deserve imprisonment?

Zeus used people. He didn't care about fairness and justice. He only cared about power. That's why he had swallowed Athena's mother in the first place. He was no better than *his* father, Cronos.

Morpheus felt like an idiot for ever trusting his king. Why, oh, why hadn't Morpheus trusted his father? If he had, maybe he and Iris would be safe, and none of this would be happening.

When Morpheus reached the throne room in the palace of Hades and Persephone, he found it empty. He followed the sounds of voices to one of the meeting rooms, where there were many gathered, including his parents. Hades and the Furies and Pete were there. Apollo and Artemis were there. Poseidon, Than, and Therese were there. Huddled in a corner, near the flickering fires of the Phlegethon, were two Asian kids fast asleep. Hermie and Hestie were each lying on a bed in the middle of the room, where the table usually was, and they were *glowing*.

Morpheus forgot that he was beneath the helm. He stared with wonder at the glowing bodies of his cousins and of the blond boy hovering in the air above them, who Morpheus now realized must be the son of Zeus, Poros.

Artemis said, "That can only mean one thing."

Poseidon glanced around the room. "Poros is stronger than Zeus."

Morpheus wasn't sure what he had heard. He felt as if he was in the Dreamworld witnessing a bizarre nightmare. Dazed, trembling, perplexed, he fell to his knees. He wanted to tell his family the truth, even if it meant that the Maenads would rip him to shreds every year; but, he couldn't bear the thought of his sweet Iris paralyzed at the bottom of a river for all eternity.

And yet, if he *didn't* tell his family what Zeus had made him swear to do, what worse thing would Zeus do to *them*? Was it right for Morpheus to put his and Iris's happiness above all of theirs? And could he really trust Zeus *not* to harm Iris, even if Morpheus kept his word?

"The mortals are in danger because of my presence," Than said. "I better go."

"No," Pete said. "I'll go. I'll take them to Tartarus and keep them safe. You need to stay here, with your family."

Pete took the hands of the Asian kids, and the three of them disappeared.

Family. That's what this was about. Pete was right. They all needed to be with their family, and Zeus was definitely *not* family. Family members didn't threaten, torture, and imprison one other.

No, Zeus was not to be trusted. Morpheus had to tell his family the truth. But what would it matter, in the end?

He covered his face with his hands and wept. He was convinced that they were all doomed, whatever path he chose.

***

Hypnos was thrilled by the transformations taking place before his eyes. Therese and Than's twins had fulfilled their destinies. A power shift from Zeus to Poros had been the result, and now, the rebellion had a fighting chance.

Hip smiled across the room at his brother, once again in his rightful role as the god of death. He was altered since the last time he had served, having aged to an appearance more like their father. But his dark wavy hair and solemn blue eyes reminded Hip of the boy he'd once been, of the boy Hip still appeared to be. It was strange and jarring to think about it.

Beside him, Therese, also older in appearance than she'd been the last time she was the goddess of animal companions, looked just as radiant and fierce, her red curls falling about her shoulders and quiver full of arrows, her green eyes determined and expectant. She hadn't hesitated in the fight against the loyalists, as if she'd never stopped fighting. Hip was happy for his brother and relieved that Than and Therese would return to the pantheon and live eternally with their Underworld family, who'd missed them. Even their children, Hermie and Hestie, could now join them, thanks to the power of Poros.

Smiling, Hip said to Than, "It will be quite a treat to finally visit with my niece and nephew outside of the Dreamworld."

"It's a miracle," Therese murmured, still in shock over the unexpected transformation of her children into gods.

As pleased as Hip was, he was worried for Morpheus and Persephone. He wouldn't rest until his son and mother were safely returned. He could tell by Jen's expression that she was feeling the same. He was about to suggest a rescue plan, when he noticed drops of blood falling from thin air, creating a trail across the room.

The other gods noticed it, too. In a flash, Hades held the helm of invisibility, and beneath it, on his knees and covered in blood, was Morpheus.

Jen screamed into her hands as Hip rushed to Morpheus's side. Jen followed, the three of them on their knees in a huddle of misery.

Hestie sat up in her bed. "Morpheus!"

"Oh, my gods!" Therese flew to the other side of Jen.

Hip couldn't believe how much blood covered his son's beautiful bronze skin and the black curls on his head. It was now on Hip's hands. He stared at it, half-dazed.

"What happened?" The stern voice of Hades brought Hip back to his senses.

With his head bowed, Morpheus cleared his voice and said, "Zeus…he…"

"He took your wings!" Jen cried.

"How barbaric!" Apollo scoffed.

"But why?" Tizzie asked.

"Leverage," Alecto said with disgust.

"He made me swear…" Morpheus began, his silver eyes troubled.

Apollo raised his hand. "Don't break your oath."

Morpheus looked at Apollo and the others with disbelief. "But if I don't tell you…"

"We already know what he wants from you," Poseidon said, with a toss of his long, sun-bleached hair. "He wants you to spy."

Morpheus turned to Poseidon, searching his turquoise eyes. "How did you…"

"Don't say another word about it," Apollo said again.

"I can't believe Zeus would do this to you," Jen said to Morpheus. "After you obeyed him and everything."

"I can," Artemis said with a scowl, her forest green eyes narrowed.

"I'm so sorry." Therese stroked Jen's long, blonde hair, trying to comfort her.

Hip could only gape, still unable to process what had happened.

"What about Persephone?" Hades asked. "If she doesn't have the helm, she must be exposed."

Hip was afraid of the answer.

New tears rushed from Morpheus's eyes, and his chin quivered. "Zeus…he swallowed her."

Hades stumbled back and fell into a chair, his face pale.

The room filled with gasps. Hip could barely process the looks of shock on the faces of the others in the room. Speechless, he stared in horror at his father, who seemed suddenly crushed. The giant, confident leader Hip had always looked up to was now hunched over in his chair on the verge of weeping.

Hip couldn't bear to see his father like this. It was almost as disturbing as the image of his bleeding son. How had things come to this?

"This is an outrage!" Poseidon shouted. "We won't tolerate it, Hades. We'll get her back. I promise you."

"Don't make promises you can't keep, brother," Hades managed to say.

"Poor Mother!" Meg wailed. "I can't bear it."

Tizzie flew to Meg and threw her arms around her. "We'll get her back. I know we will."

Thanatos crossed the room to his father's side. "Poseidon and Tizzie are right, Father. We *will* get her back." He turned to Hip. "And we'll get his wings back, too," he said of Morpheus. "I didn't return just to be defeated. We have power on our side." Than turned to Poros. "We have destiny on our side." He glanced across the room at Apollo. "We have foresight." He turned to Poseidon. "And we have the most powerful brothers." Then he met the faces of every single person in the room. "The time for change has come, and we are that change."

***

Hermie was moved by his father's speech, but he was still trying to understand what had happened to him. Hermie's body was *glowing*. He was sitting up in the bed, gazing at his hands, wiggling his fingers. He was feeling a little creeped out.

We're gods, Hestie's voice said directly into his brain.

She hadn't spoken out loud, but he'd heard it as clearly as if she had. He stared at her transformed body, glowing like his. Her red hair seemed thicker and shinier, and her muscles more defined. Was he more muscular, too? He checked his abs and gaped. Yes. He was a lot more buff than he'd ever been.

Can you hear me? he said to his sister telepathically.

Looking at him, she nodded.

I feel funny, he said.

Hermie noticed tears in his sister's eyes as she said, *We'll get to be with Mom and Dad forever.*

He hadn't thought of that. Everything was happening so fast. But it was true. He smiled as he realized it. They would be a family forever.

But he frowned as quickly as he had smiled. What would it mean to be a god? The others were talking about a revolution. Would this mean that he and Hestie would be expected to go into battle? Their parents had trained them to fight ever since they were babies, but he'd always thought of it as a sport, like live action role play. He wasn't sure if he had the guts to wield a sword against a real person, much less a god. He wondered if it was possible to be turned back into a mortal.

Thinking of being mortal reminded Hermie of Mina and Jinsoo. Pete had taken them to Tartarus, where all the evildoers go. He hoped they weren't freaking out. He wished he could go with them and tell them everything was going to be okay, though he wasn't convinced that it was true.

He wondered where Prometheus was and then remembered someone had said he was with Hecate, who was recovering from being tortured by the Titans. He'd heard that even her father, Perses, had participated in her suffering. Hermie shuddered. Torture seemed to be a common theme among the immortals. Hermie hoped Prometheus would return soon and take Mina and Jinsoo someplace away from here—someplace safe, if such a place existed.

Artemis crossed the room and stood before Hades. Like Therese and Apollo, she wore a quiver full of arrows. "I imagine your first thought is of rescue."

"Yes," Hades said.

"But we can't rush in," Artemis insisted. "We need a plan to overtake Mount Olympus."

Poros moved to Artemis's side. "I agree. You might not want to hear this, Lord Hades, but Persephone is safe where she is."

"She's been *swallowed!*" Hestie cried, as if that fact hadn't already been known.

"My mother survived in my father's belly for centuries," Poros continued. "She could hear everything Zeus said. She could even hear his thoughts."

"Persephone could be of use to us where she is," Apollo said.

"Telepathy is impossible with someone who's been…" Meg's voice trailed off.

"And think how miserable she must be!" Tizzie cried, just before her white wolf howled.

Poseidon crossed his arms. "We know firsthand. Don't we, brother?"

"It's *pure* misery," Hades said, looking as if he were in a daze.

Hermie had to agree. His Grandma Persephone must be terrified, lonely, and uncomfortable, if not in outright pain. Could she breathe? Could she see? Could she move? She must feel like she was buried alive. He shuddered again.

"We have to get her out of that tyrant as soon as possible!" Alecto's red hair became flames, and her snake, coiled around her neck, hissed.

"We have to get her out," Artemis said, "but not yet."

Hermie frowned. "But when?"

"Let's give her time to know Zeus's mind," Apollo suggested. "Then, once we do free her, she can help us with our next move."

Poseidon turned to Apollo. "Being swallowed has a way of…changing a person."

"We can't leave her there, Father," Meg pleaded.

As if in agreement, her falcon squawked.

"We need to think of a way to free her as soon as possible," Hades said.

"Uranus," Hip said. "That's how I recovered Ares's leg from the dragon. Uranus gave me an herb from Circe's stash."

"Maybe he can tell us where to find more," Hermie's mom suggested.

"With the helm, Morpheus can sneak it into Zeus's cup before Hebe serves him," Poseidon said.

"Why must it always be Morpheus?" Jen complained.

Hermie glanced at his cousin, feeling sorrier for him that he'd ever felt for anyone or anything. He'd been mutilated, his girlfriend was imprisoned, and now he was expected to play the dangerous role of double agent in a war between gods.

"Poseidon is right, I'm afraid," Hades said. "We'll have to use Morpheus in the same way Zeus meant to."

"Are we sure we can trust him not to play both sides?" Artemis asked.

"What?" Morpheus gave Artemis a surprised look and then glanced at the faces of the other gods in the room for the first time. "I wouldn't do that. I swear."

"But you've sworn your allegiance to Zeus," Poseidon pointed out. "Even if it was under duress."

A chill crept up Hermie's spine as he recalled the way Morpheus had turned him over to Zeus. If Morpheus hadn't done that, things might have turned out differently.

Apollo turned to Hades. "I sense the boy is telling us the truth, but we need to keep him ignorant of our strategies, so that Zeus can't force the information out of him. We've said too much in front of him already."

"We'll have to tell him something, though," Hip said, "or Zeus will know that we're keeping him in the dark."

"And if Morpheus is no longer useful to Zeus…" Artemis's voice trailed off.

Nausea formed in the pit of Hermie's stomach. He loved his cousin, even after all he'd done. Hermie knew Morpheus had only been doing what he thought was right.

"Wouldn't Zeus leave him alone?" Jen asked, hopefully. "Morpheus wouldn't be able to spy for us, but he'd be safe."

"Not if he'd already heard too much of Zeus's plans, I'm afraid," Hades said.

"Then let's keep him here," Jen said. "He's just a boy."

"I'm almost twenty," Morpheus argued.

"You're still so young," Tizzie agreed with Jen.

"I *want* to go, Mom," Morpheus said. "Iris is still there, and Persephone. Zeus put Demeter into my cage, and she didn't even do anything wrong. If I don't go back…"

Hermie covered his mouth. He wasn't sure what shocked him more—that Morpheus wanted to go into danger, or that Demeter had been imprisoned.

"He's imprisoned Demeter?" Meg asked.

"Oh, no!" Hermie's mother cried.

"He's lost it." Poseidon turned to Hades. "Our brother has lost it. Who knows what's next?"

"We need a plan," Hermie's father said.

"Send Morpheus to the Dreamworld, so we can get on with it," Poseidon said.

Morpheus looked to his father and mother.

"Just for now," Hip said.

"I'll go with him," Jen offered, before taking Morpheus's hand.

Prometheus and Hecate entered the room just as Morpheus left with his mother. Hermie gasped at the sight of Hecate. She was covered in cuts and bruises, and dried blood surrounded her eyes.

The Furies and Therese rushed to her side, asking if she was okay.

"I'll be fine," Hecate said with a half-smile.

She didn't look fine to Hermie. Tears filled his eyes, and he swiped them away. He was an effin' god, but he'd never felt more afraid.

EVA POHLER

Eva Pohler is a *USA Today* bestselling author of over thirty novels in multiple genres, including mysteries, thrillers, and young adult paranormal romance based on Greek mythology. Her books have been described as "addictive" and "sure to thrill"—*Kirkus Reviews*.

To learn more about Eva and her books, and to sign up to hear about new releases, and sales, please visit her website at www.evapohler.com.

www.ingramcontent.com/pod-product-compliance
Lightning Source LLC
Chambersburg PA
CBHW061237210726
48293CB00003B/808